Ugly B...

Mike Thomas was ... ...
inspiration for his ... ...
serving police offic... ... ...
published in 2010 ... ...as longlisted for the Wales
Book of the Year Award. Married with two children,
he lives in Portugal.

Ugly Bus

MIKE THOMAS

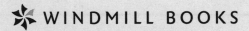

WINDMILL BOOKS

Published by Windmill Books 2015

2 4 6 8 10 9 7 5 3 1

First published in Great Britain in 2014 by William Heinemann

Windmill Books
The Random House Group Limited
20 Vauxhall Bridge Road, London SW1V 2SA

Addresses for companies within The Random House Group Limited
can be found at: www.randomhouse.co.uk/offices

The Random House Group Limited Reg. No. 954009

www.randomhouse.co.uk

A CIP catalogue record for this book
is available from the British Library

ISBN 9780099559238

Typeset in Dante MT by Palimpsest Book Production Ltd,
Falkirk, Stirlingshire
Printed and bound by CPI Group (UK) Ltd, Croydon, CR0 4YY

MIX
Paper from
responsible sources
FSC
www.fsc.org
FSC® C018179

Penguin Random House is committed to a
sustainable future for our business, our readers
and our planet. This book is made from Forest
Stewardship Council® certified paper.

For M.F. and our little monkeys.

'And my existence, while grotesque and incomprehensible to you, saves lives . . . You don't want the truth . . . I have neither the time nor the inclination to explain myself to a man who rises and sleeps under the blanket of the very freedom I provide, then questions the manner in which I provide it. I'd rather you just said thank you and went on your way . . .'

Colonel Nathan R. Jessup,
A Few Good Men

'The strength of the disease should be well estimated and if you see you are able to cure it, set yourself to doing so without reservation; otherwise leave it alone and attempt nothing.'

Machiavelli,
Discourses, Book 1, Chapter 33

She's barefoot.

Somewhere during the long and tortuous journey she'd lost one high heel, hadn't even noticed, had continued to stumble onwards as if afflicted with a limp and it was only after some time and when a distant, dull ache formed in her hips did she look down and see the pale and bluish skin of her left foot at odds with the dark varnish on her toenails. She'd stopped for the first time, stopped even though she was terrified of not being able to start again if she did, stopped because she had to, because her hips burned, her stomach roiled with sickness and her foot had lost all feeling so she'd placed a steadying hand against a tree, felt the rough and cold bark catch on her fingernails as if the tree wanted to keep her there, wanted to suck the last of the warmth from her body, then she'd pulled off her other shoe, thrown it aside, placed both feet on the frozen ground, the crystal-lised blades of grass crunching and crumbling beneath her, and cried again. She'd cried because – despite the drink and the drugs – what had happened was still so raw and so real yet barely believable and she'd cried for being so stupid, so naive, and she'd cried because they were her favourite shoes and she'd lost one and thrown the other away and when she'd realised she was crying about something so trivial she'd laughed, almost manically, desperately, and that had made her cry even harder. She hadn't known how long it had lasted because when she stopped it was still the blackest of black nights and time was nothing there so she'd straightened, wiped her icy hands over her face, scraped her sodden, matted hair from her eyes and pushed on.

Pushed herself on in spite of the pain in her belly and the stabs of nausea and the muffled, nagging fear that if she made it, if she got to where she wanted to go, she wouldn't know what to do anyway.

But she made it.

And now she's barefoot and standing, shivering in her little black dress, in the park across from the building. Watching the empty offices, imagining the glow from the fluorescent lights is reaching across the street to embrace her, to warm her somehow. Her scabbed and ruined feet aren't numb any more, they're just not there. She can't feel them, can't feel anything below her knees, as if her feet were lost somewhere along the way, discarded and abandoned without her noticing, just like her expensive high heels, and she marvels at it, at the irony, because on nights out she always berates other women for removing their footwear to pace along filthy streets and here she is having done exactly that.

Though not through choice.

She hasn't been allowed that luxury.

She places one unfeeling foot in front of the other and leaves the shadows of the park behind, moves through the cones of amber street light and the parked cars and the dead and chilly silence of the road then pauses at the bottom of the steps, places a shivering hand on the frosted rail, steadies herself. Breathes. Breathes deeply to calm herself. Looks up at the building, at the brightly lit sign above the entrance doors.

For a second or two she thinks about turning and limping away. Away from this place of shelter and safety. Thinks about walking, walking until somebody, anybody, finds her somewhere and holds her and wraps her in their arms and shushes her, knows instinctively what has happened, knows just what to do, tells her everything will be all right, everything will be fine now because at last her ordeal is over.

It is over.

She climbs the steps. Lifts a quivering hand to her eyes and wipes at the streaked mascara with the heel of her palm. Runs ragged nails through her blonde and grubby hair. A pathetic attempt to make her look less pathetic.

She would laugh if it wasn't all so horrible. So grotesque.

On frozen feet she ascends the steps, the ache in her hips and stomach swamped by a lurching, tumbling sensation in her chest as she finally succumbs to shock, to the cold, to the exhaustion.

She falls to her knees. Grips the metal railing.

Lifts her head, neck straining, mouth letting slip a faint whimper.

Squints at the brilliant light of the sign, the sign that was all she could think about as she forced herself onwards for miles, for hours, for ever.

The sign that reads WELCOME TO TRINITY STREET POLICE STATION.

She lowers her head and cries.

CODE 1 – ON DUTY

PS 6263L Martin Finch

Martin . . . I wish I'd tried twice as hard at everything.

His father had said it to him. Christmas Eve, six years ago.

He couldn't recall what was on the television but it had been a relief just to stare at something other than a face he didn't recognise any more. He sat next to him, had sat next to him all morning while listening to the laboured breaths, the weak chuckles that were echoes of a man long gone, chuckles that he hadn't heard in an age, that had made him want to weep. They had brought his hospice bed down into the lounge to make him more comfortable. To make *them* more comfortable. They prayed he would last until the big day. Prayed he would slip away quietly right then so he wouldn't suffer further. Felt guilty for thinking both. And all the time he had wondered how on earth this was happening to his dad.

He wished he could remember what the programme was, wished he'd taken more notice. If he could just recall what they had been watching, it would give him something good to cling on to. A memory not of narcotic analgesics, benzodiazepines and morphine hydrochloride. Not of his distended abdomen, his hairless, sickly features, his ever-decreasing bouts of lucidity. Not of seemingly endless visits from family members who spoke of him as if he were already dead.

Just a recollection of his father's hand in his, his quiet laughter, enjoying a Christmas television programme together. A moment. Something good.

Martin . . .

When his father had whispered his name he'd squeezed his cold hand. Still too frightened to look at him. At his engorged face, the listless eyes. The sallow skin. Because if you don't look, it isn't real.

I wish I'd worked twice as hard at everything.

Then he'd sighed, an almost contented sound. Martin had laced his fingers with his father's, continued watching the television. Only when his mother walked up to the bed and gave a low moan did he turn to see he'd slipped away. There was nothing there any more.

He'd held his father's hand until the programme finished.

Even now he marvelled at the randomness of it all. The cruelty. This man who'd done his thirty, who was still walking the streets on his final day, who got out clean . . . and then it took him. Like it was waiting there all along, a filthy animal crouched inside him, until he handed in his warrant card and let go. Gastrointestinal stromal tumour. It ate into his bowel, his chest. Gone, eighteen months after putting his ticket in. Eighteen months into a pension he'd worked his entire life for. At his funeral they'd lined the roadside in the drizzle, right up to the crematorium, Number One dress, tunics and white gloves and bulled boots. So many people. Too many. Uniforms spilling out of the tiny chapel, on to the grass verges, stood erect and listening as his favourite hymn wafted out of the front doors before being carried away on the January breeze.

He'd never realised how many people his father knew. How respected he was. It was the moment Martin realised what he wanted to do with his life.

He'd desperately wanted his father's collar number, had almost begged for it when, two years after his father died, he joined up. But it had long been given to another recruit.

And with that Martin knew he really was gone for ever. As if nothing he'd done ever mattered.

He saw his father in himself all the more now. Same little dark eyes in a baby face. Those thick eyebrows he hated so much, the thatch of wild black hair that he could never seem to keep under control. The squat body shape Samanya always laughed at. *You're all legs, hubby*.

Martin looked down, away from the bedroom mirror. He held the epaulettes at his midriff, one in each hand. Rubbed a thumb over a set of chevrons. His stripes. Still so new. Three silver arrows that were supposed to empower him, were meant to give him an air of authority. He slipped one on to each shoulder, fastened the buttons. Took a deep breath and looked at his reflection again. Shook his head. He didn't feel empowered: he felt a fraud, a boy pretending to be a man, and sometimes – usually in drink, and with Samanya, and when the alcohol induced a little more candour than he would have normally liked – worried that he would be found wanting when the time came.

So this is for you, Dad. Twice as hard at everything, yes?

He glanced at his watch. Nearly one p.m. Time to go.

He was checking his kitbag in the hallway, making sure the overalls, the utility belt, the flame-retardants were all in there, when the lounge door opened.

'Very smart,' Samanya said. 'I could jump you right now.'

'Why thank you,' he said. It was their joke, of course, as there was no way on this earth his wife was capable, but he grinned anyway. He tilted his head, exhaled on to one epaulette, pretended to buff it with his fingertips. His mouth felt dry. 'Very smart and very late,' he said.

Samanya stepped towards him. 'Looking forward to it?'

'Always said I like a challenge . . .'

She smiled. 'Well, I'm very proud of you, Mart. Really.'

He glanced at her as he shrugged on his civvy jacket; her dark hair was lank and greasy, her olive skin wan and bloated. She looked so tired. Fed up now. 'You're the one we should be proud of.'

'Ah,' she said, waving it away. 'Look, just enjoy it out there, okay? Show those people what you're made of.'

'Those people. Right.'

'Don't take any crap from them, that's all,' she said, moving towards the kitchen.

Martin followed her, nodding to himself. 'I'm just going to sit back and see how things go. I'd rather make my own mind up about them.'

She was pulling trays from the refrigerator, jars from cupboards, her eyes far away, ringed with dark circles. He watched as she arranged cold turkey and pickles on a plate, pulled at her bottom lip as she thought something over, then reached for tomato ketchup, chocolate biscuits, peanut butter. Thought some more. Grabbed a banana, added it to her strange buffet.

'You're the sarge,' she said, not looking at him as she buttered two slices of wholemeal bread. 'I'm sure you'll be . . . you know . . . okay . . .'

The sentence petered out as she stared at her food concoction, cocked her head, pulled at her lip again, thinking. Lay four chunks of turkey on one of the slices, spooned pickles, peanut butter, squirted ketchup, broke open the banana, chopped it into discs and placed them on to the pile. Dropped the second slice of bread on top, wielded the knife, started slicing around the sides of her sandwich.

'Crusts, yuk,' she said, then lifted the plate from the worktop triumphantly. The sandwich was fanned with chocolate biscuits; her dessert, no doubt.

'Yuk indeed.' He gave a quiet chuckle. 'I'm sure I'll be

okay too. I'm just glad we're one man down for the shift. God bless disciplinary suspensions.'

'One less for the new boy to deal with.' She smiled, drifting back towards the lounge and eyeing her Christmas leftovers.

He sighed. 'It's just a shame I couldn't bed in a bit before such a big day. The football match alone is bad enough, but with everything else . . .'

She was nodding in agreement, and gestured at his kitbag sitting at the side of the small tinselled tree they'd erected in the hallway. 'Still no locker?'

'Second day on the team,' he shrugged. 'Still a hobo.'

Samanya laughed, and he took a step towards her. She caught the look.

'I'll be fine,' she said.

'You're sure?'

'Yes, I'm sure. I've got blanky and remo at the ready.'

He glanced through the lounge door, saw the blanket splayed on the settee, the television remote control on the arm of the chair. The 20th Century Fox fanfare was blaring from the TV; a Boxing Day afternoon film was about to start and she was all set to settle down with it.

He tipped his head towards the television. 'Anything good?'

'Star Wars.'

'Original trilogy?'

'One of the prequels.'

'Oh dear.'

'Yeah,' she said, and held up the plate. 'Hence the comfort food.'

'I could stay, Sam,' he said, and brushed his fingers through her hair. 'Just in case.'

She rolled her eyes, mock-exasperated. 'You can't stay.

People are relying on you. So stop fussing and just go, will you?'

'Is that a lawful order?'

She balanced the plate on one hand, saluted with the other. He resisted the urge to point out she'd got it wrong.

'Make me proud,' she said, reaching for him with her free hand. 'Make *us* proud.'

Us. Martin placed his arms around her hips, pulled her towards him. He bent at the waist, pushed his backside out, gave her room. It was almost second nature now. It was odd, and not a little terrifying, to think that soon he would be able to hug her standing upright.

He kissed her neck, let her go. 'You'll ring me straight away?'

'Straight away,' she said.

'Is your phone charged?'

'You're going to be late, remember?'

'Promise? If anything happens?'

'Get out of here, will you?' she laughed. 'I've got a date with Jar Jar Binks.'

He placed his hands either side of her stomach, over the bump. So warm. So huge now. He looked up at Samanya, back down to her belly.

'My boy,' he said, and thought about his father again. Thought how good a father he really had been. How he wanted to be just as good to his own son.

Martin dropped his hands, hoisted his kitbag from the floor, wondered – hoped – if she'd ring in an hour, would tell him in panicked tones that her waters had broken, that he had to come home straight away, that he wouldn't have to deal with a TSG serial – the old Thick and Stupid Group – whose reputation preceded them.

Samanya was at the door and waving him off as he peeled

away from the kerb. All he could think about was the van of gorillas he was about to spend twelve hours with.

That, and something else his father had once said.

Human failings are contagious.

PC 443L Andrew Mills

For Andrew, breaking point had been reached around four hours earlier, and a mere half an hour after Claire had left the house for the shopping trip with her irritating best friend.

Never the most patient sort, Claire's children had succeeded in driving him into a murderous rage – mainly due to their inability to comply with the most simple of instructions or orders – and petrol had been added to already-roaring flames by the fact that his wife, despite him drilling it into her before she left, was now Very Fucking Late home.

As a result, he was to be late. And still nowhere near ready, being incapable of dealing with her five-year-old and three-year-old while simultaneously folding some clothes into a kitbag then taking a quick shower. He likened her offspring to demented flies, circling and bugging him all day. Stepdaddy duty, with its routine of day-glo television and garish toys and the attendant requests for biscuits, hugs, wees and poos, was a skull-crushingly boring chore. Or, as he often told Claire, tag-team mental torture: if it wasn't the girl, it was the boy under his feet and bothering him.

He had given up waiting for feelings of paternal love to emerge about a year before, around the same time – a month after their wedding, when the reality of taking on somebody else's children had finally hit home – that he'd realised marrying Claire had been a horrendous mistake. He'd been played, had been blinded by the rigorous and frequent sex

– often four or five times a day – and had grinned like a loon as he'd said *I do* to the woman he'd admired from afar for so long, almost unable to believe he'd finally captured her. She was a Bury girl, and he a Bury boy, and he'd loved her throughout their school years in Radcliffe, had loved her when he was shipped abroad to lie in sand and take potshots at towelheads for kicks, and had known he loved her still when he'd returned home and settled in Cardiff with his then-girlfriend because whenever they'd fucked he'd close his eyes and picture Claire.

It was on a rare trip up north to see his family that he'd bumped into her in their old local, his eyes widening as she appeared by his side at the bar of the Victoria. *Alraht, Andy, 'ow the bloody 'ell are ya?* she'd chuckled and for a moment he'd lost the ability to speak, such was the sheer joy that had shivered through him. He'd found his tongue eventually and they had talked, and talked, and she forgot her friends and he his, and he formed what he hoped was a solemn expression as she told him of her recently failed marriage and the bastard husband who'd left her stranded with two young children, and at the end of that night he'd found her tongue as they'd swayed in the shadows of the hanging baskets at the doorway of the pub and he'd ordered – nay, commanded – himself that he would never let her go again.

The stupidity of it all – his stupidity at being suckered – made him angry the moment he opened his eyes each morning, and the fury only grew throughout the day.

And he was so late. Late and working on Boxing Day. And it was the local derby match, Cardiff and Swansea, the Bluebirds versus the Jacks, notorious for problems and already listed as Category CIR. Plus they'd had intel about some kind of demo so it was all likely to go, as Andrew called it, *rather bendy*. Furthermore, the briefing was at four and he'd wanted to arrive in good time to pitch up at the gym for their regulation training hour, quickly followed by securing some decent refs; if late, the divisional plods on backfill were likely to scoff the best of it.

Then there was the bingo. If he missed that he truly would go postal.

All these thoughts were whirring around Andrew's primary-colour-addled brain, further confusing an already permanently confused mind, when he heard a familiar engine noise and *squee* of brakes. His anger grew; he peeked out of the window, hands on head, fingernails scratching at the stubbled dome of his buzz cut, and watched as Claire tried to reverse their car on to the hardstand outside the house. One, two, three attempts. Four. With each crunch of gears and pathetic, erroneous readjustment, her silhouette wrenching at the steering wheel, he could feel his blood pressure rise higher still – until finally she gave up and abandoned the car with one wheel on the weed-ridden lawn.

He watched, vaguely aware of his right eye twitching uncontrollably, as she walked up the drive, juggling bags. The happy shopper with her post-Christmas goodies. Already spunking his cash. The bank holiday cash he was about to earn. Her retail therapy. Her MasterCard makeover.

Priceless.

He was waiting at the front door for her. 'For Christ's sake.'

'*Forkrice sake*,' his stepdaughter mimicked. 'Hiya, Mummy.'

Andrew watched as Milly pirouetted, humming to herself. He was annoyed with himself for recognising the tune: *Toy Story*'s 'You've Got a Friend in Me'. He'd played the film on a loop all day, hoping it would entertain or at the very least distract the kids while he fucked about on the Internet, but the ruse had failed spectacularly: they'd treated it as background music, an accompaniment to their terrorising, with the net result that Randy Newman was now lodged permanently, maddeningly, between his ears.

Claire eyeballed him. He backed his gangly frame into the lounge, the bristles of their fake Christmas tree digging into his backside as he brushed against it; he heard a faint tinkle from one of the pound-store ornaments that hung from its branches.

She dumped the bags. 'For Christ's sake what?' she shrieked. 'What's the problem now?'

Neither child registered any surprise or upset at the outburst.

'Half one,' he shouted and shifted his sleeve back, looked at his wrist. There was no watch there but that wasn't the point. 'It's half past fuckin' one, woman. What the fuck?'

'Oooh,' said Milly, sitting on the settee. 'Andy, you swore again.'

'Fuck,' said Tom, hanging off Andrew's legs and tugging on his jogging pants.

'It's Boxing Day,' Claire said.

Well, that's all right then, he thought. *Silly me.* 'I've got to work.'

'Well, blame your lot for closing off half the roads in the city. And it was the bloody sales, okay?' She pointed at the bags, smiled at the children. 'You've got to see. Come on. Some of the stuff there I wouldn't normally dream of buying, but when it's twenty per cent off you've got to give it a go, haven't ya?'

Course you have, love.

The children squealed, ran to her. She pulled out clothes, accessories, make-up, shoes. Shoes just like the pair she already had upstairs. The ones she'd worn twice. A tiny backpack for Tom. Toy jewellery for Milly. Andrew waited. Waited for something. Claire kissed the children. They hugged her. They laughed together. She rummaged in the last bag. Her face lit up. He held his breath, the fury subsiding a little.

Claire pulled out a magazine. 'And this is for Mummy to read in the bath later. Heaven . . .'

'That's lovely,' Andrew said, finding it increasingly difficult to speak. 'Give me the keys.'

'Let me just put this stuff aw—'

'Now.'

'Don't talk to me like that, please.'

Here we go. Here we fucking go again. More insubordination.

He grabbed her arm. Dragged her into the hallway. She struggled. Tried to pull free. The children were still in the lounge with their gifts, so that was okay. He didn't want them watching. Watching him stamp his authority. *Who does she think she is? Rocking up late. Late, with nothing for me. Look at the trouble she's caused again.*

He took a good handful of hair. A dirty-blonde knot in his fist. Twisted it, pulled her down and on to the stairs. *Sit. Stop your squealing.* He bent at the waist. Pushed his face into hers. Felt the heat of her skin. Heard her quick breaths.

'Be home on fuckin' time next time,' he told her. He tried not to raise his voice. Kept it low. He was mindful of the kids. More menacing too. Always a bonus.

'Let go of me, Andy.' Her face flushed, sweating. Eyes closed.

'If you'd just do as you were told, woman,' he whispered, teeth bared, 'then I wouldn't have to keep doing this.'

He gave the hair one last yank. Let go. Pushed her head away from his.

'Gimme the keys,' he said, and gave her a quick dig in the belly. She *oof*ed. A barely audible sob as the air rushed from her lungs.

Better there, darling. Nobody can see the bruises.

Andrew snatched the keys from her shaking hand, left her on the bottom step. The naughty step. He walked upstairs, opened his kitbag, checked his Level Ones. The overalls stinking. He'd forgotten to make her wash them after last week's public order training. The petrol bombs and shield cordons at the old RAF base. Lobbing bricks at the SMT. A right giggle, he'd thought at the time. Only problem was now he'd smell like a burnt tramp for the rest of the day.

He had a quick shower and shave. Slipped on clean under-wear and socks. Grabbed his kit. Waved to the kids. Ignored his wife ignoring him. Left.

Loping across the lawn, Andrew speed-dialled the man. 'Yo, Vincenzo!' he said.

Vincent sounded slightly miffed. And slightly out of breath. Then he got it.

'No way,' he said into the phone. 'Now? Are you serious?'

Vincent was serious.

'You're fuckin' insane,' he laughed, licking at his uneven front teeth as he pictured his colleague. 'Yeah . . . yeah. Enjoy. But you'd better be quick. And I want the full griff when I see you, right—'

Vincent had cut him off, and he felt slightly wounded about it for a second or two, but consoled himself with the thought of sitting next to his bestest bud for a shift, shooting the shit and putting the world to rights: a taste of how it used to be back in the day with the guys on the unit, when things had been more regimented, more ordered, when he'd known his place and what he had to do, before life had become horribly confusing and terribly disorganised. Before Claire.

Andrew slipped into the car, dropped the mobile phone on to the passenger seat, patted his overalls pocket: the notepad and pen were there, ready.

'Fuck It and Drive On,' he said to himself, the old unofficial army motto.

He started the engine, accelerated away.

Three hours to bullshit bingo.

PC 3301L David Murphy

David sounded the car's horn and braced himself.

He'd got the call from him that morning, was caught off guard, quite probably still drunk from the colossal amount of single malt he'd sunk the previous day. A fair and troubling distance from the town of Lucid, he'd said, *Yeah, no problem, Al, you can grab a lift with me*. It was only as he was putting down the phone that the enormity of it had set in and he'd winced, sinking back in the settee, wondering how on earth he was going to kill forty minutes in the car with Dullas.

Five years working together but other than at incidents he'd never spent any time alone with him. Just the two of them, stripped of the faux matey facade the uniform seemed to carry with it. No beers on rest days, no doubling-up for cinema trips or an evening at a restaurant with their respective wives. No sitting on a riverbank together, pretending to fish while they bitched about the latest phoney stat-fiddling diktat from senior management up at the Dream Factory of HQ.

Paired up in the van, surrounded with equipment and radios telling them where to go, and they were fine. Buddies in the work environment. There was that bond. The siege mentality. The small talk at boring firearms incidents, the ribbing each other as they POLSA-searched a murder scene, the war stories at demos while ducking the lukewarm piss-filled Coke bottles the dog-on-a-string crusties were lobbing at the front lines of the cordon. Take that away and . . .

Alan Redding.

The most boring, tedious man in Christendom.

Known less than fondly as Dullas. Because . . . well, because he was dull as fuck.

He watched Alan skulk down the oh-so-clean driveway that cut the neat lawn in two, the pathway edged by carefully trimmed miniature hedging. Mr Average Suburbanite with his nondescript features and inoffensive haircut, his unremarkable frame wrapped in a thick coat and jumper. On the low garden wall, facing out into the street, was a sign that read THOU SHALT NOT PARK HERE. To lower the chances of grumbles of complaint he brushed the pasty flakes from his belly, quickly scooped up food wrappers and drinks cartons that littered the footwells, and braced himself for his colleague's opening burst of good humour and festive cheer.

Alan slumped into the passenger seat, closed the door, said nothing. *Oh dear.* David spied a hideous Christmas jumper lurking beneath Alan's civvy jacket: a chunky woollen effort in emerald green, with delightfully jovial snowmen ringing the waist area. The happy faces were decidedly at odds with their wearer's expression. Woven into the fabric was a phrase, partially obscured by Alan's coat:

> esus
> s for life
> ot just fo
> hristma

David decided not to comment.

'Good day yesterday, Al?' he asked, and glanced towards the rear seat. His own jumper lay there, a bloody crimson horror, reindeer pattern knitted into the chest. His present from the kids, one he'd unwrapped before quickly producing the rictus grin he saved for such occasions where running – screaming – from the room would be frowned upon. He'd worn it to the car, waved as he'd pulled away from the house, checked the rear-view mirror to be sure his brood had disappeared inside then stopped in the middle of the road. Off came the reindeer, tossed into the back. As he'd resumed driving, he'd made a mental note to slip the thing on before he got home. He pictured it: walking in at half two in the morning, no jumper, one of his munchkins wandering about looking for a drink of water and seeing him *sans* present . . .

His wife Sandra was a ripe and volatile brunette who, until they closed the place down, had graced the bar on the top floor of Markham police station, her plentiful breasts regularly and pleasingly separated by the shaft of the Brains beer pump as she poured pints for the off-duty – and sometimes still on-duty – coppers. This was before David wooed her with the promise of a better life, whisking her gold lamé sandals down a narrow gap between the chairs of the local registry office. Like him, she'd gone a few tumultuous rounds but was yet to be knocked to the canvas for the full ten-count. He saw himself in her, and was smitten. Sandra doted on their children, repeatedly telling David she would kill for them if necessary. She said this with such conviction that he often considered her ready to plunge a fork into his eyeball if he deigned to raise his voice to them, so she would be less than pleased if he upset the children over the season to be jolly, of all times.

It wasn't worth thinking about, and besides, he couldn't afford to get divorced. Again. There were two Christmases to go before he escaped the job, and he had no intention of losing yet another chunk of his pension for services rendered.

Alan yawned. 'Good service, if that's what you mean.'

David resisted the urge to blurt *God-botherer*. He'd meant nothing of the sort; he'd been thinking whisky, a turkey the size of an emu, dozing through the Queen's speech before drinking yourself into a drooling semi-coma. Drinking until he was incapable of, as Sandra frequently put it when dissatisfied with his bedtime performance, *getting any wind in it*. A traditional family Christmas.

'Right,' David said. 'And sorry about . . . you know.'

Alan was silent, staring at his house. The Redding family car sat on the driveway, a black plastic sack taped across the driver's side window. David gently pressed the accelerator, hoping the revving engine would snap his companion out of his little fugue state.

'"Every sin brings its punishment with it,"' Alan said.

David tried not to groan. 'Take much?'

'The usual. Radio, CDs. Had a go at the steering.'

'Window'll cost you a pretty penny.'

Alan looked at him, his neck colouring. '*Really*. Thank you for that, David.'

With Alan it was always *David*. He wished he would just call him Dave, or even Flub like everybody else, but the inability to refer to anyone by anything other than their *complete first name* was, along with his aversion to robust language, another one of Alan's peculiarities.

'Sector lads all over it?' David asked.

Alan shrugged. 'Didn't tell them I was job.'

'Why not?'

'Why bother? They thought I was just a MOP so gave me the usual flannel about increasing patrols in the community and getting CSI down to dust and dab, but you know it won't come to anything. I just wish . . . Christmas, you know? Why Christmas of all times? I've got . . . I've got enough on my mind as it is, so this . . .'

Alan was eyeballing his house again. David waited for him to finish. He didn't.

David exhaled. 'Shall we rock and roll?'

'She's stopped eating chocolate.'

'Chocolate?'

'Chocolate. Stopped. She loves her chocolate.'

David shook his head. 'What are you talking about, Dullas?'

'Please don't call me that. I've told you all not to call me that.'

But we do, thought David. *When you're not in the room, anyway.* 'Sorry, Al. It's just you're not making much sen—'

'Lisa. I'm talking about Lisa.'

'Erm . . . that's a good thing, isn't it?' If David was blunt about it, Alan's wife was a tad on the heavy side last time he saw her. *Then again*, he thought, patting the mound of flab that hung over his trousers, *who am I to talk?*

Alan turned to him. 'Is it, David? Is it really? Don't you know?'

'Know what?' David caught himself grinding his teeth.

Alan looked up, probably towards his beloved deity of choice. 'It's a *sex substitute*,' he said. 'The chemicals and all that. The *chemicals*.'

David just let it hang there. 'I really don't know what to say, Alan. Is there a point to this?'

'It means she doesn't need chocolate any more. Don't you get it? Don't you?' Alan turned away, checked his house again.

'Well, good for you,' David said, hoping it was the right thing to come out with while wishing they could move on to a topic that he actually understood. Hell, he'd even go for a bit of religion right about now. 'Keep her sweet and all that.'

Yet Alan was silent again, pique over, staring out the window at his damaged car, at the front of his home. *He's worse than ever today*, thought David. *At least he didn't have to spank the plastic for three ex-wives and Chrimbo presents for five kids*. He could strangle the shits that put in Alan's car window. Rather than suffer the atmosphere further he turned on the radio and pulled away from the kerb.

'All this,' Alan was muttering. 'All this and a new sergeant.'

On this point they were in agreement. 'Yarp,' said David. 'Don't know what the job's coming to. He seems all right but . . . he's just too young to be an onion. And so *tiny*.'

Alan was staring at him. '"All right"? We met him four days ago. For one shift. An hour touring the city centre in the van then he cleared off upstairs for tea and buns with the inspector. I'm starting to wish Jim had never retired.'

David eased the car on to the ring road that headed towards the city centre. 'You? Missing the old stripy? Bugger me.'

'We didn't see eye to eye, granted. But this kid they've shunted on to the group . . . Give me Jim and his juvenile ways over an onion bhaji who looks like he should be revising for his O levels.'

'They don't do O levels any more.'

'You know what I mean, pedant.'

David smiled, more at the memory of Jim and his *juvenile ways* than Alan's description of their new *sargey*. Like the time Alan returned from leave to find a dead and particularly fragrant rabbit hanging by its neck in his locker, Jim having run it over with the van on a night shift a week earlier. The times Jim would turn Alan's locker upside down just because he was bored. And the numerous times he'd place Alan's Tupperware tub – sandwiches, yogurt, fruit and all, meticulously prepared by his wife – into the microwave while Alan was in the traps having, as he called it, *a movement* and heat it on high power for five minutes, gleefully clapping his hands as an incandescent Alan pulled out the resulting sludge of plastic and scorched banana skin. Then when he'd moan they would cackle and shout out in unison: *It's not bullying, it's character building!*

'Anyway, think how useful he could be,' smiled David. 'Get him into the pub after work, I could rest my pint on his head while I play the fruity.'

'It's not funny.'

'He won't be around long enough to cause any bother. Six months, tops.'

'Six months is a long time,' Alan said, and there was something in his voice that made David wonder if they were still talking about the same thing. He was gazing out of the window once more. 'A lot can change . . .'

Balls to a fine for speeding, David thought, accelerating to sixty in a thirty zone.

He tried to improve the mood. 'Couple of beers at Lewis's later to Stella-brate twelve hours of double bubble, you'll be feeling a lot more chipper.'

'We'll have to dump the new boy,' Alan muttered, breath fogging the glass. 'We don't even know him. We take him to Tackleberry's house party while on duty, he'll be reporting us to PSD at the first opportunity.'

'We'll sort something.' David nodded, drumming his fingers on the steering wheel as he waited at a junction for a green. 'Kids enjoy themselves yesterday?'

Alan rubbed at his eyes. 'Lisa's parents picked them up

for an overnighter just before you arrived. We've got family around tomorrow so she's . . . cleaning.'

David chuckled. 'Wish I could offload my youngest two for an afternoon. I'm sick of Disney cartoons and bloody squeaky-clean heroines. I'm actually looking forward to mixing with the public just so I can feel a little grubby.'

'Clean is good,' Alan said, so quietly David had to turn off the radio to hear the rest of it. 'Belle in *Beauty and the Beast*, Snow White . . . women of virtue. Proverbs thirty-one – "a wife of noble character . . . she is worth far more than rubies".'

David squeezed the wheel. 'I've told you, mate, the only time I do God is when I've got to give evidence in Crown and only then to make the jury think I'm telling the truth. But I would do that Belle bird. Very nice indeed.'

Alan was looking at him now. 'But she's a cartoon character.'

'And you wouldn't?'

'It's a ridiculous suggestion,' Alan said, flapping his hands about.

'Come *on*,' David laughed. 'You would, wouldn't you? If she was real? A delicate virgin type, with that singing? Imagine her belting out those hymns you love . . .'

David felt he might faint when Alan cracked a reluctant smile.

'She is rather attractive, I must admit,' said Alan.

'I knew it. Who else? Snow White, yeah? Come on, we've got to have three. You know what Vince says: always choose three women to work on, and you can guarantee you'll go home with one of them. It's the Rule of Three.'

'It's nonsense.'

'I bet you'd do Snow White.'

Alan closed his eyes. 'Yes,' he whispered. 'And . . . Ariel.'

'You talking about the fish?'

'She's a little mermaid, actually. A very pretty little mermaid.'

'Mate, whatever. But, you know, there are going to be complications with her. Know what I mean? You and . . . a mermaid? It's just not going to work out.'

'David, you're talking about me sleeping with cartoon characters. It's absurd enough as it is. So does it really matter if one is a mermaid or not?'

The car slowed, David dropping down the exit ramp from the ring road and towards the city. 'Fine,' he said. 'That's our three then. Belle, Snow White and that mermaid thing.'

'It's *Ariel*, she's not a *thing*.' Alan was almost shouting. 'All right, bloody hell. Calm down. Ariel it is.'

David agreed with him, though.

She was pretty tasty for a fish.

PC 1219L Alan Redding

It was already busy.

Already chaos. The Civic Centre full of plod.

Personnel carriers. Minivans. Prisoner vans. Pandas. Spotter wagons. CCTV trucks. Horse boxes. Dog vans. Shake-and-bake mobile tea trailers.

Response officers on cancelled rest days. Beat bobbies. Neighbourhood teams. The black rats of the traffic department. Mutual aid vans drafted in from neighbouring forces. The force chopper circling overhead. PCSOs. Specials. Mounted. Medics. PSUs. FITs. ARVs. EGTs. Tac advisors. The other TSG units. Dog handlers with their snarling land sharks. Bosses with their fake grins and limp handshakes. Fluorescent tabards. Armadillo long riot shields. Round riot shields. Kitbags and batons and public order gear everywhere. Hundreds of officers, gathered in groups and cliques, stamping feet in the cold, outdoing each other with war stories as lukewarm tea was gulped from polystyrene cups.

Alan had been in the job for twenty-two years and still couldn't get over the resources deployed to deal with a bunch of frustrated white-collar workers out to get their kicks. Those estate agents who understandably hated themselves. Frustrated bank workers who despised their bosses and bottled their anger ready for Saturday afternoons. The call centre supervisors, those cubicle monkeys who did the hard sell for your car insurance, your personal loan, your satellite television package or mobile phone, those people whom you loathed and they knew it, who loathed you, and themselves, every single minute of their miserable working lives. In a few hours they would be here. Descending upon the city centre, shirts and ties swapped for casual gear, for loose-fit denims, puffa jackets, baseball caps. Burberry scarves to hide their faces, mobile phones to arrange the meet.

The Civic Centre closed off, the city centre shut down, just for a football match.

Everything, everyone else, disrupted. Road closures. Diversions. There was never this fuss for rugby. It wouldn't be needed. And it left everywhere else empty, of course. No plod anywhere. He pitied the poor woman out in the suburbs who would step through her front door this evening to find some crackhead rifling through her jewellery.

Don't call us, madam. We ain't got anyone to send.

As if the derby match with its *increased risk of disorder* wasn't enough to contend with, the spooks at the regional Counter Terrorism Unit had provided wonderful news: analysis of *soshul meeja* had uncovered plans for a large-scale demonstration outside the stadium.

Alan rubbed at his eyes, wishing he'd called in sick, or opted for the day off instead of double time for the bank holiday shift.

I should be at home, he thought.

David was navigating the rows of police vehicles, still muttering about the Rule of Three. He had moved on to actresses, and was vacillating between two for his final slot, because '*Jolie's clearly a crazy cow, she'd let you do all sorts, the dirty mare, but Aniston is obviously a good girl, shit actress but a good girl and I think she's the type that if you were lucky and you scored she'd look after you for the rest of your days, it's just a shame about that shovel face of hers*' and Alan just nodded and tried to tune him out.

David banged the steering wheel. 'Decision made.'

'Oh good,' said Alan.

'Forget those two. Lindsay, innit? Old Li-Lo?'

'Li-Lo. Right.'

'Now she's as dirty as the Jolie girl and likes a beer or nine so will get you into the good Hollywood parties. And the clincher? *Bisexual*. Just picture it: you, Li-Lo, one of her girl pals, you'd be swimming in bodily fluids, mate. Can you picture it?'

David was beaming.

'Yes. It's a joyous mental image,' said Alan.

'Sweet, right?'

'Like nectar. We're here, by the way.'

David grunted, snapping himself out of his daydream where, Alan assumed, he was engaged in an unlikely *ménage à trois*, and steered his car towards the road closure.

'Looky looky, here's one of your friends,' David said.

Alan eyed the PCSO, some skinny kid of about nineteen in an ill-fitting uniform, standing in front of the row of police cones. He felt a flicker of anger, of frustration, but the emotion was quickly swept away by a profound sense of pointlessness at railing against it all.

David seemed keen for him to bite, though.

'It's a plastic plod,' he said, nudging Alan's ribs with an elbow. 'Attack, Al.'

Alan watched the badly dressed PCSO trudge towards the car.

'No? Blunkett's Bobby? C-3PO?' David was wittering. 'Come on, Al, you're normally straining at the leash when you see one.'

'My bothered bag is empty.'

'But it's a PCSO. Police constable's stolen overtime? Go for him, mate.'

The community support officer was at David's window, his malformed forehead pressing up against the glass as he scrutinised the car's occupants.

Alan sighed. Thought of Lisa at home alone. 'Just let the scales fall from your eyes. Pretty soon there will be more of them than there are of us. And then the MOPs will have something to complain about.'

David held up his warrant card to the kid gurning through the glass. The PCSO hovered for a moment before shuffling back to the line of cones, adjusted his uniform trousers at the crotch in full view of a dozen senior officers who would never take him to task, then moved one of the cones aside and waved them through.

The basement car park, the underbelly of the nick. Drab concrete struts, air-con ducts, electrical cabling, NO SMOKING signs. Water dripped from above; the floor was flooded again. All the bays bar one were full, so David abandoned the car in it: the slot normally reserved for the chief inspector of the Minorities Support and Diversity Unit.

'Not like she'll need it today,' David said, killing the engine. 'Hasn't worked a Christmas or weekend since her probation. Fuckin' ESSO rankers.'

'Careful,' Alan said to him. 'There's the boy.'

David followed Alan's nod of the head. The new sergeant was waiting at the foot of the steps that led up to the locker room with its compact but filthy gymnasium, where it had already been agreed – during the hour the new boy spent with them on the last shift – that the team would meet to get a little exercise in to warm up and, Alan worried, *bond*.

Alan thought Martin looked about thirteen. Fresh-faced and innocent. With peculiarly bushy eyebrows. His gear was piled at his feet – kitbag, NATO helmet, PPE.

'Bit keen, isn't he?' whispered David, hoisting his canvas bag from the boot.

'Hit-the-ground-running type,' Alan said. 'In early, get on the front foot.'

'Yeah,' David muttered. 'A tosser.'

They walked towards Martin, who raised a hand.

'All right there, Sarge?' David smiled, and Alan looked at him in disbelief.

'Okay, boys?' Martin grinned, giving Alan's Christmas jumper a quick once-over.

Boys? thought Alan, gesturing at the ridiculous pile of personal protection equipment leaning against the kid's knee; he had far more than was necessary for today's gig. 'No locker to store your stuff yet?'

'Ah,' Martin said, laughing oddly and waving the question away.

Alan waited, but the kid said nothing else.

David swiped his fingers at his chest, clearing a stray flake of pasty. 'Must be an unlocked one somewhere up at HQ. Or half empty, at least. When we get back there tomorrow you can bin any kit that's left inside, use it yourself. RHIP and all that.'

Martin screwed up his face. '"RHIP"?'

Alan and David exchanged a look.

'Rank has its privilege, Sarge,' said Alan, shaking his head. 'You know?'

'I'll be fine,' Martin chuckled, that weird snort of a laugh again. Alan could hear the boy's dry tongue clicking against the roof of his mouth and knew he was nervous. The sergeant turned to him, caught Alan staring.

David looked him up and down. It didn't take long. 'Not planning on staying around then?' he smiled.

Martin gave those thick eyebrows a quick twitch and

laughed along as he glanced back and forth at the older men. Then nobody said anything. His inane chuckling petered out and he looked down at the waterlogged floor.

'Don't worry,' said David. 'Thrush'll be here soon. Bit of time lifting some iron and then he'll make us all a nice brew before the nonsense starts.'

Alan was already making his way up the steps, fiddling with his redundant car keys in one pocket. If his own car had been there he would have skipped the weights and the kitting-up, skipped the bingo and driven back to the house. Nobody would notice if he was missing for an hour.

Nobody really notices me anyway, he thought.

There was a familiar high-pitched whine; Alan knew Andrew was about to scream down the ramp – late again, which would set him off from the outset – and still hadn't fixed the fan belt on his useless car. He pushed open the locker-room door, David following, the new onion behind him and asking cheerfully, 'Why Thrush?' and David saying, 'It's because Andrew's an irritating cunt,' the boy not laughing this time.

Alan opened his kitbag. Fished out his wallet. Eyed the photographs slotted into the front sleeve. 'Everything will be fine, Alan,' he promised himself in a whisper. He said it again, and again. 'We are two become one flesh, okay? And "what God has joined together let man not separate".' He slipped Lisa's photo out of its compartment, touched it to his forehead, felt its tacky surface stick to his skin, closed his eyes. He was vaguely aware of people standing behind him. Knew they were watching. Found it hard to care.

'"Because marriage should be held in honour among all,"' Alan breathed, '"and let the marriage bed be undefiled, for He will judge the sexually immoral and adulterous."'

He heard the boy's voice, quiet and concerned and not a little anxious: 'Is he okay?'

Alan opened his eyes. Stared at Lisa's photograph. That easy, contented smile, the like of which he hadn't seen for so long. His head swam.

'Yeah,' said David, seemingly from far away now. 'He's just having a bad day.'

Alan knew it. Swore to himself.

Everything would be fine.

PC 88L Vincent Vinyard

Vincent thought: *I'm looking pretty good here.*

He'd been a little concerned after gorging yesterday: alone again for Christmas, just like he'd wanted it, maxing out on booze and junk food and junkier television, a rare day letting everything go, letting everything out, where nobody told him what he could or couldn't do. Thinking of Christmases with his parents, working through those memories of his dear old mother short of a skag fix and clucking, his old man on the sauce and pacing, hands clenched into fists before the first presents had been opened . . .

Vincent knew he'd be missing the workout with the team at Trinity Street nick so had risen early, beasting himself at an empty gym. Cardio work, mostly. Thirty minutes on the treadmill, on an incline at maximum speed for an intense all-over workout. Rowing machine at full tilt for another thirty. Cooled down with a two-kilometre static cycle ride. Honed his rectus abdominis and external obliques with crunches, sit-ups, twists. Eased off with a ton of leg raises. He had to keep his body fat percentage down. Keep that eight-pack ripped and tight. It was the only way he could see what he was doing properly.

His skin looked mighty fine; the self-tan was working a treat. Vincent was more than a little sceptical when Herc recommended it, given that most of what the guy said was bunk and any gear he sold in the gym was usually weak East European knock-off stuff, like that counterfeit Winstrol that made everyone's tits tender. Vincent especially liked the tan's colour dial: twist the cap to get the right shade. Brilliant. Topped with a handful of Imedeen Tan Optimizer capsules and he was glowing. He felt lovely, and couldn't stop looking at himself in the mirrors on the dressing table, which was always a plus when he was struggling.

Like he was right now.

He drifted.

Thought about the supermarket.

A month ago.

Jingles playing like they had been since early October. Tinsel in the hair and hats of the staff. The rows of seasonal offerings, the crackers and streamers and booze and party food, stacked high and screaming at him. In his left hand he'd held an inedible fusion of water, twenty-four per cent tomato, reconstituted beef, hydrogenated vegetable oil, salt, flavour enhancers, stabilisers, emulsifier, ascorbyl anti-oxidants, all the E numbers you could dream of. A convenient, microwave-friendly feast for the abandoned.

His right hand had gripped a pathetic noodle meal. Ready-made. Cooked, blast-dried in a protective atmosphere, may contain traces of nuts. Sucked of any calorific value and ordering him to be good to himself. The instructions were simple: just add hot water and stir for effect.

The irony had not been lost on him.

The aisle, the store, that cavernous hellhole of fluorescent strip lights and catatonic shoppers, the PA bleeding Christmas tunes that stabbed at his eardrums. He'd been there because he had to be. Standing next to the refrigerated mausoleum for once-nutritious foodstuffs because he'd known it was time to move on.

It had been just after lunchtime; her timing was impeccable, her routine completely predictable. She'd stepped into the far end of the ready-meal aisle, knuckles white as she gripped the trolley. Ring on her finger, clothing cheap. Chain-store items that aimed to replicate the Pradas, the Jimmy Choos, the Westwoods – the things she'd once taken for granted and which now, thanks to her underachieving husband, she could only covet – and to the trained eye failed miserably. The trolley had been loaded with organic this and premium that, a nod to better days and which he knew she'd be hitting the credit cards for. Her children buzzed around her calves and Vincent had watched as her pinched, exhausted face scanned the shelves. Already he knew her life: one of appointments she had to keep for others, of quick and easy fixes, of responsibility, of drudgery and self-neglect.

She was the loneliest woman in the building.

In that aisle and searching for something.

Something for herself.

Something easy.

He'd paused as she noticed him, saw the flicker of recognition, the glimpse at the carefully selected cardboard-covered chilli in his left hand; she remembered him from a week earlier, in that very aisle, when she was with that morose and wearisome husband of hers, when Vincent had been on an errand for Lucy, and when he had engaged her – effortlessly charmed her under her other half's nose – in conversation about some triviality he could not recall.

Before he'd dropped the junk food back to the shelf Vincent had hesitated long enough to make it seem as if he were thinking it through, actually wrestling over which disgusting faux gastro meal to purchase in order to make his life that little bit easier. It had worked. He'd seen it in her eyes. They were kindred spirits. Casualties of failed or miserable marriages: weary, alone, desperate.

Vulnerable.

He'd looked directly at her, dipped his head ever so slightly, just a hint of a nod. She'd caught it, had glanced down at her offspring then given him a shrug and a tired smile.

What can you do? it said.

But it said more. And Vincent had known what he could do. How easy it would be. He'd stepped closer to her.

Are you who I think you are? he had asked.

And that was all it took.

Of course, Vincent still had The Lucy Problem. He'd driven home straight after sealing the deal with the woman in the supermarket.

It didn't end well. Lucy had cried, standing in their hallway. Her green eyes bulbous. Pale grey snot oozing from one nostril. Handmade Christmas cards Blu-tacked to the wall, her children's comically deformed snowmen and misspelt greetings hovering behind her.

What d'you mean, it's over? she'd asked him.

I'm losing myself, he had told her, before looking down for a moment. Her tears, glistening between their feet on the wood floor. Vincent's bags at his heel.

Lucy had used both hands, clenched to fists, to beat at her own chest. Her voice had risen to a shriek: *Losing yourself in what? What the fuck is that supposed to mean, Vince?*

He'd looked at the woman he'd shared his life with for a year and forced himself to feel nothing. It was always better that way. Better for him, anyway.

Lucy had grabbed at his upper arms; he remembered feeling the throb of desperation as her fingers dug at his flesh. *Please. Please, Vince. What's going on?*

He was an automaton. Removed. *There's someone else,* he'd said, and not for the first time he had marvelled at how coolly, how cruelly, the devastating sentence slipped from between his lips.

Lucy had recoiled, hands falling away from him. Her head had dropped.

'No,' she'd said, as if that one word, her blunt denial, would make everything right again. Vincent had known without reservation that it wouldn't. When he said nothing Lucy had looked up, face creased with anger. 'You swore to me,' she'd said. 'You told me you'd never do this to anyone again. After everything I've done for you . . .'

And Vincent had thought about that. He really had, standing there with her in the hallway. He'd thought of their time together and what the woman had done for him. His eyes had closed and he'd seen images of her children. He'd remembered how she had coaxed and cajoled them to like him, even love him over time. How she had rebuilt her life around him. How he became the paterfamilias.

He'd opened his eyes. Lucy's mouth had been moving but he heard nothing. It hadn't been her fault, him leaving. It's not you, it's me. Better to leave before the kids loved him too much, before he really hurt them. And he hadn't trusted himself not to. He'd shuffled towards the front door, knowing he would not see Lucy, or her children, again. To smother the odd ache he had felt in his stomach he'd pushed down on his diaphragm as if to curtail a bothersome fit of hiccups.

You Judas, Vince. Yes you.

He wasn't willing to lose himself in her any more. He had needed to move on, to be cleansed, to make amends. As he'd opened Lucy's front door and stepped out into the November chill he'd thought of the woman from the supermarket. With her, he'd the chance to start afresh.

To make everything all right again.

Flash-forward a week after leaving Lucy.

A restaurant.

Dimly lit, white stucco walls, heavy wooden tables laden with flaccid crackers, a guitar-strumming greaseball crooning ghastly carols into a microphone in one corner. Vincent couldn't remember if he had chosen the place because the gloom masked how cheap and dirty it was, or because it meant Supermarket Girl couldn't see his expression of self-loathing.

She had talked with her mouth full of pasta, excited about being out alone for the first time in whenever. Vincent had watched with mild disgust as her crooked teeth chewed at the penne, half listened to the redundant but interminable anecdotes of her offspring.

He'd suffered it. The gag-inducing niceties. The vacuous small talk. He'd tolerated those torturous moments because they were always the path to better things, to the pay-off. He'd nodded agreeably to whatever inanity she was spouting, and while she prodded at her food had allowed himself to glaze over then decide that this one wasn't worth the aggravation. One night out to hook her and from then on it was business only. *You are my convenience meal*, he'd thought while watching her . . .

Vincent's mobile rang, jarring him from his memories.

Right in the middle of everything.

'Yo, Vincenzo!' Thrush bellowed in his ear.

Vincent brushed him off. Ended the call. Threw his phone back to the bed.

He was struggling here as it was.

'Who was that?' she asked.

He'd forgotten where he was for a while.

What he was doing.

'Work,' he said, and continued working. His concentration

was slipping. He was losing rhythm. Falling out of the groove. He checked the mirrors again. Saw his bronzed arse, his thighs. He loved the way his buttocks moved, how sharp and beautiful they were, carved like the cheekbones of a pubescent, heroin-chic supermodel. And sitting above them were the *pièce de résistance* of his abdominals. His eight-pack. Flat, delineated.

Vincent found it hard to understand why people let themselves go. It wasn't rocket science. Eat less. Train more. Eat right. Train smart. Look after yourself. A couple of salads wouldn't hurt. He looked down at her, pushing herself back on to him. The marbled whiteness of her legs and back. On all fours and . . . juddering. She certainly hadn't looked that poor in the supermarket but Vincent supposed clothing could hide a multitude of sins.

'Oh my,' she breathed. 'I think I'm coming.'

Really? thought Vince. *How nice. Because I'm going. Soon. I'm late.*

'Yes. That's it. My God. My God . . .'

He watched, as if from a distance, as her necklace swung beneath her neck, the pendant hitting the pillow she was in danger of swallowing. St Christopher. The patron saint of travel. Of bachelors. *How apt*, he thought, and briefly pictured Lucy again, grizzling as he'd walked out of her life.

He was bored now. To amuse himself he timed his thrusts to each of the woman's cries but nothing was happening; she'd squeezed out a couple of puppies in her time so was a bit roomy down there and he couldn't get any purchase.

Exercise, woman. Whatever happened to pelvic floor work?

Vincent slapped her pasty buttocks, contemplated jamming a thumb into her tea towel holder. Raising the stakes and making things a little nasty. A little more exciting.

But no. It was early days with this woman and he didn't want to scare her away just yet.

He turned and watched himself in the mirror. On his knees, the pale heifer in front of him, jiggling and wobbling, his light brown hips thrusting at her. He slowed it down so he could scrutinise his work, study himself, and it was only then that he got that tingle in the pit of his belly so he latched on to that feeling and moved up a gear, caressed his flanks, tweaked his nipples, pulled hard on his scrotum and then she was wailing and shuddering, telling him 'I've come, I've come, oh God that was so good' and Vincent was still watching himself, touching himself and then it was there, he was done, at last, and he pistoned into her, hard, to celebrate then kneaded her doughy arse cheeks until she gave a ridiculous squeal.

It feels so . . . he thought. *I feel so* . . .

Vincent stared at his reflection.

Stared for a long time.

He didn't know how he felt any more.

BOXING DAY, 1411HRS

She weaves through the crowd, the pedestrianised high street teeming with people, with families, with pockets of laughing teens outside sport stores and fast-food shops and sliding down the escalators into Queens Arcade, the chill air rich with the aroma of frying onions and hot dogs and the faint chimes of music from the Winter Wonderland in the Civic Centre.

It feels good to get out. To get away.

Her parents, staying with her and Paul since Christmas Eve, just two days but it felt like an eternity with their fractious ways making Paul ever more irritable, putting her on edge, the tension between them increasing until last night, with her mother and father in bed and Paul drunk, again, the barely suppressed rancour had spilled over and he'd sneered at her, arms wide, conveniently forgetting he'd agreed to her parents visiting, *Why the fuck are they here? They're ruining my Christmas*, and they'd fought, screamed and yelled at one another, the worst it had ever been, loud enough for her mother to come downstairs, face fearful as she asked them if everything was all right.

She'd dropped them off at the railway station this morning, telling them everything would be fine. That it was just a silly row. That it was nothing to worry about and she loved them and would see them both soon.

Her mother had looked unconvinced.

She sidesteps a toddler freewheeling around the legs of his father, arms outstretched, the coat he's wrapped in clearly new, his cheeks flushed from the cold. The father catches her eye and nods, stares at her a little too long, so she flashes a smile and lowers her head. Holds the plastic bag tight against her midriff. Ducks into the store.

Paul's gift to her. Something she'd never wear. Something she suspects was a panic-buy as he rushed about on Christmas Eve, loaded with alcohol after an early finish and afternoon spent in the pub.

The sales assistant is frazzled and sweating, the store an explosion of exclamatory sales posters, of countless rails of clothing, of jostling, rummaging bodies washed in spotlights and soft rock.

'My partner . . .' she begins, and places the bag on the counter.

A raised hand and knowing nod from the sales assistant. A quick glance at the receipt, a weary 'Exchange or refund?'

Then she's amongst the bodies, pulling out hangers, checking labels, seeing the ever-decreasing sales prices scrawled in marker pen, shifting from one area to the next, picking up handbags and peep-toe shoes then a little black dress she loves immediately but can't think of a single occasion when she'll get to wear it so settles on a hooded jacket. Functional. Useful. Something to keep out the cold.

Jacket in hand, she walks towards the counter, feels a faint tug of guilt about Paul's gift, feels her mobile buzz in her jeans pocket. Fishes it out.

Can't believe the name on the caller ID.

What has it been, a year?

'Oh my God, *Chloe*?' she says into the phone, and it's her old friend, wittering away in her ear as if they last spoke this morning, wittering away without pausing for breath and she nods along, laughs and nods along just like she's always done, 'Yeah, yeah uh-huh, oh no,' and before she thinks it through, before she realises what she's doing, before she can think about what Paul is going to say she gives a final nod.

Says: 'That'd be fab, Chlo, I'll meet you there, say, about seven?'

And she ends the call. Looks at the jacket draped over her forearm.

Looks across to that little black dress.

Smiles.

STAND BY
TO STAND BY

Martin hadn't been expecting much, given previous experience training in stations he'd visited around the force area, but he was still shocked at the paucity of equipment and poor facilities within the Trinity Street basement gym. So much so that he wondered if it actually qualified as a gymnasium at all.

He shook his head: a smattering of ancient and corroding free weights, a worn-looking Nautilus machine, a rickety Weider bench press, a running machine that looked like some seventies prototype that had failed miserably during tests and never been put into mass production – he'd never seen such an antiquated, monstrous contraption before – and a thick, cylindrical red punchbag that had split at some point in the distant past, black gaffer tape now holding the thing together as it hung, listing to one side, from an exposed roof beam. A floor-to-ceiling mirror took up one wall, creating a doubly depressing environment. The floor was covered in a ripped and tatty carpet the colour of fog, with a few crash mats dotted amongst the equipment, their navy skins taped with the same black strips as the punchbag.

All this lit with a single fluorescent, the remaining three strip lights just sad and long-forgotten plastic tubes clinging to the cobwebbed polystyrene ceiling tiles. The only thing that seemed to be new was the digital entrance keypad on the gym door, yet when they'd arrived the door was propped open by a five-kilo weight, thereby rendering the security system worthless.

Not that there was anything worth stealing, Martin reflected, unless you considered *The Very Best of Bananarama* to be of significant value.

'We normally listen to some banging choons while we train,' grinned Andrew, pointing at the chubby little CD player sitting in a pile of dust on a windowsill. Martin noted the window itself had been bricked up and skimmed over. Not that the view out into the basement car park was something to mourn the loss of, but even that would have bled some light into the room.

'Classy,' Martin said, breathing in the heavy odour of stale sweat and damp. There was no air con, which explained why the door was left open at all times. 'And . . . you actually come here *regularly*?'

'Whenever we're working the city,' said David, missing the sarcasm. 'Do our regulation hour of exercise at the start of the shift, then crack on with whatever's needed.'

'It does the job,' said Alan. 'You don't need much to get the heart rate up.'

Andrew was sniffing himself, slightly annoyed with something, his crooked nose buried in one armpit. 'You want poncey shite, Sarge, get your arse to a Bannatyne's. They can give you a Brazilian while you sup on one of them wheatgrass smoothies or summat.'

Martin laughed, despite the mild hostility. 'It'll be fine,' he said, dropping his kitbag into one corner. He saw a clump of soiled cloth there, and assumed it used to be – possibly circa 1968, and clearly the last time anybody cleaned this hovel – white in colour. It was bunched and flattened to the carpet, the dark grey flannelling now smeared with dubious pink stains.

'Communal towel,' said Andrew, pulling off his tee shirt and watching Martin study the rancid thing.

'Serious?' Martin turned to him. Andrew's elongated torso was inked with tattoos, his upper body – taut and wiry and without an inch of fat – a patchwork of tribal scrawls and what appeared to be military badges and battlefield maxims. There was also the faint smell of . . . *Is it smoke?* Martin thought.

'Course I bloody am,' Andrew barked. 'If you're using the bench for presses, lay the towel down first, innit? Keeps the surface clean for other users.'

Martin found himself nodding.

'Ah, he's used to the finer things in life,' David said, grinning lopsidedly at Andrew.

'Tch.' Andrew sucked at his jagged teeth, his long and oddly prehensile tongue darting out to grip the edge of a broken incisor that Martin hadn't noticed before now. 'This ain't HQ, bruv.'

Martin agreed completely. Headquarters had extensive, top-of-the-range exercise apparatus in a purpose-built fitness centre. During his initial training he'd spent many an hour within its bright and airy confines, watching numerous chief officers while away lunchtimes – sometimes whole afternoons – walking treadmills with glazed eyes glued to daytime television on wall-mounted flat-screens, oblivious to the state of affairs in the badlands beyond the borders of the Magic Kingdom.

'Welcome to the real world,' Alan muttered, and started racking twenty-kilo plates on to a greasy-looking weights bar. He was stripped to the waist. The strange and horrific jumper had disguised what fine shape he was in, especially for an early-forty-something: lean, toned, just a hint of belly in the midst of a solidly muscular frame. A long, thin scar – pale and faded, an old wound – ran down the left side of his ribcage and curled towards his belly button.

Alan caught Martin staring. 'Knife,' he said casually. 'Four years ago.'

'That's . . . that's terrible. How?'

'Happened up at HQ,' David said from the other side of the room.

Martin jerked his head towards him. '*What?*'

'Stabbed in the back by the bosses again,' David grinned.

Martin sighed as David and Andrew hee-hawed with laughter. Alan rolled his eyes, smiling thinly as he bent down to grip the barbell before lifting it to knee height to start a set of bent-over rows.

'So what war wounds do you have?' Martin asked David, while Alan huffed and strained in the centre of the room. 'I'm beginning to feel a bit left out here.'

'Give it time,' David winked. 'Anyway, tip-top me. No scars.'

Andrew pressed a button on the CD player; Hi-NRG eighties pop music farted from the tinny speakers. 'Listen closely when he walks. You'll hear the rattle.'

'Rattle?' asked Martin, frowning.

David sat on the Weider bench; it squeaked worryingly under his weight. 'Meds for the usual complaints. Cholesterol, high blood pressure, type two diabetes, blah-de-blah. All the good things that come with nearly thirty years of shift work. I take so many tablets I feel like a medicine bottle.'

'Maybe you should get some more exercise,' Martin said, noticing David was yet to shed a single item of clothing. 'I can spot you on that bench if you like.'

David chuckled, pushed himself up, walked over to the punchbag. He picked at the masking tape, looked at Martin. 'Never done the weights or that jogging nonsense in my career, and I have no intention of starting with twenty-six months to go before I escape, either. Not that I'm counting.'

He swung a vicious right hook into the body of the bag; there was a booming *thwack*, audible even over the music, David's fist disappearing into the bag's body, causing it to crumple then swing wildly on its chain. The whole ceiling creaked above Martin's head and he glanced upwards to find dust drifting into his eyes.

'All I've ever wanted, and all I've ever needed.' David smiled at him, and continued thrashing the punchbag with lefts, rights, jabs, still fully clothed and caring not a jot about the patches of sweat already creeping from under his armpits.

Martin watched them for a while, Alan shifting from bent-over rows to squats to lateral raises with a set of dumbs, David grunting as he hammered the poor bag, Andrew on the floor beneath the CD player and exhaling loud *choo* noises while carrying out some particularly impressive press-ups. Martin mentally counted along with him to press-up number one hundred and twenty-seven and checked his watch.

Fourteen thirty hours already, and no sign of Vincent.

'Any chance of our missing colleague showing his face today?' he asked.

David, seemingly content that he had successfully beaten the shit out of the punchbag, stopped it swinging with a bump of the knuckles and sucked in a deep breath. 'Don't think Tackleberry is allowed to come out to play with us at the moment,' he chuckled, and Andrew guffawed from the corner before flipping on to his backside to start what Martin assumed would be several hundred sit-ups.

'Quite,' said Martin. Tackleberry, real name Benjamin Lewis, was – so Martin had been advised by their inspector – a muscled, gung-ho and currently suspended PC on the team with a fondness for hanging as much pointless equipment and firearm-related apparel from his ballistic vest and utility belt as humanly possible. His nickname was derived from a character in the God-awful series of *Police Academy* films – a few of which Martin had seen on DVD as a child – who got rather upset whenever he missed out on any gunplay. This alone was enough to make Martin dread Benjamin Lewis's return to work, if he returned at all given his suspension was for unlawful discharge of a Taser. And not just any old discharge: he'd shot it into the penis of a pensioner who'd refused to alight from his Nissan Micra after Lewis, bored on a night shift, had tugged him for not wearing a seat belt.

'I mean Vincent,' Martin said.

He was met with shrugs from David and Alan; Andrew was now in the sit-up zone and *choo*ing in time to the disco rhythm.

Martin tutted to himself, batting away the itch of irritation he felt, because he'd promised himself to take it easy at first, to sound them out, especially today of all days. His new colleagues were rough around the edges, but then what did he expect? They were – *he* was now, he reminded himself – Territorial Support Group, the guys you want to see turning up to a shout when the wheel came off, the big ugly lugs who can look after themselves. And it was abundantly clear that his team were more than capable of looking after themselves. He found this strangely comforting.

In the corner of the room Martin changed into shorts and a sweat top, ignored Andrew's wolf whistles, and hopped on to the running machine. It took him five minutes to work out the archaic dials and buttons and then he was off, matching the contraption's speed to the gutsy squelches of Bananarama's 'Venus', which Andrew, for some incomprehensible reason, had placed on repeat.

He near-sprinted for fifteen minutes, lowered the belt

speed to a brisk walk, breathed heavily with hands on hips as he cooled off, then lowered the torture machine to the minimum setting and paced slowly as the conveyer belt juddered and whined.

'Pretty fast,' said Alan, stripping the bar of plates.

'If anyone legs it today you can chase 'em,' called David, and Martin arched an eyebrow at him in the mirror.

Martin turned the treadmill off, stepped to the carpet, reached over and picked up his kitbag. 'Showers?' he asked, palms up to query their location.

Andrew was in the middle of a star jump; he stopped, legs akimbo, and turned the music off. 'You're washing?'

'Now?' asked David.

'We don't normally shower after a bit of light training,' said Alan.

Martin checked the time. Fifteen eleven hours. He smiled at them. 'Plenty of time to freshen up and make a brew before we head upstairs to grab our seats.'

David stared at him. 'Or we could skip the communal nudie session and have a couple of brews *and* a Hobnob or five.'

Martin watched as Alan rubbed his face and neck with his Christmas jumper, as Andrew simply shrugged on the top half of his overalls and zipped them up. David, sweat stains blossoming from his armpits and along the length of his spine through his uniform tee shirt, sat unmoving on the Weider bench. Andrew caught Martin studying their grooming techniques and cocked his head.

'Tch.' Andrew sucked at his teeth again. 'We got the old bottle of Kouros in the van, Sarge. Few splashes of that and you'll be beating 'em off with a shitty stick.'

'Get you smelling like a real man,' grinned David, helpfully.

Martin rubbed at his eyes. 'Okay . . .' he sighed. 'I'm showering.'

He was still one short.

'Any word from Vincent yet, guys?' Martin asked.

The sports hall on the fourth floor was heaving. Rows of uniforms, thirty or forty deep, just the first of several staggered briefings before kick-off. The predominant colour was black; waves of public order overalls punctuated by the occasional fluorescent tabard. And the noise: Martin was barely able to hear his own voice over the catcalls and laughter. He thought of a morning assembly, of those cacophonous moments before the headmistress strode through the hall doors and shushed the horde of unruly children.

Martin didn't get an answer from his team. He wasn't sure if it was because of the racket or if they were being discourteous, so optimistically he decided on the former and asked them again. Louder this time.

'He'll be along,' said David, not looking at him.

'Not like he's missing nothing,' said Andrew. 'It's the usual *hurry up and wait* bollocks. All we do is hang around for hours.'

David was nodding. 'Then hang around some more.'

'Then a bit more,' said Andrew. 'Then the wheel will come off.'

'And we'll scream about like headless chickens for a bit,' said David.

A yawn from Alan. 'And then we'll go home.'

Martin sighed. He supposed he should be grateful. At least they seemed keen to get started – all three of them had their notebooks open and pens poised. Andrew, Thrush, whatever Martin was supposed to call him – and he wasn't keen on the latter by any stretch – seemed particularly fired up: grinning wildly and elbowing David as he fidgeted. But the smell. He'd caught a whiff of it in the basement but couldn't quite make out what it was at the time, or who it was coming from. But it hit him now: it was Andrew, and he stank. Martin thought it was oil or diesel with a delightful hint of smoke, and Andrew hadn't even washed after their stint in the gym. None of his team had washed, but then it was only Andrew who seemed to be cloaked in the aroma of eau de charcoal grill. Martin made a mental note to say something to him once they were out in the carrier, maybe ask him if everything was okay. Welfare issues and all that. He'd never heard of Kouros aftershave and for all he knew it smelled of medicated baby wipes, but wished he had a bottle now: anything was better than Andrew humming in their midst.

He checked his watch: coming up to sixteen hundred hours and the senior ranks would be making an appearance imminently.

'I don't suppose any of you have his mobile number?' Martin asked.

'Yep,' said Andrew, and reeled it off to Martin, a hint of reluctance in his voice.

Martin stood. 'I'll make a quick call.'

'If you see the Chief Supernintendo, ask him where the munch is, skipper,' David yawned. 'I'm Hank Marvin already.'

The team watched silently as Martin shuffled along the row, apologising for stepping on tactical boots and nudging knees with his own. He left the hall, pushing through the double doors and hopping down the stairwell. He was dial-ling Vince's number and steeling himself to deliver the first admonishment of his new posting when doors opened a flight below and footsteps echoed upwards. He looked down, saw hands grab at the steel banister. Several hands. Ascending towards him.

'Shit,' he muttered and turned the phone off.

Chief Superintendent Alasdair Da Silva was at the front of the cadre of senior officers. He lifted his head as he reached the top of the stairs where Martin stood, his eyes settling on the diminutive sergeant.

'Is it Martin? It is, isn't it?'

The Chief Super was impeccably dressed: sharp creases in his brilliant white shirt sleeves, tie clipped tight, shoes bulled to the point where Martin could see the ceiling lights reflected in the gloss. Da Silva's aftershave was heady and smelled expensive. He was tall, far taller than Martin, with a lean, muscular body shape. The black goatee around his mouth was neatly trimmed, his eyes a pale blue at odds with his dark skin. Martin knew of his reputation as a force pin-up but had never met him before now – this big player in the NBPA, the top cop who was militant about ethnic issues, Trinity Street station's treat for the female civvy staff.

Martin had heard a few other things about the Chief Super. Incidents he'd never wish upon himself. Rumours that had followed Da Silva as he rose through the ranks, as the pips then crowns appeared on his shoulders.

Tea boy, wasn't it?

Martin nodded at Da Silva. 'Sir.'

The Chief Super extended a hand and Martin shook it. Da Silva's bagmen formed a semicircle behind him: a superintendent, three chief inspectors, two inspectors. The Silver Command team that would be running the show from the control room. Over a quarter of a million pounds in annual salary, of taxpayer money, gathered right in front of him, and Martin knew not one of them would be able to make a call today without turning it over for committee discussion. Police careers were lost for ever on the basis of one split-second decision that subsequently went pear-shaped. Better to surround yourself with minions or those of equal rank. At least once the clueless media and politicians – who senior officers always seemed to bend over backwards to appease – got on the job's back about the mistake, they could blame each other and muddy the waters until it went away.

The officers watched Martin, their faces expressionless. He'd sworn to himself he would never end up like them, no matter what. No matter what tough decisions he had to make.

'I knew your father.' Da Silva was smiling down at him. 'Hell of a man. Good thief-taker in his time, too.'

The Chief Super was still pumping Martin's hand; such praise for his father from a cop who'd – *allegedly*, he reminded himself – behaved in such a way back in the day made him a tad uncomfortable. The hollowness of Da Silva's words was compounded by the fact Martin knew it had undoubtedly been a long old time since Alasdair Da Silva had come within a mile of a criminal, never mind arresting one. There was also the possibility that his father may have been on the same shift or in the same station as the Chief Super when he was a PC. Martin wondered if Da Silva knew that he was aware of his chief superintendent's past.

He smiled back anyway. 'Thank you, sir.'

'How is he? Living somewhere warm and enjoying his pension, I hope?'

Martin hesitated as he thought of his father in his last days. He contemplated lying, telling the Chief Super, *Yes, Dad's fine. He's got a little apartment in Lanzarote. No, I never see him now, he's over there with my mother four or five times a year. You should see him, he's browner than you, haha*, because he doubted very much if Da Silva knew. Yet one of his staff may have known. And then it would be more than awkward for Martin: it would make him look dishonest and Da Silva think Martin had taken him for a fool and treated him accordingly. And Martin had seen what happens in the organisation when your card is marked by a senior officer.

Politics, politics.

He opted for the less damaging option. 'He passed away, sir. Few years ago now. The big C, unfortunately.'

The chief stopped shaking his hand. Released it. His eyes on Martin, Da Silva did an odd thing with his fingers, quickly rubbing his thumb against the tips as if to clean off dust or dirt or some terrible cancerous cells that had been trans-ferred to Martin from his father.

Da Silva's smile was still there, though. He was that well practised.

'Please accept my condolences,' Da Silva said robotically, as if at a sudden death where the deceased is a career criminal who's overdosed on brown and you've got to play nice or the distraught family will complain.

'Thank you,' Martin said, and kept smiling. *Just keep on smiling, Mart.*

'So,' Da Silva said, rather too loudly, twitching his head as if snapping himself out of a mildly unpleasant daydream. He'd placed a hand on Martin's shoulder, was guiding him back towards the sports hall doors. 'How's the portfolio thing coming along?'

Martin walked with him, dredging his memory for some High Potential Development Scheme buzzwords. 'Rattling along, sir. I'm consistently aiming to deliver and perform to the highest standar—'

'May see you at the top table before you know it, eh?'
Da Silva cut across him, leaning down and grinning. His
companions chuckled together; Martin thought the effect
was somewhat sinister.

Dredge, dredge. 'Well, I'm determined to succeed, sir,
make an impact . . .'

'Very good, Martin, positive and professional,' the Chief
Super said, but he was scanning his paperwork now,
squinting at the operational order grasped in his left hand.

'And I'm keen to demonstrate commitment to my own
development and improvement . . .'

'Oh yes, of course, of course,' Da Silva said. 'Commendable
to hear you're on core message. We'll have to link up again,
have a dialogue, yes.' Martin thought he could have reeled
off his mother's recipe for fruit sponge, such was the
amount of listening going on.

Da Silva turned to one of his team, a female inspector
who had not been able to take her eyes off him. 'Can I
have a clock-check, please?' he asked her.

A clock-check. Martin said nothing, watched in mild amazement as the inspector looked at her watch, then glanced
deferentially at one of the chief inspectors, who nodded
his permission. Then she gave Da Silva the time.

Martin found himself questioning why he was chasing
further promotion. He threw a quick look down the stairwell, praying he would see Vincent sprinting up towards
them, that his missing team member would be able to slip
in behind the group and take his seat without Da Silva
noticing.

'Okay,' Da Silva said, turning to Martin at the double doors.
'Lots to do, as usual. Plenty of information and intelligence
to cascade today to make sure everyone is coterminous. Are
you and that team of yours all set?'

Martin had no idea what Da Silva was talking about. 'Coterminous'? And there was no sign of Vincent. He couldn't hide the fact that one of his crew had gone AWOL; Da Silva was too switched on not to notice, and even if Martin was giving him too much credit there would be one of the Chief Super's underlings to point out that Martin's serial was missing a body.

Martin swallowed. 'I'm just waiting on one, sir.'

'Oh,' Da Silva said, his voice light and matter-of-fact, but his annoyance was betrayed by the hand falling from Martin's shoulder. One of Da Silva's companions gave an awkward cough.

'Who?'

'PC Vinyard, sir.'

Da Silva's face tightened for a fraction of a second. The ever-present smile evaporated. 'Oh,' he said again, and his eyes flicked towards the female inspector.

Martin waited. Nobody said a word. Da Silva seemed away with the fairies so he found himself looking from the Chief Super to his coterie of rankers, thinking the situation had suddenly taken a turn for the surreal. The female inspector had lowered her head slightly, one hand raised with fingers twisting a stray lock of blonde hair. Her left hand was splayed at waist level. Martin thought it possible she was staring at the expensive-looking ring on her wedding finger, but her fringe had concealed her eyes.

'Sir?' he said to Da Silva.

'Ah, best you get going, Martin.' It was the other inspector, a whippet-thin chap whom Martin had seen on the force news pages a few times. Runner. National level. Won. A lot. He was glancing at Da Silva, back to Martin. 'I'm sure you'll address your officer's no-show.'

Martin's shoulders slumped. 'Of course.'

He left Da Silva and his support network outside the double doors, slunk back to his seat.

Silence when Da Silva made his entrance. The odd squeak of a chair, the shuffle of tactical boots on wood floor. Two hundred pairs of eyes on him – already showing the Thousand Yard Stare of Contempt specially reserved for SMT briefings – as he strode towards the front of the sports hall, gliding to a halt in front of a large PowerPoint screen where he continued to ooze *presence*. His acolytes fanned out around him. The inspector, the runner, glanced at Martin, at the door, pointedly checked his watch, then spoke.

'I think we're all just about here . . .'

Martin lowered his head.

The inspector talked about deployments in the stadium. RV points. Meal break times. How the refs would be distributed. Mundane stuff for his portfolio, no doubt. Martin was already on the first rung of that particular ladder. *Leadership qualities*. Tick. *Demonstrates flexibility and adapts to new and challenging situations*. Tick. *Speaka da corporate lingo*. Tick.

His part complete, the inspector stepped back. The sports hall dimmed as he introduced the Chief Superintendent. It was a near-theatrical moment: Martin half expected the beam of a spotlight to appear and bathe Da Silva in a brilliant white circle.

The Chief Superintendent floated to the front, the PowerPoint screen washing him in a ghostly blue. He smiled, and Martin swore Da Silva's eyes were boring into the empty chair next to Andrew.

Bloody Vince, Martin thought.

Da Silva took a breath, began to speak.

And then the doors opened.

Yet they didn't just open. They were double-door efforts

on brackets, a health and safety special that closed ever so slowly after you'd walked through them, and those brackets desperately needed oiling because as they closed and as the first syllable died in Da Silva's mouth there was a high-pitched squeal, long and drawn out and excruciating and everyone had turned to gawp. Not one person in the briefing audience was looking at the Chief Super any more.

Not one person except Vincent, who'd just walked into the sports hall.

He pulled a comedy *oops!* face and shrugged, tiptoeing in an exaggerated fashion across to the rows of chairs while officers shook their heads and grinned, muttering and smiling at him, one of them laughing out loud before smacking Vincent on the backside – *you naughty boy, you* – and then there was more disruption as he shuffled along the row to take a seat next to Thrush. *Andrew*, Martin corrected himself. He was aghast as Andrew and Vincent elbowed each other and sniggered, Vincent wrinkling his nose as he sniffed at Andrew's clothing.

Vincent caught Martin's eye. Mouthed, *Sorry, Sarge.*

When Martin glanced up he found Da Silva's eyes narrowed and murderous, locked on his team, on Vincent. He checked Da Silva's companions. As one they were staring in the same direction as the Chief Super, the lesser beings of the hive mind emulating their leader.

He could sense the collective anger from where he was sitting. Knew he had to be seen to do something about the matter.

'Thank you for gracing us with your presence,' Da Silva said, his voice husky with rage. There was a ripple of laughter but Martin knew it was of the nervous kind. He watched as Vincent turned to the Chief Super and opened his mouth to speak.

Martin cut him off: 'Apologies, sir,' he said, standing.

Da Silva and Vincent both snapped their heads towards him.

'What the actual fuck?' Vincent whispered, and Martin shot him a look.

The Chief Super let his blue eyes rest on Martin for a moment. An uncomfortable silence filled the gymnasium. Martin found himself thinking about his lounge, wishing he could see the rest of the afternoon out watching a shitty science fiction film with his wife.

'Accepted,' said Da Silva eventually.

Martin took his seat. Looked at Vincent, saw his expression of disgust. *Well, let him be disgusted*, he thought. *Because next time he's two hours late I'll take the time off his card as well.*

He watched as Vincent shook his head, pulled his notebook and a pen from a pocket, leaned back to listen to Da Silva's briefing.

Martin was pleased to see his intervention had worked wonders on Vincent's attitude.

Vincent bristled, and mentally filed away what the sergeant had just done. He'd settle that score another time. He was busy: never the sort to let an opportunity to get one over on somebody pass him by, while Andrew was busy gurning away as Da Silva talked, Vincent used the occasion to sneak a peek at his colleague's notebook.

The bingo was about to begin and he was ill-prepared. Not like him, but then other matters had eaten into his preparation period that afternoon. Ol' Thrush had pushed the boat out, though; his list was particularly – and surprisingly, given his limited intellectual capabilities – impressive. Vincent would never admit this, of course. It would shift their dynamic, a dynamic where Vincent had Andrew in a position where he could ask him – command him, even – to do anything and everything that took his fancy. Andrew liked commands. He *understood* commands, if little else. He especially liked Vincent giving them to him. Altering the balance of power in their relationship by just a fraction would upset Andrew's world view, his equilibrium – not that he would know what the word meant – and when Andrew got upset . . . well, it didn't bear thinking about.

Vincent could see the blonde hairs clinging to Andrew's overall sleeves. They looked bleached. Faded. Claire's hair, no doubt. *Bit of a domestic before work, Thrush?* Sounded about right. Vincent had never known a shift pattern to pass without Andrew *putting the missus right*. He assumed his colleague had taken her to task for not cleaning his kit properly: the man honked. He checked Andrew's list.

Human rights
Risk Assessment
Diversity
Community
Targets
Statistics
Best Practice
Performance
Health and Safety
Inclusiveness

A rather fine selection. Vincent stole five and scribbled down another five to make his bingo ten, mindful not to let the others see he was breaking the cardinal rule by doing it during the speech. He thought about adding a further 'community' or three, given that rankers could barely speak in briefings or in front of the media parasites without mentioning the word half a dozen times. It wouldn't count, though. Duplication. Bingo rules is bingo rules. *Well, most of the time.*

Vincent tuned in to Da Silva, crapping away at the front of the hall.

'. . . So as you can imagine I am particularly concerned about the possible media implications following recent meetings between these two football teams, and the negative coverage we, our partner agencies and, unfortunately, our communities have received. Even with the added complications of the demonstration I am convinced we can avoid any of the unfortunate incidents which have blighted previous derby matches, and project a positive image of *our* community to the wider *sporting* community. I'm assured our media officers have taken ownership of this, and that we are going to release some of the *good news* items we will accrue from today. We need to be area-focused, use best practice and have a can-do attitude. I expect you all to take pride in your role, project a positive image and ensure coterminosity in terms of our force vision, values and performance, because the people and communities of our great capital city are always at the core of my thinking. Professionalism is *crucial.'*

Community, best practice, performance. Vincent crossed each one out and silently thanked his idiot companion for unwittingly allowing him to crib. He was pleased to find two of his own selections in there, too. *Partner agencies, values.* He had no clue what *coterminosity* meant, and suspected Da Silva was a little shaky about it too.

He watched Da Silva hold court, delivering his speech with dead eyes and deader tone. The usual rhetoric and bullshit. Drilled into these wannabe ACPO clones, the Association of Conniving Political Opportunists, prior to them disappearing for their final lobotomy and indoctrination at the College of Policing. You could cut and paste the repetitive, vacuous nonsense they all came out with.

Da Silva had spoken for ten minutes, saying nothing whatsoever about the impending match in terms of orders, instructions and policy. Nothing at all for the boots on the ground to work with if the lefties and righties actually turned up and started thumping each other across the police lines.

Nothing new there at all, then.

Vincent noticed Da Silva watching him, eyes motionless over a mouth that continued to form empty words. Watching the team. He could imagine what he was thinking, behind that slick facade. *He's probably wishing he could stab me with his ballpoint pen. Wondering who I think I am, the Johnny-come-fucking-lately waltzing in here with nary a sorry to him or his suck-ups. He knows I think I'm better than him, knows I'm right to think that, too. And that fucking onion, apologising on my behalf . . .*

He couldn't help but smile. Da Silva, second-longest-serving member of the regional Superintendents' Association and – so Vincent had heard – one step away from ACPO and all the riches that it brings. Those things Vincent would never experience: the free job motor, the PA, the Monday-to-Friday eight-till-fours, the police holy grail of the designated parking space with your name on a fancy sign. All those riches, all that power, and yet Da Silva could never discipline Vincent for anything, because if he did, if he even dared try, Vincent would dig out his old notebooks and make an appointment with Professional Standards and turn to the pages he'd bookmarked back in the day when he and Da Silva were on shift together. He was certain the rubber-heel squad would take great interest in the notes Vincent had made, and the evidence he'd bagged and tagged and hidden away in his locker, as he shadowed the senior PC on the shift – a younger, rather warmer Alasdair Da Silva.

The jolly japes Alasdair used to get up to. The toms and the bookies. The appropriation of items during search warrants. The debts. The money he'd had to find, somehow. Anyhow. Even if it meant stealing it from the shift tea kitty. He got pinched for that. Never charged though. Da Silva had played the race card and, post-Macpherson, management quivered with fear at the thought of being labelled racist. Better to let things slide and get on with protecting your own little empire within the empire.

Vincent had more on him, though. Much more.

Fun times. Recorded meticulously. You had to have insurance. In the job as in life. People turned turtle on you. Walked away. Abandoned you. Did your legs. Vincent learned that the hard way. He would never be caught out again, no matter what it took.

All the real power. Vincent knew he had it, rank or not.

He drew himself back to the present, realising he'd stopped listening to the Chief Super, had let himself fall behind in the bingo. Thrush was already on an eight. He still had five. *Damn!* There was forty in the kitty, too.

'. . . absolutely crucial,' Da Silva was saying. 'But let us not forget that today is for both sets of fans to enjoy themselves and the surroundings our fair city has to offer. We have the resilience and capacity to—'

'*House!*'

Vincent turned when he heard the strangled shout.

It was David. Half standing, notebook in his hand. A look of pain slowly emerging on his face as he realised what he'd done, and where he'd done it.

'PC Murphy,' Da Silva said quietly, menacingly. 'You have something to contribute? Or a question to ask on behalf of Serial 502?'

There were sniggers. Their new sergeant had gone pale, head slightly bowed and his glassy, unblinking eyes fixed at a point on the floor between his boots, like a child refusing to look at something terrible in the vain hope that somebody will make it go away.

'How's . . .' David was stuttering. 'How's the, erm . . . How's the away crowd going to be escorted, sir?' He sat. Looked at the young stripy, then joined him in staring at the floor.

Nice one, Flub, Vincent thought. *Jammy bastard for*

winning, though. So he'd lost this one. No matter. He would sort it out with Thrush later. The old Ways and Means Act while on patrol. There was always some throbber of a MOP who would cough up.

'As per normal, of course,' Da Silva said, teeth gritted. 'Coaches and vans in convoy, then round up the pub stragglers and anybody else on foot from the railway stations. Containment, then we walk them in. And I'm sure we're all in the loop in terms of ensuring arrests are kept to minimal levels.'

Vincent was in the loop on that one all right. Every single grunt in the sports hall was totally *looped up*. Da Silva was saying: *You bottom-rung bastards had better not lock up too many of those chav fans because it will spike my crime figures for the BCU. And if that happens, I can wave goodbye to my nice five-figure bonus from the Home Office come April.*

Da Silva was wrapping up. He looked miffed. Vincent knew the Chief Super well enough to know he wouldn't be able to let his late arrival, or David's outburst, go unpunished. He wondered how Da Silva would deploy the kick to their collective testicles.

'Good luck, ladies and gentlemen, I wish you well,' Da Silva said.

And then Vincent caught the slightest quiver at the right corner of Da Silva's mouth: a self-satisfied sneer threatening to curl the lip upwards, but – via much practice in social and professional situations where best behaviour was expected – never quite appearing. He'd seen it many times over the years and knew Da Silva was about to fuck with them all.

So here it comes.

Da Silva smiled. 'I hope you have a quiet one.'

There was stunned silence in the hall. Then a few low groans.

Da Silva motioned for the lights and headed towards the doors.

Vincent shook his head. *You don't say the Q-word in the police. It's the law. You say it and everything goes to hell in a handcart. It curses the shift, or the operation, the entire fucking day. And if the wheel does come off, Da Silva will still expect us to keep a lid on the figures so his lump sum isn't affected.* He sighed. Looked across at Abbie, following Da Silva as he strode across the sports hall. An inspector now. Da Silva's wife now, of all things. New hairdo for Christmas too, by the look of it. Lowlights in that blonde hair of hers. Vincent thought she'd done well for herself, marrying the force golden boy. Getting herself nice and entrenched with the power players.

Vincent wondered, amongst all the noise and shouts and laughter that now echoed around the hall, that when all this was done, when he'd done his thirty and Da Silva had done his and they were recently retired plods, MOPs who happened to bump into each other at a pub one evening, if Da Silva would come over all magnanimous and let peace break out. He pictured it: standing there quietly at the bar as Da Silva talked about letting bygones be bygones, nodding calmly as his old chief super bought him a pint or three, listening to him talk of burying the hatchet, that it was all water under the bridge, that they needed to *engage* now they were older and wiser. Da Silva telling him he'd forgiven him for keeping the arm on him all those years over the whores and the thievery and the corruption, even slipping in a couple of buzzwords as he spoke because, you know, old habits and all that.

And Vincent would sing the praises of Da Silva's wife,

of lovely Abbie, always so well groomed and immaculate, so sensible and career-minded, the respected inspector who quietly and efficiently went about the business of supporting her husband while his career went stratospheric.

Da Silva would nod in agreement, thank Vincent for the compliments, tell him he would pass his kind words on. And Da Silva would buy a fourth then a fifth round because he'd retired on a far bigger lump sum and it was his way of reminding Vincent how important he once was.

Vincent would sip at his drink, then beam as he told Da Silva of the occasion – while Abbie, still a sergeant at that point, was prepping their wedding – where he fucked her bandy in the property store at Streppey Road nick, fucked her so vigorously she drew blood when she came, when she almost bit through her bottom lip. Or that other time just after Da Silva's honeymoon when – newly promoted, thanks to the *kind words* provided by her husband, and those shoulder pips of hers barely out of the box – Abbie bent Vincent over her knee in the Da Silva marital bedroom while the Chief Super was at work and spanked him until he whimpered, spanked him until his arse cheeks burned and his ears rang while she demanded he call her 'ma'am' as he begged her to stop. And Da Silva would blanch, and gag on his whisky, and feel unsteady on his feet as Vincent regaled him with how she'd talked about dear Alasdair watching them fuck, how all those times over all those months she'd breathed into a rutting Vincent's ear and said things Da Silva would never hear because – and Abbie had told him this – Da Silva was pretty limp when it came to bedroom activities.

Vincent pictured all this. He'd already forgotten about the pain of losing the bingo. Just knowing what Da Silva didn't was a victory in itself.

'Where were you?'

Vincent shook himself.

The boy-sergeant, face warped with frustration, was crouched in front of him.

Vincent closed his eyes and gave a sigh, like it was oh-so-much effort. He paused, dragged it out. 'I've apologised,' he said, eyes now open but not meeting Martin's.

'No, *I've* apologised,' Martin said.

'Well, I didn't ask you to . . .' Vincent looked directly at him. '. . . *Sarge*.'

'The Chief Super wasn't impressed.'

'I can fight my own battles.' Vincent felt his cheeks redden. 'Always have, always will. And fuck Da Silva. Shouldn't be in the job anyway.'

'That doesn't mean you can just turn up whenever you feel like it.'

Necks were craning in the other rows. Alan, David and Andrew were watching intently. Vincent could see the boy felt awkward; hunching down at Vincent's feet probably hadn't been the best idea because to the others it looked deferential, like he was a student officer begging the forgiveness of an old sweat after a major transgression in the custody suite. Vincent was pretty happy with that.

'I was busy,' said Vincent.

'Doing what, exactly? You're two hours late.'

Vincent looked away. 'Laying a bit of pipe, y'know?'

David coughed; Vincent saw him place a hand to his mouth out the corner of his eye.

Martin squinted. 'What?'

'Vince is a qualified plumber, Sarge,' Andrew said, leaning forward. 'All above board. The job knows about the business interest. He does some work outside work and all that . . .'

Martin was looking from Vincent to Andrew. 'A plumber.'

'A master plumber,' said Vincent.

'Best pipe-layer I know,' nodded Andrew.

Vincent watched as Martin stood, shaking out his right leg to rid himself of the pins and needles he'd obviously suffered while squatting. The sergeant panned his eyes across his team members, as if realising something was off, that he was the butt of some unspoken joke between the old lamp-swingers.

David was clicking his fingers next to Vincent's ear.

'Dollar,' David demanded.

Vincent muttered under his breath as he pulled the notes out of the leg pocket on his overalls and slipped them into David's eager hand. David gave a whistle and grinned.

'Don't spend it all on food this time, tubs,' Vincent said. He noticed Da Silva had already left the hall; his drones filtered out after him, Abbie once again looking anywhere but at Vincent.

'Speaking of which, where's the refs, Sarge?' Andrew was asking the new guy. 'I needs to eat, like.'

'*You* need to eat?' David said. '*I* need to eat sharpish, so I can take me tablets.'

Alan snorted behind him. 'Of course, David. Of course.'

Vincent noted the stripy was watching David count the fivers he'd just handed over.

'Did I miss something?' Martin asked.

'Briefing tradition,' Andrew said. 'You can play next time.'

Vincent could see the boy disapproved.

'It's just a bit of fun,' said Alan. 'No harm in it. Been doing it for years.'

'Really,' Martin said. He was looking at Vincent as he spoke.

Vincent cocked his head. 'You a bit miffed cos you didn't have the chance to win, Sergeant?'

'No, Vince. I'm a *bit miffed*, as you put it, because this is my first week on the team. And I have eyes on me. And you were late. And then you play some stupid *bingo* game in the middle of the Chief Super's briefing? And then David stands and calls frigging *house*?'

'I thought he recovered quite well though, in all fairness,' said Alan.

Andrew laughed. 'Flub, give the sarge a tenner, for God's sake.'

Martin was shaking his head, confused. 'Flub?'

'He means me,' said David. 'Fat lazy useless bastard.'

'Charming.'

'Term of endearment. My viewpoint is, I may not look that busy most of the time but on a molecular level I'm a hundred fuckin' miles an hour.' He shrugged, pocketed the money. 'Get *in*,' he smiled.

Vincent watched the new boy, looking at each of them, silent and thoughtful. There was a hint of amusement on his features now. Softening a little, at last. Seeing the funny side of things, like his old man used to do. But he could guess the kid was ruing the day he ever accepted the supervisor's position on the group, and probably thinking he might have shot any further promotion prospects to shit in the last half-hour.

'Downstairs,' Martin said abruptly. 'Conference room two.'

'Are we having another briefing?' Alan asked.

The boy glanced at him. 'No, Alan,' he said patiently. 'The food is there. Packed lunches. Can you go pick up five of them, please, and meet us at the van?'

Alan mumbled to himself as he skulked off. 'Saves me having to load up the shields, I suppose.'

Andrew was at Vincent's ear as they left the gym, wittering away about swapping sandwiches, asking if he didn't mind Vincent having his tuna ones, or if Vincent had egg salad could he keep it away from him as the last lot gave him the shits and he didn't want that over New Year, and Vincent ignored him, kept walking towards the double doors, around the scattered chairs and clumps of plods, past the Area Two TSG boys blacked up and ready to bring it, past two plonks sitting chatting to one another and as he closed on them the brunette, a broad twenty-something with muscular calves, she stopped talking to stare at him and Vincent thought, *I'm sure I've been there, can vaguely recall her riding me like a pony sometime last year after a public order training day or search refresher course*, but began to doubt himself, doubted if he'd been there at all yet couldn't fathom why she was looking at him with such hatred, why her friend – chick solidarity and all that – was doing likewise and he was checking his mental Rolodex, all those nameless faces reeling by and the brunette's wasn't there so he decided he couldn't have fucked her because surely he would remember.

Then the brunette mouthed *Wanker* at him.

And Vincent realised he had been there after all.

He pushed open the double doors, amusing himself with the memory of pounding Supermarket Girl into a sweaty mess, and turned to Andrew. Raised his right hand, held his forefinger and index finger under Andrew's nose.

'Smell that,' Vincent commanded.

Andrew sniffed, recoiled. 'Eurgh, what is it?'

Vincent winked at the glowering brunette.

'It's love, my friend,' he smiled. '*Love*.'

Alan had assumed loading the shields, the CBRN kit and the first-aid medic pouches would be more important. Maybe ensuring the mesh shield for the carrier windscreen was going to work this time, or that they all had PPE – the NATO helmets and speedcuffs, the stabbies and CS spray, the selection of batons, some of which were withdrawn from use years ago and were now considered illegal – or that the new boy would have lined the team up and checked them down, briefed them again on their remit of pre-match public order patrol, which licensed premises they were visiting to monitor for hoolies. What the plans were for stadium evac, for segregation of opposing groups if the demonstration materialised, for bubbling in the away fans or even where to deposit prisoners should they be unlucky enough to pick any up. But oh no, here they all were in the basement, going through the ritual at the side of the van, the shields and everything else yet to be loaded, any team briefing temporarily suspended because *this* was more important, apparently.

He wished he'd thrown a sickie, but he'd bottled it, and now here he was standing next to Andrew, the stinking idiot, smelling like the nozzle of a petrol pump despite a few liberal squirts of the communal Kouros bottle, his plastic bag in his hand and The Ritual had begun.

They open bags, check contents, and for a twelve-hour shift it's typically pitiful, the quid-a-head special: one pack sandwiches, one can of fizzy drink, one bag of crisps, one piece of fruit, one chocolate bar. The sandwich filling varies, but only between egg mayo or tuna and onion or already-curling ham. The drink is Coke or Fanta or Tango, the fruit an apple or blackening banana, the chocolate a Mars or Snickers, and what you end up with is pot luck, a lottery, and nobody, in all the years the police service has been feeding its troops, has ever been happy with their lot. So The Ritual begins.

A circular huddle at the sliding side door of the carrier, hunched over the bags, jostling to avoid a reeking Andrew, eyeing everyone else's food, checking their own, making hasty mental calculations, sizing up their chances if it comes to a haggle, or a bargaining session with the lucky swine who got the rare cheese and pickle, aware that whispered deals have already been struck: *What you got in them sammiches, bro? What drink you got? I'm not a banana fan, they gets me bloated. I refuse to drink Fanta cos they created it for the Nazis in World War Two doncha know*, and David doesn't drink Diet Coke so he'd traded with Vincent for his full-fat orange Tango, Vincent had used this as a bartering chip to ensure Andrew handed over his apple to add to the one he'd already got and Andrew didn't mind because he *don't really do that fruit shit* and anyway would kneel and fellate Vincent if asked but this meant Andrew was now down a food group so as a sweetener the sergeant gave him his Mars bar with the proviso that Andrew swapped his tuna sandwiches for Martin's slice o' pig nasties, the kid being one of those trendy types who didn't eat meat but could tolerate fish.

This took ten minutes to resolve to the satisfaction of all parties and it could have been Armageddon outside and still the van wasn't loaded. And Alan could have driven home while they sorted the food; he was past caring what he ate. He was stuck there in the madness, the money he was earning already spent on replacing his car window. *Just try, Alan*, he thought. *Try and remember everything will be fine, try not to let it matter, just remember, 'lay not up for yourselves treasures upon earth, where moth and dust doth corrupt, and where thieves break through and steal'.*

He heard Vincent. 'You spazzing out on us again, Dullas?'

David was clicking his fingers in front of Alan's face. 'Aaand . . . back in the room.'

Alan thought how wherever he was, he always found himself looking out the window wishing he was somewhere else.

'Don't call me Dullas,' he said to Vincent. 'That's the last time I tell you.'

He watched as Vincent rummaged through his food bag, laughing to himself. 'I think we'll have to keep the Taser away from you today. You're as twitchy as Thrush.'

Andrew was behind him, chewing on a hunk of gooey chocolate, a pained expression on his face as he gestured to the onion. 'You're a veggie that eats fish. What's that all about?'

'I'm pescatarian,' Alan heard the new boy say. The kid smiled, holding up the packet of tuna sandwiches as if that would explain all. 'It's not vegetarian, but pretty close. Fish, plus lots of fruit and grains.'

'Sounds thrilling,' said David.

Vincent snorted. 'We'll have to stop off and get you some Trill.'

Alan saw the kid's cheeks pinking, but there was a laugh anyway. 'Don't knock it, guys. It's pretty healthy.'

'Healthy is good,' said Vincent, and looked down at his bag of food. 'But I sense junk food coming on for these guys.'

'Post-match kebab?' asked David.

'Affirmative,' said Andrew. 'Vincenzo?'

'If I must,' sighed Vincent.

Martin's face twisted. 'Kebab? They're a fast track to a heart attack.'

'You jest, surely?' said David. 'Prime lamb, unleavened bread, lots of healthy salad. I can't see the problem, meself.'

'Do you actually have any vices, Sarge?' asked Andrew.

He nodded. 'Fags.'

'Steady,' Vincent said. 'SMT hear you say that, you'll be on a diversity course first thing next week.'

'Didn't figure you for a smoker,' said David, and fished his beat-up packet of twenty Benny Hedgehogs from an overall pocket. 'Good on you.'

Martin sighed. 'Jacked them in a month ago. Been trying to quit for years but things, you know, things changing at home . . . I've been using the patches but I must admit to one or two sneaky smokes. Accidental ones.'

'You devil, you,' said David drily. 'Couldn't do it myself. It's all about balance, see. Drink in one hand, ciggie in the other. Otherwise I fall over.'

'You're using them patches all wrong, mate,' Vincent offered. 'Stick them over your eyes instead, you'll never be able to find your smokes.'

Andrew cackled loudly.

'Anyway,' Martin said. 'What about loading this thing and getting out of here?' He slapped the bodywork of the Mercedes Sprinter twice, *bong bong*. In other words: *let's change the subject*.

Andrew was still chuckling as he followed Vincent to the PSU store.

'Pescatarian, right,' he mumbled, clearly none the wiser. Alan wondered if the new sergeant had realised that thinking caused Andrew some considerable pain. Here was a man who could hide his own Easter eggs. The fool genuinely believed it when Vincent told him that gay people were physically incapable of whistling. Alan was convinced a very important brain function broke down or was beaten out of Andrew during his army training. Despite leaving the Royal Marines years ago, anything other than a direct order resulted in him getting confused and agitated, swiftly followed by him going off on one. His Mr Stick routine was already more than a little tiresome as far as Alan was concerned. Clouting some poor drunken MOP due to an itchy truncheon finger was simply not the done thing any more. Just look at that G20 bloke who snuffed it. Frightening stuff.

All those cameras about nowadays, Alan thought, *it's so easy to get pinched*.

It took another ten minutes to load the carrier, rack everything in place, select whatever personal equipment they would need then dump the remainder in the boots of their cars. The radios were dead throughout due to the poor signal in the basement, which meant the wheel could have come off outside without any one of them knowing.

At least we have the food sorted, he thought.

'All aboard the Fun Bus,' Vincent grinned, sliding open the side door of the van. He rolled up his plastic food bag and clambered inside.

Alan palmed the thick green button on a box affixed to the wall next to the roller shutter door. There was the familiar hum then a loud clatter of machinery and metal sliding upon metal as the door jerked and ratcheted upwards, before slowly disappearing into a slot in the basement roof. Alan felt cold air on the back of his legs as he walked back to the carrier. He climbed in, took the seat at the back of the van near the shields, as far away as possible from Andrew in the driver's seat, from Vincent in the chair behind him.

'BINGO seat for me,' said David, slipping into his usual position halfway along the interior of the carrier.

'"Bingo"?' said Martin. 'You taking the mick after what—'

'It means *bollocks, I'm not getting out*, Sarge,' laughed Vincent. 'Kind of suits old Flub, don't you think? Lazy bastard never wants to deal with anything.'

'Less of the old,' David smiled, settling in comfortably.

Martin, *sans* locker, and seemingly unwilling to leave anything behind, slipped his kitbag into a space behind the front passenger seat and pulled himself into the cab; he'd elected to sit up front.

'Bring it,' Andrew barked, an excitable child, and jammed his boot on the accelerator.

The carrier lurched up the ramp, equipment rattling and clanking against the side panels next to Alan. Artificial light gave way to darkened evening; the sun had set long before, and probably while Da Silva was boring them in the sports hall. Knots of shoppers drifted away from the city centre, wrapped in scarves and thick coats, homeward-bound and laden with bags from the Boxing Day sales.

'Okay,' said Martin over the noise. 'Let's see how you guys go to work.'

Don't try and ingratiate yourself with them, kid, thought Alan. *Not that way, at least. It just encourages them. And that's the last thing you ever want to do.*

'Thought we might go for an Eddie,' shouted Vincent, and Andrew turned slightly in his seat, gave him a high-five over the back of the chair, a *woo-hoo*.

The new boy was nonplussed. Alan saw him glance at Andrew, at Vincent, receive a blank, so shifted in his seat to obtain an explanation from David, but David had already dozed off. Alan was surprised to see he hadn't eaten the entire contents of the food bag yet; it sat on his meaty lap, untouched.

'Van term,' Alan yelled, feeling a mild pang of sorrow for the kid. 'He means an Eddie Cochrane.'

'I don't get it,' Martin shouted, voice high over the engine and the noise of shields butting the rear doors, of empty drinks bottles rolling about the floor, of radios suddenly squawking into life.

'Eddie Cochrane. *Cock run*. It means to drive around looking at the skirt.'

The kid gave a tiny shake of his head. He didn't ask anything else, just turned around and stared out of the front windscreen, his shoulders sagging a little.

He'll learn, Alan thought. *Quicker than he likes, too, I'll bet.*

BOXING DAY, 1708HRS

She's hungry and thinking about preparing some food before she leaves when she hears a key in the front door.

Hears a skitter of claws from the kitchen as the door opens, the hiss of passing traffic briefly blowing into the house. 'Hey, girl,' he's saying, his voice light and cheerful, 'how's my girl, how's my girl?' then the lock clicks and keys tinkle and soft, excitable pads accompany his footsteps along the hallway.

'I'm home,' he calls from the foot of the stairs and she notes the change in his tone, pauses, standing in her underwear in front of the bathroom mirror, towels about her feet, scalp still hot from the hairdryer, make-up finished, the room warm and humid, foam from her soak popping quietly as it continues to evaporate in the bathtub.

She thinks of the telephone call, thinks how she should have thanked Chloe and politely declined when she rang, should have *uh-huhed* along as her friend griped about the latest waste-of-space guy who's cheated on her and just said no when she asked her to go for drinks, to help drown her sorrows, to spend a few hours slagging off the male species but she didn't, even though she hasn't seen Chloe for the best part of a year she didn't because she can't let her down, can't say no to anybody when they're in trouble, can't say no even if it is likely to cause difficulties in her own life.

His footsteps on the stairs. Climbing slowly. Pepper whimpering after him; he trained her not to go upstairs because he hates the hairs everywhere. A final whine then a slow patter of disappointed paws back towards the kitchen.

She meets him on the landing. He gives her an approving look, whistles, brushes his fingers against the skin of her upper arm, tells her she looks fantastic. Then the confusion, the look of suspicion, and she decides she was right not to ring him at work and discuss tonight, her night out with Chloe, because that would have meant an argument over the telephone followed by another argument when he arrived home and she is so tired of the rows and the bad feeling and the constant tension. Better for him to find out now, when she is about to leave for the evening, after she's been able to bathe and get ready in peace.

'Going somewhere?' he asks, a pointless question, but she nods and explains about Chloe and he follows her into the bedroom where her new little black dress hangs from an open wardrobe door, her favourite heels resting on the carpet below it, and he tells her how much he hates her old friend and thought she was *history* and he's pacing back and forth in front of her as he talks, not looking at her, counting off the number of times Chloe has *performed like this*, as he calls it, on his fingers as he strides and asks her what on earth she thinks she's doing striking up the friendship again, after everything that has gone before and all the problems Chloe has caused.

She lets him rant and pace while she slips on her dress, picks up her shoes, calmly takes a seat on the edge of the bed, buckles the expensive heels around her feet, pushes herself up from the bed and leaves the room. Walks downstairs, Paul following, still talking, snapping a 'Don't bother coming home if you're pissed', Pepper at her ankles, sniffing and circling as she clacks into the kitchen, Paul at the doorway as she lifts her clutch bag from the worktop, checks the contents, her stomach growling, no time to eat, or rather plenty of time to eat but she can't stand it here one minute longer so she brushes past Paul and ruffles the dog's ears and opens the front door and before she steps out into the cold night air she turns.

Worry on Paul's face now. 'Please be careful.'

'I can look after myself, thanks very much,' she says, and closes the door behind her.

COMMUNITY
ENGAGEMENT

It was three hours to kick off.

The carrier chugged the main drags of the city centre, Andrew letting it slide along in first gear. Shop windows, dressed for Christmas, threw staccato bursts of light into the cab of the van. Frost on the roads, the pavements already. There was little civvy traffic; the odd taxi cruised past them with its FOR HIRE sign illuminated in vain. The rest of the hackney drivers had either called it a day, or lined the roadsides outside fast-food restaurants where they gossiped and smoked in the plummeting temperature, waiting for the evening rush but still hopeful of a stray punter. The Boxing Day sales junkies and teenagers spending Christmas money had evacuated the capital an hour before; the combined effect of the shops closing early and the impending derby clash had emptied the pedestrianised streets and arcades as quickly as shoppers had emptied stores of bargains.

It was *the lull.*

An hour, at most. An hour after the consumers finally bled away, leaving the streets deserted. Before the new patrons of the city centre arrived. Before the first sightings of scarves covering faces and replica away shirts. Before the known prominents took their places in the pubs to slug Peronis while orchestrating the meet-ups.

Before the fun and games before the game.

Martin had sat through the NCALT online training package for public order. He'd formed shield cordons and passed the fitness test in full Level Ones while a student constable, taken part in the training days, took the bricks on shield and helmet and walked puddles of fire that crept up his legs and warmed – to the point of being worryingly uncomfortable – his groin area. Wrestled with the hulking old sweats during cell clearance techniques and in the Angry Man modules, even taken a firm dig to the chin when he'd lost concentration and a smiling trainer saw the opportunity to punch him under his raised visor. He'd flown through the PSU refresher course before taking his new role as TSG sergeant.

But that was all it was. Training. Controlled scenarios. Safety words that would bring a halt to proceedings. Martin felt adrenalised already, just by touring the deserted city in the carrier, yet couldn't understand why the rest of the team were so silent. So calm. David had even managed to grab a sneaky snooze.

Then it dawned on him. They'd seen it all before, and for real. They knew what was coming. There was nothing for them to get excited about, at least not in the way he felt excited. He supposed it was more a sense of dread they felt, of foreboding, with a tiny undercurrent of antici-pation.

The van rocked and rolled around him and he wondered if he would stay on the department long enough to come to see it as a comforting environment, or even another colleague of sorts, a team member as integral to a successful shift as any of the living, breathing ones. It was clear the rest of the group felt that way: only now, during this quiet moment, did he notice the personal touches, the methods they had used to mark their turf and make the carrier a home from home; the affection they felt for the rickety five-year-old wagon was plain to see. It was also born of necessity, he thought, given that they spent a considerable portion of their lives within the bubble of its tinted windows and metal bulk.

It's hard to spend time with anything you hate, Martin thought, turning to face the main seating area of the carrier. Passing street lights threw light into dark corners, shifting the shadows: a flash of old, defunct uniform hanging off a headrest, of discarded paperwork and news-papers, of fast-food wrappers, of magazine clippings pinned above the sliding door with their pictures of scantily clad women and extreme sports and, bizarrely, a gruesome shot of a serene-looking elephant sitting on the head of a – clearly deceased – circus trainer with *Flub takes a rest* scrawled next to it in biro. A battered FM radio sat next to him in a moulded pocket on the dashboard and he knew they'd have music blaring if he wasn't there. The carrier was lived in and used, worn but comfortable, the sour and musty air of almost-permanent human occu-pation now softened somewhat by the not entirely unpleasant aroma of the eighties aftershave they'd sprayed over one another after setting off. He smiled at the chees-iness of it all. They were dinosaurs all right, and their lack of self-awareness amused him no end. He would bet his next wage packet they considered DCI Gene Hunt to be an all-round good egg. The carrier was filthy though, and in desperate need of a clean, something Martin promised himself he'd arrange for a few weeks' time, once he was more settled, because he wouldn't be able to tolerate it for much longer than that.

He checked his companions: Andrew slumped in the driver's seat, one hand draped across the steering wheel, his bored expression betrayed by the ever-roaming eyes. In the murk of the van's passenger compartment: Vincent, hunched forward behind Andrew, elbows on knees, one of which was jiggling, head turned to the side window as he gazed out to watch an empty world drift by. David a shadow behind him, face down, awake now and eating, the packed lunch all but gone, sandwich box and chocolate wrapper crumpled on the seat next to him. And in the darkness at the rear of the carrier, Alan. Quiet, still. A barely visible shape in the gloom. Surrounded by shields, fire extinguishers, helmets and a palpable air of melancholy.

His fears hadn't exactly been allayed after speaking to the department inspector the previous week, when he'd referred to Martin's new team as *the Borg* – because they flew about in a cube-shaped object, thinking with one brain. *Mischievous* was the description he'd used, but there had been an odd smile on the inspector's face as he'd said it. It was early days, though. Martin appreciated they had their banter – not that he'd been included, really – and granted it was a little coarse, but in reality it was nothing he hadn't heard before. It would take time to gel. That was the way it was.

He just had to keep giving his best.

His father used to tell him, *As a copper your working day is spent giving your best to strangers*. Martin agreed; whether colleagues or MOPs or what they now had to call *customers* and *service users* – prisoners, to his father's generation – he often gave so much that he had little left when he got home.

He checked his phone. Nothing from Samanya. He reminded himself to ring as soon as they were plotted up. Just to be sure.

'What's the griff then, skipper?'

Andrew's question jolted him from his thoughts. There

hadn't been much in the way of conversation since the start of the shift – he sensed they were being guarded around him, which he understood the reasons for perfectly well – and since they'd left the basement it had died completely, so he'd drifted off.

He slid the operational order out of an overall pocket, clipped it to the file he was holding and flipped through it. 'Basic remit for our serial: maintain public order inside and outside the ground. No other schedule, besides RVing with Bronze at the railway station around nineteen hundred hours. Last batch of away fans arrive then. We're assisting with bubbling them to the stadium.'

'I do love a bit of kettling,' smiled Andrew.

Martin nodded. 'Quite. Other than that, it's just trying to keep a lid on things.'

'You mean hoping it don't go tits up.'

'I mean staying flexible and providing resilience for unexpected incidents.'

Andrew sniffed. 'Fancy way of saying the same thing. What about this demo? They expecting it to go ahead or what?'

Martin flicked through the paperwork he'd been given. 'It's CTU intel, really. They've flagged up chatter over the Net which points to possible problems before kick-off.'

'Not as if we haven't got enough to deal with already.' Andrew shook his head.

'EDL or WDL, yeah?' asked Vincent from behind them. 'Bitching about the new owners of the club, I'll bet.'

'Not quite,' said Martin, angling the printout towards the window to catch some light from passing shops. 'The Welsh Defence League is now defunct, apparently. Looks like . . . Casuals United? Whoever they may be.'

'They're English Defence League all right,' crunched

David, packet of crisps in one hand. 'The football hooligan branch of it, anyroad.'

Martin quickly scanned the Counter Terrorism Unit's report and nodded as he turned to Vincent. 'You're right. They've been whipping up a load of nonsense about the chap who bought the club in August.' He flicked over a page, noting that they were all listening to him talk for a change. 'Dr Mousa Belbeisi, real estate and investment magnate worth blah blah blah, Jordanian Muslim, businessman based in Abu Dhabi . . .'

'Ploughed twenty-five mil into a bankrupt footie club,' said Andrew.

'Thirty-two million,' corrected Vincent.

'S'right,' nodded Andrew quickly. 'Thirty-two.'

David stretched, crumpled up his crisp packet. 'And the Casuals nobbers see this as further *Islamification of Europe*, and are protesting about it, right?'

'Correct,' said Martin, still studying the paperwork.

'And they believe the Muslim owner has poisoned their beloved club, which is why they're in the bottom three, right?'

'Again, correct.'

David chuckled. 'And it's nothing to do with the fact their team are shit and couldn't score against a pub side, yes?'

Martin dropped the printout to his lap with a wry smile. 'You don't need me to brief you on this, do you?'

'We kind of got it when we found out Da Silva was running today's gig,' said Andrew. 'If it all goes off and there are complaints that we're just as racist as the hoolies, he'll be wheeled out in front of the cameras as a friendly ethnic face.'

Martin pictured Samanya, and wasn't sure which way the conversation was going so thought it best to keep quiet.

'"Thick TSG plods know what they're doing and what's going on" *shock*,' Vincent mumbled, and resumed looking out of the window. 'Somebody ring the *Daily* fuckin' *HateMail*.'

'These clowns we're talking about, they'll use any excuse to get out there and protest,' said David. 'It's always somebody else's fault as far as they're concerned. Team struggling in the league? Must be the *bloody Muslims*, innit?'

Martin laughed at that.

'It's not the EDL or Casuals you need to worry about anyway,' said Vincent, his right temple pressed against Plexiglas. 'They only ever rock up with about two hundred people, tops, and most of them are too pissed or stupid—'

'Or both,' interrupted Alan from the rear.

'Or pissed *and* stupid,' Vincent continued, 'to know why they're there. The problems always start when Unite Against Fascism arrive.'

'That UAF lot.' Andrew steered the van through the bollards at the castle end of Queen Street. 'Stirring it up every time.'

David was studying the overripe banana from his lunch bag; after a few seconds he'd obviously declared it suspicious and dropped it back inside the plastic. 'The most violent hippies I've ever had the misfortune to deal with.'

Martin shuffled his papers, placed a boot up on the dash. 'Should be interesting to see what they've done to the stadium, anyway.'

'You used to go to matches, then?' asked Andrew.

Martin nodded. 'My father was a season ticket holder,' he said, and smiled sadly, a faint but familiar ache in his chest. 'Used to take me when I was a kid. He'd be gutted to see them near the foot of the table.'

'Right,' said Andrew, his voice hesitant, and Martin noticed him checking the rear-view mirror. He glanced over one shoulder, found Vincent and David listening in.

'He was job, too.' Martin turned back to the windscreen; the pedestrianised shopping street stretched before the carrier, cold and devoid of people. 'Not sure if any of you knew of him. Mark Finch? Worked the city his entire career. Well respected, unblemished record, handful of commendations. A good man . . .'

The words caught in Martin's throat and, alarmingly, he felt he might cry, right there in front of the most feared bunch of knuckledraggers on this side of the force, if not the whole force. He squashed his lips together, fought against it, eyes hot, blurred.

'Sound like a good man all right,' said David from behind him, and Martin was thankful, even if he hadn't meant it. He closed his eyes for a moment, let the carrier rock him.

They trundled along a ways.

'This will do,' he said to Andrew. 'Pull over here.'

'Foot patrol?' asked Vincent. 'Bit parky for that, Sarge, isn't it?'

Martin opened his door as Andrew brought the van to a halt. He was glad to feel fresh air on his face, freezing temperature or not. 'It's our remit. Pre-match public order. High visibility and pub checks. Just normal lids for now, guys. Makes us more approachable.'

David swallowed the last of his drink, crushing the empty can with a brawny hand. 'If we're wearing tits people will talk to us, you know.'

'What you reckon?' Andrew turned to Vincent. 'Ten minutes before the first SFQ?'

Vincent grimaced. 'The public won't last ten minutes before asking us a stupid fucking question. Five minutes tops.'

'True dat,' nodded Andrew, killing the engine and climbing out.

Martin jumped down from the cab, slipped his helmet on to his head. The carrier's side door slid open; he watched Vincent and David swap glances as they dropped to the pavement, fastening fluorescent tabards over protective vests.

'You can stay put if you like,' Martin said to Alan, who had emerged with a sullen face and mind clearly elsewhere. 'Keep an eye on the van. We'll give you a shout if we need transport urgently.'

'Suits me,' said Alan, thrusting his upturned hand out to Andrew.

'You lucky mother,' said Andrew, dropping the keys into Alan's palm.

Martin looked around. The street was still empty. He turned the collar of his overalls up against the icy wind that whistled along the shop fronts. 'Vince, Andrew, pair up and cover Queen Street and the railway station. Keep an eye out for the usual suspects.'

'Pubs?' asked Vincent.

'David and I will do the rounds and check for nominals. Perhaps he can teach me a thing or two on the way, no?'

Martin smiled as he said it, but was convinced he saw David's face stiffen.

'Enjoy,' Alan said, already disappearing into the warmth of the carrier.

Martin watched him pull the driver's door closed, heard the engine roar to life.

'Lucky, lucky mother,' Andrew muttered.

'Okay,' said Martin. 'Let's take the air.'

Vincent and Andrew were both happy that the new boy had doubled them up on foot, albeit for different reasons.

They weren't happy to *be* plodding about in weather cold enough to turn nipples into battleship rivets – their old sergeant was of the *stay in the van till the shit hits the fan* mould, and neither used to complain about Jim's wait-and-see attitude – but Vincent felt he had dodged an especially vexing bullet with the new onion electing to pair up with Flub. The thought of having to be on his best behaviour for the next hour while he puppy-walked the sergeant, of all people, had been enough to make him feel nauseous. Dealing with Andrew and his incessant crapping on was a doddle by comparison; he'd easily managed to fire off a few filthy texts to whatsername as they walked because all it took was a few *yeah*s and *I know, Thrush*es to keep Andrew thinking he was paying even the slightest bit of attention.

This, Vincent thought absent-mindedly, *must be what it's like to be married.*

Andrew was just content to be at Vincent's side.

'So?' Andrew asked.

Vincent was head down and just about to send a spectacularly vile message to his new fuck buddy, telling her what he planned to do the next time they RV'd. He knew she'd be shocked, possibly angry for a day or two, and the thought made him smile. But the anger would give way to curiosity, and that to a tremor of excitement, and after that he would ignore her calls and texts and let her stew in her own juices for a week or so, until by the time they met she would be more than amenable: she would be desperate to carry out his suggestion. Vincent believed they were all the same in the end, despite their initial reluctance to plumb the depths of sexual depravity. He frequently found that supposedly rock-solid principles quickly became rather rickety once they'd crossed that first line. Moral compasses soon lost their north.

'So? So what?' Vincent said. He'd already regaled him with a blow-by-blow – literally, as far as certain parts of the engagement were concerned – account of that afternoon's activities, and the retelling had led to him deciding to continue the assignation via text sex. He was mildly irritated at the interruption.

'So are you going to tell the new boy that you knew his old man?' asked Andrew.

Vincent pressed 'send' on his phone, watched the message disappear. 'No.'

'No?'

'Not yet.'

'Why not?'

Vincent thought about it for a few seconds. 'I don't know. Insurance, maybe.'

'Flub worked with his father too. He might mention it.'

'He won't. He's the same as me. We'll sound the kid out first.'

'Got to have some insurance, right?'

Vincent felt his mobile vibrate, checked the text message: *You are disgusting. Do not contact me again. IT IS OVER.*

He grinned. 'Yeah, right.'

'Thought so,' beamed Andrew.

They walked on, listening to the chatter of radio traffic

on their Airwave handsets, the comms girls in the command room updating Silver with the locations of the team buses, of opposing fans, of pockets of prominents sighted making their way into the city centre on foot, in cars, by train. Thrush talked, and talked, and talked, repeating war stories Vincent had heard a hundred times before, embellishing them to the point of ridiculousness, Thrush forgetting Vincent had actually *been there* when some of them had happened and therefore knew he was bullshitting. Vincent nodded anyway and pulled his fireproof balaclava partway up his neck and over his mouth; the cold combined with Thrush's nasal monologue were making his teeth ache.

They'd been pacing the centre for half an hour when the first football shirts began to appear. Groups of two or three home fans marching down the main shopping drag, then half a dozen more from the bowels of the railway station. A twenty-strong knot of supporters decamped from a minibus on the forecourt of the Hilton Hotel, their shouts and cheers puncturing the quiet, the noise at odds with the preceding calm.

'Game faces on,' Vincent said.

'Right,' said Andrew.

The supporters bundled past them, jostling and jumping on one another, cloaked in a noxious cloud of lager and sickly sweet Burberry aftershave.

'*Scuffers!*' one of them yelled.

'Fuckin' peeeeegs!' another shouted, laughing as he carried out a ridiculous boogie before them, elbows flapping as he taunted them from the middle of the road.

Andrew racked his ASP and stepped towards the dancing fan. 'You watch I don't push you over and kill you, cunty-bollocks.'

'Steady, fella,' Vincent said, grabbing Andrew's utility belt to pull him back. He cared little about Andrew using the baton on a few of them, cared even less about Andrew's hurt feelings, for that matter. In truth he simply didn't care about anything. He just despised the paperwork. 'Let 'em shoot their mouths off. D'you really want to spend the next five hours filling in forms?'

'Fucking fuckers,' Andrew grunted, his cracked tooth catching on his bottom lip. 'If I had my way they'd have a 7.62-millimetre through their melons.'

'You're not patrolling the Shankill Road any more, Thrush,' Vincent chuckled.

The group bowled along, moving away in hysterics, slapping each other on the back as they bragged about getting one over on the *po-po*.

'We lost face there,' Andrew said through gritted, buckled teeth.

Vincent shrugged. 'Who cares? It's nothing personal. It's just the uniform.'

'This country's gone down the shitter,' said Andrew, bending down to hit the pavement with the ball of his extendable baton. The shaft of the ASP disappeared back into its handle. 'No respect, like. I'd never treat anyone like that.'

I'm sure your missus would completely agree with you, thought Vincent.

So they walked, and Andrew talked. When they came across a vagrant, slumped in the shuttered doorway of a travel agency, Vincent was relieved to have a break from what appeared to be Andrew's discussion with himself.

The old guy's nose was bloodied, his bottom lip split; claret oozed down his chin and on to a charity shop fleece that was ripped at the neck, exposing a rug of slick, grey chest hair. Vincent could see he was wearing four or five pairs of trousers, and his right shoe was worn through at the front. A gnarled, yellowing toenail poked through the hole in the scuffed leather. There was a foul, bitter stench enveloping him, so pungent that it made Vincent recoil, his nostrils burning as if he'd snorted a toot of CS incapacitant.

'What happened here, matey?' asked Andrew, peering at the vagrant's chest. Vincent could see him studying a faded green tattoo on the old chap's pudgy left pectoral: it looked like a globe surrounded by laurels, the number 45 inked into the flesh just above his pale, wrinkled nipple.

The tramp's eyes couldn't fix on anything, rolled in their sockets. 'Dem lot. Dem lot. Dayfookindunme,' he burbled through stubbled lips. 'Dayfookindidmeindabastards.'

'Which lot? The football fans? They did this to you?'

'Christ, Thrush,' said Vincent, checking his phone again. 'Who cares about this pikey twat?'

'Igotnuttin,' the old guy was saying. 'Butdaystilldunme-overdabastards.'

Andrew looked at Vincent, back at the tramp. 'Are you Corps? Four-five, yeah? One of the lot who yomped to Stanley? I'm ex-Booties meself, Granddad. Afghan in nought-one with Forty.'

Vincent watched as Andrew gleefully pulled back the sleeves of his fluorescent, his overalls, pushed the inside of his forearm under the vagrant's pained face, showed him the commando dagger tattoo that stretched from the crook of his elbow to his wrist.

'Bagram?' the old man coughed, and wiped at the bloody bristles on his chin with the back of a knobbly hand.

'Bravo Company, all the way to Kabul,' Andrew grinned.

'What a touching reunion,' Vincent muttered. 'I think I may weep.'

'He might be a rum rat but he's still a veteran, Vince,' said Andrew, looking up at him. 'Served his country and they treat him like this on the outside. We should go looking for the muppets who did it. It was probably that lot from the minibus.'

Vincent held Andrew's gaze for a moment, looked down at the tramp. 'Fuck him.'

'That's harsh, man.'

Vincent stepped away from the writhing man on the floor; the smell was too much for him to bear. 'He pays nothing into the kitty. You think this cockgobbler has ever paid council tax? Paid our wages, like we always hear?'

'He served in the Falklands.'

'You might think you're kindred spirits just cos you're both ex-forces and stink like a pair of bombed-out shithouses, but you don't owe him anything,' Vincent said, and leaned down to the battered man. 'You ain't got no police credit. We can't help you.'

'Vince . . .' said Andrew.

Vincent was already walking away. The old guy forced himself up on to one elbow, coughed a clot of blood up and spat it after him.

'Yabastard,' he retched, and collapsed backwards.

'Come on, Mother Teresa,' Vincent called, shoving his phone into a pocket.

Andrew followed him along St Mary Street, through an eerily quiet chippy lane – the wrappers and sea of polystyrene cartons yet to make their appearance – and on to The Hayes where they plotted up outside the entrance to the St David's 2 shopping arcade. They waited and watched.

Less high visibility, more an easy target for abuse as the growing number of fans passed them by.

'Flub,' Vincent said eventually.

Andrew was busy checking the shop window displays for watches he could never afford. He dug his hands, gloved but still freezing, into the pockets of his overalls. 'What about him?'

'He won the bingo.'

'Two jammy bastards on the group tonight. I mean, look at Dullas. Warming his boring arse in the van right now, he is.'

'We need cash for the food,' said Vincent, turning to him. 'You know Flub isn't going to stump up for any of us. He'd rather pocket it for himself and use it to keep his sixteenth wife and fifty-seven kids sweet.'

He gave Andrew a look, arched an eyebrow, waited for the rusted, rarely used cogs to begin turning.

'Fishing trip?' Andrew asked after some thought.

'Ways and Means Act, paisan.'

'Count me in,' said Andrew, elated that he'd guessed correctly, but Vincent wasn't listening any more, was scanning the ever-increasing crowd of football fans.

They stood in silence for a while, watching the groups of blue- and red-shirted supporters walk by, ignoring the sarcastic comments and occasional robust language directed at them. Vincent could sense Andrew's frustration and willed him to rein it in. If he saw the telltale twitch in his colleague's eye he knew he would have trouble restraining him; as yet, thankfully, it hadn't come to that.

Ten minutes passed. Then: 'Perfect,' Vincent smiled.

'Wha . . . Who?'

It was clear Andrew had drifted away; Vincent assumed

he was replaying whatever punishment he'd meted out to his wife that afternoon. Somewhere, Vincent knew, deep in the musty recesses of Andrew's mind, he'd be feeling a smidgeon of guilt and wishing he was home in order to make it up to her like he always did: lager, takeaway curry, a nice 'n' punchy Jason Statham film followed by – and Andrew had actually told Vincent this – a good, hard shafting that frequently ventured – upon his suggestion – into watching hardcore porn while he informed Claire how much he enjoyed imagining her being fucked by another man. Or three. Before falling asleep and assuming she would be up with the kids at stupid o'clock the next morning.

Something classy like that, anyway.

Vincent shook his head at his colleague. 'That muppet over there.'

Andrew appeared to focus, immediately saw the *muppet* Vincent was talking about: some runt of a fan in an alternate away strip. Barely into his twenties. Tall and skinny and drunk, yet still attempting a cocky strut despite the problems he was having putting one Superga-trainered foot in front of the other in anything approaching a successful manner.

Vincent leaned in to Andrew, holding his breath so as not to breathe in the unbearable cocktail of Kouros, stale gym sweat and week-old petrol bomb. 'Make sure we're out of camera shot.'

'Aye aye, Captain.'

They approached the boy slowly, calmly. If the CCTV cameras – and there were so many in the city centre – picked them up, anyone watching would assume they were two plods making sure a drunken, stumbling young lad was about to be shown the error of his ways and directed to the nearest taxi rank in order to get home safely.

'*You*,' barked Vincent to the boy as they neared him. He reminded himself to keep his hands at his sides, not make any aggressive moves that might be picked up on if ever a complaint was made and the recordings viewed by the rubber-heelers from Professional Standards.

The boy was munted. 'Wha?' he asked.

'There's no way he's going to last until kick-off,' Andrew sniggered.

'Ideal,' said Vincent.

They used *officer presence*, the first step on the Home Office-prescribed ladder of police / public contact within the National Decision Model, to back the kid into a shop doorway.

'Whatchoo want?' the kid asked, head rolling on his neck. Lager fumes wafted across to them, yet despite this he'd obviously caught a whiff of Andrew's more powerful perfume: Vincent saw the slight flare of the kid's nostrils followed by a tiny flinch.

'Had a few, have we?' asked Andrew.

'I jus' goin' to the match,' the kid slurred. 'Lemme alone.'

'Did you just call me a cunt?' Vincent asked.

The boy scrunched up his face. 'Eh?'

'You cheeky little bastard. Name.'

The kid staggered, blinked at them. Vincent could see that somewhere in the alcoholic haze there was the faintest realisation that these two coppers might be about to cause him a few problems. 'What you want my name for?'

Vincent raised his hands, palms out, as if to calm the young man down. *Good for the cameras.* 'You're drunk in a public place. And abusive. Christian name.'

'Oooh, steady,' whispered Andrew. They weren't allowed

to use *Christian name* or *surname* any more, according to the chinless whelps from the force diversity department, in case it offended people from other religious backgrounds. Or offended one of those busybodies who seemed to make a living out of being professionally offended on other people's behalf, even if those people weren't actually taking offence anyway.

'Wayne,' the boy muttered.

'Surname Kerr?' asked Vincent, a thin smile on his lips.

'Kerr?' asked the kid, missing it completely. 'Nah, it's Donlan. . .' He gave a hiccup, corrected himself: 'Donaldson.'

Andrew listened to Donaldson finish giving his details, ran a person check by the command room. Vincent heard the results through his earpiece.

'Surprise, surprise,' he said. 'Pre-cons for public order. Like to get pissed and gob off at Old Bill, do you?'

They were crowding Donaldson now. He pressed his back against the glass door of a Waterstones bookstore. 'You only in the five-oh cos you was bullied at school,' he blurted.

'Yawn,' said Andrew. 'And don't tell us: if we weren't wearing the uniform you'd give us a fuckin' shoeing, right? Maybe I should strip off right now and we can go toe to toe.'

Vincent nodded. 'And then when he loses, he'll ask for our numbers because he's going to have our badges.'

'You,' the kid slurred, 'you pricks always swap your numbers anyways. Me ol' man says you fit everybody up.'

'Which means your daddy's a shit too,' said Andrew.

'You failed the attitude test,' said Vincent. 'You're nicked. Section Five, matey.'

He grabbed Donaldson's arm; predictably the boy began to struggle. *Your old man taught you well*, thought Vince. It was a pathetic attempt anyway. The alcohol and his confusion at the confrontation meant he was subdued and cuffed to the rear in moments.

'I ain't goin' to no fuckin' cells, man,' Donaldson protested.

'CCTV,' said Vincent, quietly. Andrew nodded.

They walked the boy off The Hayes and into an underpass at the rear of the NCP car park: a camera blind spot.

'This is your choice,' Vincent said to the boy. 'Night in custody, miss the match, charge sheet in the morning, court in a few weeks. Or . . .'

'Or . . .' echoed Andrew with a grin.

Donaldson was barely able to stand. Handcuffed and wobbling, he looked from Vincent to Andrew and back again. 'Or wha'?'

Vincent flicked his eyes to Andrew, forced himself not to smile. Those cosseted, clueless politicians and their ridiculous ideas for dealing with crime. 'Or you pay an instant fine right now, and you walk.'

The boy fluttered his eyelashes as if to clear away some of the drunken fog. He closed one eye, looked up at his captors. 'Wassa fine then? How much?'

'Twenty quid,' said Vincent.

'Fuck me,' Donaldson squeaked. 'That's some dollar. I ain't working at the minute.'

Andrew snorted. 'Don't tell me: depression? Back injury? Wannabe DJ?'

'Easier to lie in bed all morning and leech off the state?' asked Vincent.

'I bet you've got a bigger fucking telly than me,' said Andrew.

Vincent was nodding. 'Plus the Xbox, Sky subscription,

mobile, fancy trainers and season ticket, and people like me are paying for all of it.'

The boy looked at them, his face miserable.

'You want to see the match?' asked Andrew.

The kid nodded, an exaggerated flop of the head. 'I loves my guys, man.' He bent his neck forward, blew a kiss at the team badge on the left breast of his shirt.

'Touching,' said Vincent. 'So I take it you'll pay the fine?'

'I ain't got that much change on me.'

'Cashpoint.'

'Lessdoit.'

They marched him a hundred yards further on and stopped at Charles Street, at the rear of Marks and Spencer where cashpoints sat in the brickwork. Vincent undid the handcuffs.

'No funny stuff,' he said, barely able to stop himself laughing at how funny it was.

Donaldson slipped in his card, punched in his PIN with a finger that went in circles as he zoned in on each correct number, withdrew the cash. He handed it over to Vincent, swallowing, grief creasing his face.

Andrew stepped forward. In his hands he held his note-book. Pretended to scribble in its pages. 'Right, you have been officially dealt with and paid your fine. You can go.'

'Serious?' Donaldson asked.

'Totally,' Vincent said.

'So I get to see me guys,' the boy smiled drunkenly. 'You lot ain't complete bastards after all.'

'Don't believe everything you read in the papers,' Vincent said, wafting the twenty-pound note between thumb and forefinger.

'I don't read 'em,' the kid said. 'But respect, man. I'm gonna see my boys.'

'We're very happy for you,' Vincent smiled. 'Enjoy.'

'Peace out,' Donaldson grinned, and kissed the club badge on his shirt. With that, he was away.

'Public satisfaction,' said Andrew. 'Isn't that what it's about?'

'Fuck the public,' said Vincent. 'They're a bunch of moaning cunts who're incapable of looking after themselves. Least we've got money for some munch later.'

Casuals.

David could spot them a mile off. Clad in Fred Perry sweats and Nudie jeans. Burberry scarves and Lacoste bomber jackets. Adidas Originals trainers. No club colours anywhere, but he knew. He'd seen enough of them over the years, had even – after his second divorce, and with far too much time on his hands – taken to researching the clothes they wore. Soul Crew members. Casuals United foot soldiers. Looking to blend in, to disappear, to avoid contact with plod so they could get into the bars and clubs or, if the mood for a rumble took them, vanish into the crowd once the fighting stopped.

The District Five pub on St Mary Street. Home of the hardcore home fans. Of the Cardiff City Soul Crew, one of the most notorious firms in football. Their meeting place, normally a no-go premises for anybody in an away shirt – unless you wanted to be escorted to the Gents and battered to near-death with a toilet seat.

Tonight was different, and not a little troubling.

The CTU intelligence was on the money: team allegiances had obviously been set aside for what was considered to be the greater good: *the fight against the Muslim invasion of Europe*. Or, rather, an Arab self-made billionaire who'd decided, for some bizarre reason, to plough some of his hard-earned into the ailing, second-tier football club of the principality.

Interesting way to demonstrate gratitude, thought David.

Through the front windows he could see the place was rammed with men, knew most of them would be Soul Crew, knew the rest would be supporters of other teams – Leeds, Millwall, Bristol City, maybe a smattering of Spurs on a two-day jolly – their hatred for one another paling into insignificance when compared to the loathing felt for the *creeping cancer of Islam*, their illiterate and hazy rage focused and whipped into such a frenzy by their masters in the English Defence League that partisan rivalry became, for one night only, common purpose.

A lone female, a mousey blonde in her mid twenties, rushed back and forth, flustered and failing miserably to keep up with the orders for expensive bottled lager. The landlord – no stranger to the inside of a police cell, and a gentleman who David knew ran with hare and hounds – was plumped at the far end of the bar, his overweight frame squashed on to a stool while he absent-mindedly flicked through a tabloid newspaper and ignored his solitary staff member's plight.

David pushed through the small crowd that had spilled on to the pavement, Martin following behind. Several hoolies had mobile phones attached to their ears, calmly whispering what David knew would be instructions to subordinates and spotters, or even taunts to rival hooligan firm members who'd failed to turn up and show *solidarity against the Muslims* for an evening. It always struck him as odd how these clowns could behave like suburban gentry, engaging in polite yet occasionally provocative conversation with opposite numbers in order to meet up in a few days and beat the living shit out of one another.

As long as they avoided the attentions of plod, they didn't seem to care.

'See any you know?' asked Martin.

David sighed. He'd recognised a dozen faces in the crowd as they pushed further into the pub, heard the good-natured ribbing from some who knew his face, then the odious remarks – the northern accents, the cockney drawls – from those who didn't: supporters from other clubs who'd come to the capital looking for trouble. It was already worrying him; he hadn't seen this many hardcore guys out before a match in an age.

There may be trouble ahead, he thought.

Beneath the noise and shouts someone had started whistling the Laurel and Hardy theme tune. Within a few seconds most of the pub was at it.

'Great,' he muttered.

'I take it that's for our benefit,' Martin said over the increasingly loud tune.

David looked at his new sergeant, then down at himself. Small, skinny, fresh-faced guy; dumpy fat bloke at his side. 'Oh, it's for us all right,' he said.

Martin pulled paperwork out of an overall pocket. 'Let's see if we can find any prominents and have a word. Here.'

He offered David a copy of the intel sheet, holding it printed side out. The names, mugshots and confidential police intelligence of known Soul Crew and Casuals United ringleaders were clear for everyone in the pub to see.

David closed his eyes. 'No thanks, skipper,' he said quietly. 'I know all of 'em. And we've already walked past five of the people you've got pictured there.'

Martin turned back to the door and was met with waves and a semicircle of smirks.

'Right,' he said. 'So let's find one of the main men. Have a chat about this evening and make sure everyone's on their best behaviour.'

He made as if to walk further into the pub.

'No need,' David said, placing a hand on his arm.

The whistling died off.

'Not very clever of you,' a low voice said.

David watched as Martin turned to face the shaved gorilla towering over him: face pocked and leathered, 'ball cap on what was clearly a bald head, small diamond stud in his left ear. Late thirties but in exceptional shape. Well over six feet, his chest and shoulders impossibly broad. Wrapped in a jet-black, worn-looking Stone Island soft shell jacket and expensive-looking jeans. Pinned to one jacket lapel was a tiny, circular badge. Martin had to squint to make it out: a black-and-white figure, arms crossed, baseball cap on faceless, shadowy head, topped and tailed with CASUALS UNITED and NO SURRENDER.

Martin looked from the gorilla to the intel sheet, back to the gorilla. David knew what he'd be thinking: *funny how different they are in the flesh. How huge, in this case.*

Time for the introductions.

'Nathan,' David said.

'All right, Mr Murphy?' The man nodded at David, wiping a finger at his nose as he sniffed. 'You guys all set for tonight?'

David smiled at the thinly veiled nod to problems past and interesting times that might – or rather, would, David knowing the Casuals as he did – occur in the imminent future. 'Always ready, Nath. You?'

The man laughed quietly, a high, gurgling chuckle at odds with his massive frame.

David felt Martin's eyes on him. The whistling and shouts had stopped completely. Even the corpulent landlord had managed to hoist his jowls upwards and away from the newspaper to scrutinise them.

'Sarge, meet Nathan Telemaque,' said David. 'Nathan, this is Sergeant Finch.'

Telemaque slowly moved his hulking head to look down at Martin; conversely, Martin lifted his eyes upwards, and upwards, to meet the Soul Crew ringleader's gaze.

'Mr Telemaque,' he said. David assumed the sergeant was trying for gravitas but it sounded odd, like a boy affecting an adult's tone while addressing a genuine, fully formed adult. Like he was trying too hard.

Telemaque gave a perfunctory flick of his head in acknowledgement, sniffed again, then turned away.

'Why the house call?' he asked David, any hint of amusement now gone.

David exhaled. 'You know the score. Just doing the rounds. We don't want any trouble this evening.'

Telemaque stretched his arms wide; in his jacket he reminded David of a blackened oak tree. 'We having a quiet beer,' he said. 'Just a few of the boys.'

'Quite a few of those boys out tonight.' David glanced around. 'Some of them from out of town?'

'Family visit,' said Telemaque.

'That's a big family you've got.'

'Ah,' Telemaque shrugged. 'Derby game, right? Got to fly the flag.'

'And which flag would that be?' asked Martin. 'EDL, perhaps? Casuals United?'

Telemaque didn't look at him. 'Like I said, we just having a quiet beer.'

'Let's keep it quiet, then,' said Martin pointedly.

David gnawed the inside of his cheek.

Telemaque dropped his arms, stared at Martin. Beneath the brim of the cap his wide eyes bulged, thread veins in the whites. There was another wipe of the nose, this time with the tip of his thumb. 'Long as you stop flashing my photo to all and fuckin' sundry.'

A moment of silence. David, sensing the sudden shift in the atmosphere, the tension, looked heavenwards.

Nobody moved.

A shadow passed across Telemaque's face, and David felt the air being sucked from the bar. The boy had made a basic error, a probationer's error, by assuming these people would show deference simply because they were police, by pushing Telemaque's buttons on his home turf, in front of the majority of his own firm, in front of his *special guests*, when they were surrounded, outnumbered, and hadn't even radioed in to advise Silver that they were about to enter a licensed premises. A licensed premises called District Five, of all places.

Nobody knew where they were.

Telemaque leaned down to Martin. For a second David thought he was going to bite off the sergeant's nose. Big Nath had gone over the wall for chewing on people, usually during clashes with rival supporters when he set his teeth on earlobes and fingers and on one memorable occasion – David still couldn't figure out how Telemaque had managed it, and he'd thought about it rather a lot – biting through an away fan's jeans before chewing into the poor man's left testicle.

David tensed. Wished, for once, that Vincent and Andrew were at his side.

Then Telemaque laughed. That reedy giggle again.

'Don't kid yourself,' he said, face pushed into Martin's. 'You lot are just another fucking firm like us. 'Cept you cunts get to do it legally.'

He straightened. Sniff, wipe. Sniff, wipe. David knew the signs: the big man had probably been doing lines at his table just moments earlier.

Telemaque turned to David. 'Sure I can't offer you a drink, ossifer?'

David let go of the breath he'd been holding, reminding himself to neck half a dozen hypertension tabs as soon as he was back in the van. 'I think we'll be on our way.'

Martin followed him out of the pub, the whistles starting again as they walked, Martin's face burning – with anger, with embarrassment, David knew, because he'd done similar things as a fresh-out-of-the-box puppy PC – at such a public gaffe. Credit to the boy: he bottled it for a few minutes, putting distance between them and District Five, until the fans' jeers were nothing but echoes in his ears, until he let it go.

'We've just allowed them to walk all over us,' he seethed. 'We should have called Alan down with the van and rounded them up. It's obvious something's going to go off.'

David spun to face him. 'Fuck's sake, kid,' he snapped, then squeezed his eyes shut. 'I mean Sarge . . . But round them up for what? Drinking shit lager? I know, let's go lock Telemaque up for the offence of Making Martin Look A Bit Daft, shall we?'

Martin flinched.

'I'm sorry,' said David. 'But we would have lost back there. Lost big time. Those idiots will come again, they always do. They're incapable of staying out of trouble and we'll keep locking them up until they're too old or too fucked up to turn out for a rumble. It's the way it is, Sarge. It's the way it's always been.'

Martin jerked his head to the skies. 'It's a bloody mess, is what it is.'

'You won't find any divine assistance up there, I can tell you,' said David. 'There's only one rule you need to remember: finish your shift in one piece. Everything else in this job is irrelevant.'

They paced past Burger King, the smell of fries and

milkshakes making David moan and smack his lips, on to Kingsway where they skirted the castle, then north towards the junction with Greyfriars Road and the bleak, greying monolith of Capital Tower with its warren of offices occupied by the Crown Prosecution Service.

'CPS,' Martin said, craning his neck to look up the side of the building.

'Couldn't Prosecute Satan,' David spat, and shook his head.

Martin looked at him.

'What?' asked David.

'My wife is a CPS solicitor,' said Martin, feigning a smile.

'Oh,' said David. 'I'm sure she's one of the good ones.' He laughed quietly to himself and wandered on.

The boy walked alongside him, silent, the steady stream of fans flowing past them, the odd pocket of hardy clubbers dotted amongst the sea of football shirts, arriving in the city centre for the Boxing Day BOGOF drinks. A battered old tramp staggered past, muttering to himself, dried blood caked around his nostrils and along one side of his face. When he saw Martin and David he became agitated, jabbing a thumb at them.

'Yabastards,' he yelled before stumbling into the crowd.

'Definitely a mess,' Martin sighed.

David nodded. 'You should put a call in to the command room. There's too many scrotes floating about for my liking. Speak to the tac advisor direct, though. Keith. He knows his stuff.'

Martin unclipped his PR, hesitated. 'Not Da Silva?'

David arched an eyebrow.

Martin nodded, punched buttons on the handset for the point-to-point private call, dialled David in on the conversation. David heard the familiar electronic tone in his earpiece.

Then a male voice, *Silver Command, PC Elliott speaking* and David nodded, gave the sergeant the thumbs up.

'Keith? It's Mart Finch, Charlie Victor three zero.'

'Sarge,' Keith's fuzzy voice across the airwaves. 'Any problems?'

'Potentially,' Martin said. 'We've got Nathan Telemaque and other prominents currently swigging lager in District Five.'

'Not unusual,' said Keith. 'They spend more time in that pub than they do at home. We're monitoring on CCTV already. Seems busy out front.'

'We paid a visit,' Martin said. 'Telemaque has friends tonight.'

'Friends?'

The boy hesitated. David rolled his hand at him: *get a move on with the info* . . .

'Other firms, out-of-towners. A lot of them.'

'Casuals United,' said Keith, more to himself. 'CTU were spot on, for once. Interesting. So how many is a lot?'

'District Five has a capacity for one hundred and fifty,' said Martin. 'And the place was full to bursting.'

'Ooo-kay. This could be some party.'

'CCTV can keep monitoring the pub. But the UAF lot will be along at some point, no doubt. And that's before we even start thinking about three thousand away fans arriving in the city. We just wanted to check in with you, see if the Chief Super has any instructions.'

Keith transmitted, his voice quieter now; David guessed that Da Silva was probably in the command room, in his usual spot just behind the Tac Advisor's seat. 'We've already got the PSUs moaning about the refs. I broached that with him half an hour ago and he still hasn't made a decision.'

'I'm not surprised,' interrupted David.

'That you, Flub?' asked Keith.

'How's the movies, my man?'

A faint laugh. 'Bouncy.'

David checked his watch: nudging seventeen thirty hours. 'We're pressed for time here, Keith. I've got one in the van, single-crewed, and the streets are starting to flood with bodies.'

'Okay.' A sigh in David's ear. 'Leave it with me.'

Martin ended the call. Turned to David. '"Bouncy"?'

'Keith's got a bit of a fetish for naked, minimum-thirty-eight-double-D-breasted women firing high-powered weaponry,' David smiled. 'I borrowed one of his DVDs once. *Clunge with Gunz.*'

'Catchy.' Martin puffed air out of his mouth, the breath suffused with red from the neon bar signs. 'You sure it was the right thing to do, bypassing the Chief Super?'

'You ever been to a Silver command room?' David asked.

The boy shook his head, eyes scanning the street from under the brim of his helmet.

'Rammed with rankers and hangers-on from across the emergency services,' David said. 'And if that wasn't enough to put you off, they're letting those pashmina-wringing mung bean eaters from Liberty sit in the middle of all our confidential gubbins.'

Martin shrugged. 'It's for transparency.'

'It's because the bosses are shit scared of being labelled *something*ist, is what,' David said. 'And Da Silva's the worst of the lot. You really need to learn to go to the right people, Sarge. Da Silva doesn't care about you at all. Until you fuck up, that is.'

'Just a collar number.'

'You're not wrong there.'

The boy nodded. 'I could do with a little help here, Dave,'

he said then, looking up at him. His expression was almost despondent.

Dullas may have been right about the kid being out of his depth, David thought. *Too keen to prove himself as well. A dangerous combination.*

He looked down at Martin, could see his old man in him. Mark Finch. *Jurassic Mark*, they called him. A dinosaur, had been around for ever, since the days of Sir Robert Peel it felt like. Knew everyone, knew how to play the game. Got out unscathed too, which was rare. A survivor. Until the cancer took him, anyway.

'Your father wouldn't have needed to ask,' David said, and he hadn't meant to say it out loud, hadn't meant to say anything at all about Jurassic, at least not until they knew the boy a little more, but if he was being honest with himself he was already warming to the new sergeant.

Martin cocked his head, eyes wide. 'You *knew* him?'

David sighed. Weighed it up: stay quiet until he was certain the boy wasn't a plant from HQ, or take him on face value and let him in a little. He decided to give it up. Give the boy a chance. If nothing else it would annoy Vincent and Andrew. And he was too tired and long in the tooth to play stupid games.

He nodded, looked away. 'I'm sorry about . . . what happened to him.'

'Thank you,' Martin said, stepping closer. 'I didn't know you knew him. I've never worked with anyone who knew him.'

There was something about the shine in the boy's eyes that was unnerving. He'd moved closer again, was almost chest to chest, head pushed back to study David's features.

'We'd better get a shufty on,' he said, shifting on his feet. People were moving past and watching them; it was making him uncomfortable.

'What was he like to work with?' Martin asked.

'He was a good old boy,' said David, feeling mildly unnerved with the sergeant close enough to caress his gonads if the urge took him. He took a step back. 'Shall we head over to the van?'

'I've always wanted to know more about him,' said Martin. 'I was still a kid, really. I never got the chance to learn from him. Learn about the job, I mean.'

David decided to move. He turned and walked, Martin fell in alongside, eyes still on him. He was already regretting opening his mouth. For one, the rest of the van would take him to task for showing a little kindness to the new guy when none of them really knew what he was about. Second, Dullas's moaning would reach new and previously untouched levels. And third, and most worryingly, the kid now seemed to think he and David had a connection, that David was his means of getting to know the father he had lost.

The fucking questions would never end.

David wondered if the boy knew the meaning of the expression *feet of clay*. He wondered how he was going to deal with that, when it inevitably arose. He wondered why he had mentioned the boy's father at all.

'You'll do fine, kid,' David said, but couldn't be sure if he was lying or not.

It was like a Saturday night. People everywhere, masses of supporters drifting westwards towards their theatre of dreams, revellers queuing at pub doorways in search of their own brand of entertainment, clumps of drunks clogging pavements and roads with the now-happy taxi drivers easing through the sea of people and sounding horns to clear a passage through the morass of bodies.

'They must be bloody freezing,' David said, shaking his head as they shuffled along: a clutch of girls, barely out of their mid teens, barely clothed against the worsening chill. Bare, really.

'Those aren't skirts,' David said, ogling. 'They're more like wide belts.'

Martin smiled. 'If my daughter ever dressed like that . . .'

'You got a daughter?' David asked, incredulous. 'What, you a daddy when you were ten or something?'

Martin chuckled. 'I was speaking hypothetically. And thinking of a long way into the future. My wife is due imminently, though. A boy.'

David whistled, raised an eyebrow under his lid. 'Your first?'

'The great unknown.'

A louder whistle. 'Sarge, I love my kids, but if you think you need help now, wait till the sprog pops out and has you in his clutches.' He gave a loud cackle.

'Cheers,' Martin said. 'I think.'

David motioned for him to stop as a taxi pulled up in front of them; they watched as two women clambered out of the back seat. Both around Martin's age, but they looked oddly incongruous amongst the teeming hordes of Lolitas strutting about the street. Despite this the whoops and catcalls started, the *awright darlins* and cries of *you pair of beauties*.

The taller of the two, a stick-thin woman with hair dyed a screaming red, was already in her cups and *come on, come on*ing to her companion as she righted the sequinned silver dress that hugged her bony frame. The second woman, a blonde, was trying to pay the taxi driver through the car window, and turned towards her friend.

'Calm down, Chloe, will you?' the blonde said, checking through her clutch bag.

'Ooh, might have a cat fight here,' muttered David.

The blonde took her change, straightened up. She clocked Martin and David staring at her and lowered her head as if to check the little black dress she was wearing. When she looked up there was a thin, weary smile on her lips. David caught the nod she threw at the boy, then the look she gave to her flame-haired friend.

David turned to Martin. 'Looks like you've still got it, matey,' he said.

'Something about the blonde,' the boy said.

David nodded. 'She's a pretty one alright.'

'I mean there's something vaguely familiar about her.' Martin was blowing onto his hands.

'Oh I get it,' said David, giving him a nudge.

The boy looked up. 'No. Happily married,' he said, shaking his head.

'Yeah, right,' snorted David, looking at him with amusement. 'Give it six months with that ankle-biter of yours then come and speak to me about a happy, stress-free marriage.'

Martin's Airwave set bleeped and vibrated. David watched as Martin's curiously stumpy finger depressed the transmit button to answer the private point-to-point call.

It was Keith.

'Shout came in ten seconds ago,' Keith's metallic, distorted voice blurted into their earpieces. 'Thought you'd want to know soonest: one of the PSU vans just picked up a load of people heading over to the Cardiff City Stadium.'

Martin glanced at David, too quickly for him to hide his resigned expression.

'Let me take a wild guess: UAF?' Martin transmitted.

'Yarp,' Keith replied. 'About five hundred of them.'

'Deep joy,' muttered David.

'And it gets better,' Keith said. 'I'm watching the CCTV

covering District Five as we speak. Long old line of Casuals streaming out of the doors and heading west.'

Martin groaned. 'Towards the stadium.'

'With Nathan Telemaque front and centre.'

Martin lowered his face into one hand. 'I suppose Da Silva wants us to make our way?'

'You and every other spare body we've got.'

'Which means we'll be outnumbered ten to one.'

Keith chuckled. 'Remember the Alamo, yeah?'

'TJF,' transmitted David.

'I hear you, brother,' said Keith. 'TJF indeed.'

Martin cut the call and looked at David.

'"TJF"?' he asked.

David began to walk.

'The job's fucked,' he yawned over one shoulder.

Alan sat quietly in the driver's seat of the carrier, head back and nestled against the headrest, body limp. The diesel engine ticked over, a low growl. The Airwave set burbled and bleeped, the comms girls in Silver updating the troops about Casuals and UAF already clashing in the stadium car park. Air con blew warmth into the cab. The street was filling up, home fans drifting from the eastern side of the city, using the shopping centre as a short cut to the stadium on the west, stopping to fill up its wealth of fast-food joints and theme pubs, filling themselves up with cheap burgers and discounted drinks before the match.

Some shouted abuse as they passed, sneered at him, threw salad and ice cubes at the window, at the bodywork. Others gave him the finger, or mouthed obscenities, or beckoned for him to leave the van so they could jump him. One supporter, his face twisted and ugly and filled with hate, came right up to his window and knocked and when Alan didn't respond, thumped the glass with the palm of his curled hand and told him he was a *pussy cop* and a *kiddy fiddler* and that he was going to drag him out and beat him to death.

It barely registered with Alan.

If he was at home now he could make sure everything was okay with Lisa. They would talk things over, work things out. He would tell her that next time around he would pass the promotion board, he'd get the Blackstone's books and study hard, apply himself, she would see a change, he would move up in the world, get those stripes on his shoulders, show her he was still the man she fell in love with and *her father is wrong, he's so wrong to be telling her those things, that he's a failure, that he'll be a PC until he retires and it's not as if her father had nothing to do with it anyway, is it?* At home and at work, he'd loomed large and meddled constantly, whispering his disappointment to his daughter who now looked at Alan with contempt, pulled strings and stabbed his back behind the scenes at HQ where he constantly berated him to other senior officers. Alan knew if that happened your career was pretty much over before it began.

The things he'd done for her. The changes. The sacrifices. When they first met she was already deeply involved in the Capital Temple, had grown up with the children of the temple's pastor, a magnetic and mesmerising man whose guttural, growling sermons Alan soon came to associate with their Sunday evening *dates*. He'd never been a religious man, had even been scornful of the church and its patrons until then, but he loved Lisa and desperately wanted her to be happy, wanted her to love him, so surrendered, gave himself to her and her beloved church, forced himself to believe, to succumb, and once he let go, once he realised the profound change that was taking place within himself, and all for his beautiful wife, from that point it was inexorable.

And now . . .

Alan knew something was very, very wrong and it was all he could do to stop himself grabbing the steering wheel and driving home to confront her.

The signs. They were all there.

The new hairstyle, the dye job.

But she's always said she wanted to see what she looked like as a blonde.

The diet.

But then, isn't everyone on a diet after Christmas?

The new underwear.

But she was always complaining how her old stuff was tatty.

She'd been so distant lately.

But her mother's been ill and Lisa's worried about her.

These thoughts rattled back and forth in his mind, making his head thrum.

Those vile creatures, smashing my car window. I'm stuck here now. Stuck here in this madness, the money I'm earning already spent on replacing the glass, on paying a grease monkey for the privilege of calling him out on Boxing Day.

He tried not to let it matter. Tried. Balled his hands into fists.

'You chickenshit copper!' the fan shouted, cheered on by his companions, but Alan wasn't listening as he blinked away the image of his wife cowed on the floor by their bed, hands raised, fearful, the dark shadow of the criminal falling over her as she screamed.

The supporter stood at the window for a moment, not quite sure what else to do. The plod sitting in the driver's seat wasn't biting. He hadn't moved.

The fan waited a few more seconds then shrugged and walked away, his mind already wrestling with the more important decision he had to make: McDonald's or KFC.

EMBRACING
DIVERSITY

It didn't take long for Martin, once in the job, to realise that his father had shielded him from most of the unpleasant aspects of police work. It was always the funny incidents and practical jokes with colleagues on his relief that he shared with his fascinated son, even after a night shift where, exhausted and clearly desperate for his bed, he'd still pull Martin on to his knee and spend half an hour thrilling him with the exciting things he'd got up to, Martin's mother pottering about behind them, humming as she prepared breakfast.

His parents had done a pretty good job of shielding him from most of life's nasty little secrets, to such an extent that by the time he entered university to waste three years studying for a dry and uninvolving policing and criminology degree – all he'd wanted to do, and desperately so when his father died during his first year, was join up – Martin realised, one awful December evening, that he might be a little on the naive side.

That people weren't all as open and honest and friendly as he'd always thought. That his parents had made a mistake in wrapping their only child in cotton wool for most of his life, before sending him off to uni where he'd have to fend for himself for the first time in eighteen years.

That evening – his nascent relationship with Samanya in its second month, and at a pub in the town centre, away from the drinking games, thrashing music and pool tables of the student union – was the evening when, for a while, he came to love and hate his parents in equal measure.

Loved them for protecting him. Hated them for protecting him too much.

They'd chosen the pub for privacy, for a quiet booth in one corner, for easy conversation and a cheap bar meal. For a different atmosphere, something outside the bubble of student life with its lectures and *Loose Women*, its pasta packets and budget courgette bakes and squabbling over who did the dishes in the house he shared with five other guys.

An hour had passed, Martin held captivated – he was already in love – as Samanya talked about her law studies, her family, her plans, and for a blessed moment he'd forgotten about his dad's illness, about the impending trip home for Christmas where he'd have to confront the terrible reality, and not noticed the voices at the bar getting louder, not noticed what they were saying and who they were saying it to.

Only when a shadow had fallen across their table had he looked up, still smiling, still holding Sam's hand, to find the two men standing over them.

You fucking that wog, mate?

Sam's hand had squeezed desperately at his. Martin's smile had died and he'd nervously asked them if they really thought that was appropriate language in this day and age and the men had cackled drunkenly but there'd been no humour in the laughter and Martin, mouth dry and sticky, an odd tremble in his legs, had demanded they apologise immediately.

Then they'd set upon him.

As he'd cowered into the curve of the booth seat, Sam screaming somewhere above him, the fists and trainers and even a pint glass and its contents raining down on him, he'd cursed his overprotective parents, cursed himself for bringing his girlfriend to this place, cursed his naivety, his mistaken belief that all people had at least a little good in them.

Most of all he'd felt ashamed: curled on the musty fabric, the pain from the blows to his body and head had been dwarfed by the ache of guilt he'd felt, because for the tiniest moment he'd wished his dying father dead.

And because when that horrible question was asked of him he'd instinctively withdrawn his hand from Sam's.

Pulled it away, as if abandoning her in order to save himself.

Later that night, his scalp stitched and cracked ribs troubling him with every breath, he'd gripped her fingers, swearing that he'd never allow any of it to happen again.

Now, Martin felt the same sense of shock as he had in the days and weeks following the assault in the pub, albeit on another level. Shock at the ferocity of abuse, the intensity of hatred, the pointless violence, the ignorance on display as he stood, surrounded by people and placards, and once again wondered if he would have been better equipped to deal with this kind of thing if his father had just told it like it was. If he'd skipped the amusing war stories and tall cop tales in the kitchen and cut straight to the misery and death and horrendous things people do to one another. Classroom training packages and observing from a distance while mentally ticking promotion boxes didn't really cut it in terms of preparation and experience. But, he supposed, dead babies and mutilated domestic violence victims do not breakfast conversation make, no matter how jauntily you tell the tale.

He finally understood, though. He wouldn't dream of

telling Sam or his son, when he was old enough to ask, about the things he'd seen in the job. His own father had obviously made the same decision.

'Hold the line!' he yelled, wiping a gloved hand to clear the globule of phlegm from his visor. He was stunned that it had even happened.

'You fascist fucking *pig!*' the woman screamed at him, the abuse made all the more absurd and troubling by her clipped and refined accent, because if somebody as well heeled as this had turned on them with such venom just for keeping people separated, then he dreaded anybody a little more hardcore showing up. Martin looked her up and down through smeared plastic: forties, neatly dressed in quilted jacket, herringbone trousers, cashmere scarf and light brown bobble hat, a delicate touch of make-up. She reminded him of his old deputy head teacher, except his old dep head never once spat in his face for wearing a uniform.

The spitting across the police lines started within minutes of them plotting up in the car park outside the stadium. Plotting up with their thin blue line. And it really was thin. Thin to the point of emaciation. They'd mustered – he'd done a head count – sixty-six bodies to link arms and stand between the hundred or so Casuals lunatics and their immediately more vocal – and more aggressive – opposites in the Unite Against Fascism camp, which had swelled along their march. They'd picked up all sorts, from the soup kitchen rough sleepers to drinkers looking for a pre-nightclub giggle, to number more than six hundred. No dog handlers available. Two mounted plods, whom Martin was incredibly relieved to see when they trotted up, their horses skittering to and fro between the front lines, just about keeping a lid on it in one spot before it all kicked off again thirty feet away.

Nearly eight hundred people, the majority of them out for a spot of bother, corralled and compressed into the disabled parking area beneath the Canton stand, the chaos bathed in the soft white glow of external security flood-lights.

'Hold the line with what, exactly?' shouted Andrew, his NATO helmet shaking from side to side in disgust.

'You're just the EDL's army.'

'You fuckin' UAF allies.'

The chants from both sides. The spitting and eggs and placards swatting at helmets. The thin line between, and they'd become the object of hatred for both simply because they were there, and had the temerity to keep them apart.

Piggies in the middle.

Martin hooked his arm into Andrew's elbow, into Vincent's on his right, pulled them close, steadied himself against the crush. *Always stay on your feet. Never go to ground if you can help it.* Drilled into him, into all of them during basic training. He'd seen the videos, of officers falling to the ground during scuffles. Of the packs of teenagers swarming the poor plods' prone bodies, stamping and kicking heads as if they were footballs, indifferent to the fact that just one of those kicks could kill.

The woman who'd spat at him was jostled to one side, lost in the melee, her snarling mouth dissolving into a sea of snarling mouths. An egg landed on Andrew, spattering his fluorescent tabard. Cheers rang out. Fists flew, from in front, from behind, Martin amazed that most of the violence was coming from the supposedly peaceful Unite Against Fascism counter-protestors. They'd chanted and shouted about freedom, about democracy, about fear and prejudice, but to Martin it seemed – with their behaviour, which was far worse than anything the Casuals were meting out – they'd become what they hated, that they were everything they opposed.

'Patchouli-oiled hypocrites,' said Andrew, flinching as another set of knuckles scraped the side of his helmet. It connected with a skinhead behind him, bringing about another push and retaliatory punches. 'They think they're better than the hoolies so twatting 'em is okay.'

'They're winning though,' shouted Vincent.

'Well, we're getting ripped to bits here,' said Andrew. 'There's not enough of us.'

Martin checked along the cordon: David and Alan barely visible amongst the outstretched arms and grabbing, grappling hands; David was shouting something at him but Martin heard nothing. The noise was incredible. The heat of bodies pressed against him almost cloying. The evening air heavy with stale coffee breath, with lager fumes.

'Should we draw batons?' he yelled at Vincent.

'You're the stripy, you make the call,' Vincent barked.

Andrew rolled his eyes at Martin before thrusting his head forward to butt a scowling, struggling protestor in the chest with his helmet. 'Back off, you fuckin' hippy.'

'You Nazi scum!' the man screamed, and the crowd behind him surged forward again.

Fighting against the mess of writhing limbs, Martin craned his neck, looked over one shoulder. Saw Nathan Telemaque alone on the fringes of the car park, pacing back and forth, mobile clamped to his ear. Like he was nothing to do with any of it. Like he was an innocent passer-by, stopping to goggle at the mini-riot taking place. He was a hundred yards away but Telemaque's amused expression was clearly visible as his mouth moved against the phone, eyes shifting beneath the brim of his cap and surveying the carnage.

Arranging. Orchestrating. *He must be*, thought Martin. A second later he was convinced: Telemaque's right hand pointed to one of the mounted officers; within a second over a dozen Casuals shifted in that direction, looping around the back of the crowd, putting pressure on a point in the police cordon where officers were isolated, were battling hand-to-hand to keep people apart.

Just for a moment Martin felt a flicker of envy. At Telemaque's prowess for marshalling his troops. At his organisational excellence. At his ability to make split-second decisions under pressure.

He lowered his head, felt a numbness in his chest, his arms. His legs, shaking like that night in the pub with Sam.

'You going to make the call or what?'

Vincent at his right ear, voice hoarse.

'We need to . . .' Martin said, but trailed off. He didn't know what they needed. They were losing control. He was the only substantive sergeant on the line, and he was losing control.

More noise, louder still, shouts and shrieks from further along the cordon. He looked in that direction, saw one of the police horses rear up, spooked, saw placards and signs hitting the animal on its flanks, its head, people pulling at its rider.

Saw David break away from the line, push towards him, visor tucked down as he ducked the hands and bottles being thrown.

'God's sake, kid,' he bellowed, and snatched Martin's Airwave set from his vest, the set Martin used for direct contact with Silver Command.

'*Code Red!*' David screamed into the radio. 'Urgent assist-ance required at the stadium car park. Repeat, *urgent assistance required at the stadium.*'

Martin heard the shout go out in his earpiece. The comms girls broadcasting it on all channels across the city. David dug the PR back on to Martin's vest, eyed him with contempt, stalked away.

''Bout time somebody did somethin',' said Andrew.

Martin listened to the acknowledgements, the call signs on their way to the shout, the divisional officers cutting short their burglary visits and house-to-house enquiries, their dumped stolen vehicles and pub fights, the traffic black rats peeling away from the link roads and motorways, the rest of the mounted section abandoning crowd-control duties nearby and giving their ETA as three minutes, one of them even joking about making it at a canter, and Martin wished he'd just called it in himself.

Just pressed that button and asked for further units at scene.

Just made a decision.

He looked for Telemaque again but he was nowhere to be seen.

The reinforcements made short shrift of the crowd, dispersing them across the car park and into the night. Horse charges, divisional prisoner vans blocking roadways, response officers acting as arrest teams to snatch ringleaders.

Within ten minutes of David's call, it was over.

So simple, in the end.

Martin walked amongst the rubble and broken glass, the pieces of wood, the clusters of officers talking up the rumble, still adrenalised, their voices high and excitable. He stepped on a placard, looked down.

STOP THE HATE inked on the bright orange rectangle in marker pen.

He thought of Samanya.

'Is everybody all right?' he asked, edging up to the team

where they hovered at the side of the carrier, the sliding door open, David sitting on the metal step and leaning back on his elbows. Andrew slouched at the front passenger door, his long forearm hanging over the wing mirror, eggshell glued to his chest.

Vincent was hunched near the back wheel, NATO resting between his thighs. 'We're fine,' he said without looking at Martin. 'Just thankful somebody took control of that clusterfuck.'

'No offence, like,' Andrew said, without conviction.

Martin's face suddenly felt hot, flushed. He turned to David. 'I appreciate what you did,' he said quietly.

'No bother,' David said, and pulled on his cigarette, not caring whatsoever about Martin or anybody else objecting to the smoking in public and while on duty.

'Where's Alan?' Martin asked.

Andrew unclipped his helmet strap, took the NATO off and rubbed at the sweat covering his scalp. 'Playing nurse,' he said, motioning towards a line of Portaloos tucked in one corner.

Alan was hunched over somebody, PSU medic kit open at his feet, dressings and sprays on the tarmac. Whoever was lying on the ground was clearly unhappy: Martin could hear angry shouts and see the person's legs fidgeting and twitching.

'Need a hand?' asked Martin, stopping behind his colleague.

'Maybe a muzzle?' said Alan over his shoulder.

The casualty was a teenager, an Asian lad, no more than eighteen, nineteen. A deep gash ploughed across his forehead from the left eyebrow and into the hairline; his face was slick with blood from the wound, despite Alan's best efforts. He turned to Martin, eyes flicking to his epaulettes.

'You're in charge, are you? Are you?' Loud, agitated.

'I'm in charge, yes,' said Martin, and sunk to his haunches to speak to the teen.

'So why did you set the horses on us? Look at my head, man. Just look at it! Knocking us all over? It was a peaceful protest—'

'You think that was peaceful?'

'*It was a peaceful protest!*' the teen screamed and sat upright, Alan placing a hand to his chest. 'Peaceful until you lot got involved. You let those Nazis have a go at us. You're all the same. All the same.'

'We couldn't let you fight each other. There's no need for viol—'

'*You're all the fucking same, you racists.*'

Martin shook his head. 'You don't know me or anything about me, my friend.'

'Friend? I'm not your friend. *Fuck off, you Nazi pig.*'

Alan sighed, holding the straining teenager against the ground with the palm of his hand. 'I'd give up if I was you.'

Martin stood. Stared at the teenager. Thought about explaining all to him. About Sam, about the countless other times when comments had been made, when looks had been thrown their way while out shopping, or in restaurants, even at the student union bar during those early years. All those times he'd been left frustrated and angry for not speaking up. For not confronting people.

He thought of the pub again.

Turned away.

As he walked back to the van, the teenager's voice rang in his ears.

'*Stephen Lawrence! Stephen Lawrence! You're all the fucking same!*'

Andrew shifted aside as Martin opened the passenger

door and climbed into his seat. As he pulled the door closed, he caught Andrew and Vincent exchanging a look.

Heard Vincent mutter, 'We're bubbling the away fans in next. He'll fuck that up too.'

Heard Andrew say, 'He couldn't organise a fuck-up in a fuckery.'

Martin swallowed, sank into the seat. Checked his mobile for any message from Sam, kidding himself he was checking she was okay when really he needed something, anything, to hold on to.

There was nothing.

DELIVERING PUBLIC REASSURANCE

'Coppers put the kettle on, coppers put the kettle on . . .'

The away fans, surrounded by police in public order kit, were in fine voice.

'. . . coppers put the kettle on, we're going to stab three.'

They'd rendezvoused with Bronze at the railway station, Andrew slapping his baton into his palm as the smiling, chatty Swansea supporters swarmed off the train. Disappointed at the lack of a bite and angered by the reproachful look from the onion, he'd sulked behind the wheel of the carrier as the containment bubble made its way westwards. He was still sulking and grinding his teeth as they passed through the Leckwith area, just a mile from the Cardiff ground.

He flipped the visor up on his NATO helmet, peered at them through the windscreen, at the backs of hundreds of shaved heads and baseball caps, at a legion of white-shirted visiting Swansea fans marching slowly towards the stadium while singing the same four lines over and over and over and it was taking all the strength he could muster not to smash his specially ordered German parachute boots – not official issue, of course, but then the job stopped paying for footwear years ago so as far as Andrew was concerned SMT could go fuck themselves – onto the accelerator and cause vehicular carnage.

It was only because the rest of the team were out and on foot, high-vizzed up and forming one of the containment lines directly between the carrier and the fans, that he decided to let his boot hover just above the pedal. Vincent, in particular, was walking right in front of the van's front grille, having argued quite reasonably that it was bloody freezing outside and he was taking that spot so the engine would warm his backside.

'If I see your eye going . . .'

Andrew turned to Alan in the front passenger seat. He wasn't even looking at Andrew as he spoke. His helmet was ill-fitting and squeezed at his cheeks, turning his ever-present expression of misery into a pained pout.

'You'll what, exactly?' asked Andrew, pushing his chin out at him and leering. 'Get all fire and brimstone on me arse?'

'I'd like,' Alan said, closing his eyes, 'one shift to go by without you losing the plot. You've been hyper since the protest. We're just here to shepherd the away fans to the ground then go for tea and biscuits. It's not the Gulf War.'

'It's still game on,' said Andrew. 'That hippy lot might have sloped off home but the Casuals are well up for it. You've heard the intel reports over the PRs. They're still hanging about. They lost that rumble. You know they won't let it lie.'

'They may not even show their faces again,' Alan sighed, exasperated.

'It's *the* derby match,' Andrew laughed, pointing at the bubble of supporters lined in front of the van. 'And they've got three hundred away fans to have a go at right here.'

'Well, let's keep a little faith,' said Alan.

'Robust policing'll sort 'em out if they do,' said Andrew, excited at the prospect of further aggravation. 'Firm but fair, innit? We should've gone in hard in that car park and it wouldn't have got out of hand like it did. If I wanted pussying around and listening to sob stories about nasty neighbours growing their trees over an old dear's fence I'd transfer to a community team.'

Alan opened his eyes and looked at him. 'There's robust, then there's you who holds the force record for CS spray discharge and ordering replacement batons because you've already bent four from overuse.'

'Love it,' Andrew beamed.

'It wasn't a compliment, you buffoon. You're going to do something someday that will end up with you gripping the rail in Crown. Then it's a fast track to a few years over the wall and the rest of your life wasting away watching Benefits TV all day with whichever woman you decide to shack up with next.'

Andrew very nearly said something. Something that would have quietened his companion quicker than a Taser would drop a raging football hoolie. The only thing that stopped him speaking, the only cogent reason that bubbled through the mire of his jumbled and angry thought process to stop him destroying Alan in five short and terrible words – *Vince is fucking your wife* – was that Vincent had expressly told him not to.

Vincent would abandon him for doing his legs. He disposed of everyone and everything that became troublesome to him, especially women. From conversations in the carrier over the years, Andrew knew it was something to do with Vince's parents, and what he'd learned from them when just a kid, but the finer points of it were vague to Andrew because he hadn't always listened. Night shifts, when most of the small talk and sleep-deprived banter took place and where people inadvertently opened up more, was when he slept in a shield rack at the back of the van, wrapped in his old Marines bivvy bag and purring like an infant. A lot of it Andrew didn't really understand anyway, so it was easier if he didn't dwell on it.

But he didn't want to lose Vincent. Not ever. Being around him gave Andrew a taste of what his life used to be like. The fucking about. The freedom. The glory years.

So he squeezed against the spasm in his right eye, grimaced as if suffering some terrible ache there, and spat: 'Watch your mouth, Bible boy.'

'You'll take us with you, you know,' said Alan. 'The whole van. Take us down.'

'Rubbish.' Andrew nodded towards the away fans. 'Wish I was out there now with me stick. Get in the bubble, few whacks for effect, they'd soon stop performing.'

'It's just banter,' sighed Alan. 'If you can't take it . . .'

'. . . you're in the wrong job. Yeah, yeah. Don't go swinging the old blue lamp, Al. I've got the years in too. But I'm telling you: drop one of that lot with a Taser, let his pals see him doing the Curly Shuffle round the floor for a minute, they'd soon stop singing that shite.'

'Ah, "Behold",' said Alan, '"How good and how pleasant it is for brethren to dwell together in unity".'

'Please don't start with that,' Andrew said. 'It'll tip me over the edge, I swear.'

'You could do with getting some of it in your life, my friend.'

Andrew shifted in his seat and leaned forwards, his freak-ishly long arms cradling the steering wheel.

'Religion, yeah,' he yawned, drew it out for effect. 'Giving hope to people in a world ripped to shit by . . . religion.'

Alan raised his eyebrows. 'Profundity from you? Well I never.'

Andrew blinked, reached forward. Pinched the volume dial on the in-carrier Airwave set between a gloved thumb and forefinger. 'I dunno what you're on about and you're cooking my swede now, Dullas, so shut the fuck up, you boring throbber.'

'I have *told* you not to call me that, you . . . you . . .' Alan struggled.

'You what? Duh-dur-dur . . . spit it out, you stuttering fucktard.'

'. . . you *onanist*,' Alan blurted, but Andrew didn't hear him.

He'd yanked on the lever to drop the windscreen shield, smacked his visor down with a gloved hand, turned the volume up to maximum, the comms girl's voice filling the carrier, telling them what they didn't want to hear, telling them it was all going horribly wrong further down the containment line.

It was difficult to see them in the darkness.

The first shower came from a side street, grey shadows spinning against black sky. Martin didn't realise, didn't even know what was happening, merely thought it odd that the singing had stopped so abruptly.

Then the shout came over the radio from somebody at the front of the bubble.

'*Missiles!*'

As he heard it, the high, adrenalised warning, as Vincent and David swapped glances, the stones and beer bottles then a lone piece of timber, a garden fence post or ripped-out windowsill, began to rain down amongst the away fans in front of him. He watched, breath suddenly fogging the visor on his NATO helmet, the quickening thump of his heart loud in his ears, as people crumpled to the ground. Away fans. Officers on the right flank of the containment, their Level One kit no protection against the hail of heavy projectiles.

'*No surrender, no surrender, no surrender . . .*'

It was coming from the surrounding streets. Martin thought of Telemaque, of the tiny button on the lapel of his jacket. CASUALS UNITED. Keith had rung him after the scuffles between the Casuals and Unite Against Fascism: while the UAF had downed placards and gone home, Telemaque's hoolies had been spotted here, there and every-where in smaller pockets, retreating to pubs and snooker halls and shop doorways. Waiting for the order to gather again. Waiting for the visiting fans.

'They want to win at least one fight tonight,' Keith had said to him.

A police horse, a dapple grey that had run the lines at the protest, reared upwards, squealing, its rider – a chunky, silver-haired veteran whom Martin thanked profusely after the crowds had cleared in the stadium car park – struggling to stay in the saddle.

Just in front of Martin a supporter, drunk and as yet unaware of what was going on, pointed and laughed at the horse, the thin scar at the side of his right eye wrinkling as he cackled uncontrollably.

'Only animals I know that've got cunts on their backs,' the man cried.

He turned and made as if to high-five a companion, but the companion had vanished. The fan looked around, momentarily confused, then down, his mouth dropping open when he saw his friend pale and unconscious on the ground, an opaque bruise dusted with orange already spreading across his buddy's left temple, a half house brick next to his head on the concrete.

'How . . . ?' the fan blurted.

Then the wheel came off.

Incandescent light from above, panning back and forth among the teeming column of supporters, throwing strange, malformed shadows on to house walls. Martin squinted to let his eyes adjust to the brightness of the helicopter's searchlight. Saw the stones had become blocks of concrete and chunks of rubble. The lone piece of wood replaced by multiple lumps of timber. Hammering down on them. Arcing into the bubble, towards officers on the perimeter, from both sides of the main road.

The away fans went berserk.

'Where're the shield cordons?' Vincent shouted.

White-shirted supporters had turned to them, teeth bared, pulling at their overalls and gloves and helmets, pushing against them to get out of the containment, to get away from the relentless bombardment, but with the carrier behind them Vincent and Martin and David had nowhere to move, no way to let them out.

Martin tightened his grip on David's belt, shook his head; he didn't know. Bronze public order was silent. There were no transmissions from the Silver command room either. The PSUs meant to screen and clear junctions were nowhere to be seen.

'Not again,' grunted David, head tucked low and pushing back against the frenzied, terrified away crowd. 'Wish I was back in the bloody BINGO seat.'

A crush was forming. The containment march had stopped. People at the front of the bubble were pushing backwards, towards the rear, to escape the bombardment. Dozens of struggling bodies, then hundreds, pressing up against each other, strangled shouts and calls to *'Let us out, we're getting battered, let us out of here, you wankers'* and still David and Vincent were wrestling and holding them off, shaking their heads, telling them *'We can't, we can't let you out'* because as bad as it was now both knew if the bubble burst and the away fans spilled out into the side streets there would be butchery on a scale not seen outside a football stadium for decades.

Da Silva, despite his unhelpful silence, would be mightily unimpressed.

And there was still nothing from the Bronze public order commander.

'Fuckin' do somethin' this time,' screamed Vincent. He was bent backwards over the bonnet of the carrier, white shirts swarming him, on him, twisted faces pressed up to his visor; the bonnet was crumpling under the weight of bodies.

Martin looked skywards, at the helicopter looping in low, tight circles above them, the fast *whuckawhuckawhucka* so loud as to be almost deafening, the rotor blades so close on one pass that they ruffled his epaulettes. He followed the glare of its searchlight as it juddered, casting the chaos in an eerie, bleached glow, as if somebody was screening a black-and-white recording of a riot before his eyes. It was surreal. Unreal. He looked to Vincent, then David, the helicopter a roaring shape in the night sky, his radio suddenly buzzing endlessly as officer after officer along the bubble pressed their emergency buttons, his ears ringing, his throat tight and dry. People were punching him. Yanking at his overalls.

Martin stared at the mob of away fans encircling him. Their mouths moving, stretched and ugly and angry. He couldn't hear anything they were saying. There was noise but he couldn't understand it.

His body felt heavy, that numbness again. The tremor in his legs, just above his knees, making him feel as if they might give way at any moment. He let the punches rain down on him. It felt easier to let them do it, somehow. To let them get on with it.

'Where's Bronze? *Where is Bronze?*' yelled David, and drew his ASP, racked it, started swinging wildly. Lashing out before they were overwhelmed, trampled underfoot. Hit forearms, hands, shoulders, foreheads with the balled tip of his extendable baton. Trying to force people back. Yet the fans kept coming. Blood on some of them now. Angrier still.

'*Make a fuckin' decision for once!*'

It was loud, so loud, audible even over the beat of the

chopper's rotors, a crackled and fuzzy bark over the cacophony that startled Martin and he turned, saw Andrew and Alan leaning forwards in the cab of the van, misshapen faces peering through the flip-down grille shielding the windscreen, Andrew with a gloved hand clenched around the loudspeaker mike, pointing at Martin, furiously jabbing his finger at the glass.

Martin thought of his father. Of what David had said to him when he'd asked for help. Less than two hours before. An age ago.

He struggled a hand up through the mass of limbs and white shirts, depressed the transmit button, repeated the other officers' requests for urgent assistance, asked for instructions from the Bronze public order commander, for anything from Da Silva in the command room.

Waited.

Waited.

And nothing.

Twice as hard at everything, yes?

He elbowed a supporter's hand away from his chest, twisted at the waist. 'Take the van up to the right junction,' he screamed at Andrew. 'Chase those bastards back, run them over if you have to. And switch the van radio to the divisional channel, see if Ops Room have picked up on this. Tell them to send everyone.'

He watched, sucking in breath, as Andrew reversed away, head shaking in the windscreen as he backed off. The carrier screamed ahead, along the right side of the bubble, turned into the side street, disappeared. A handful of officers split from the containment, charged after the van, batons and CS spray canisters drawn, bellowing as they went.

The bottles and wood and stones and coins stopped coming.

With the carrier gone Martin felt the pressure of the

swell of bodies more keenly, hung on to David's belt to stop the fans breaking loose, leaned forward, pushed on his toes to hold the line. Lifted a hand. Radioed again: 'Charlie Victor three nine, take the left junction. Disperse the home fans, then block the road.'

He was sweating heavily, despite the cold. His arm shook, his muscles burned, with the effort of holding on to David, with holding back the rampaging white shirts.

Martin watched the carrier he'd radioed accelerate away to his left, take the junction opposite Andrew and Alan, blue strobes punctuating the grey evening light.

The missiles stopped completely.

Then it was as if nothing had happened, that the last five minutes had been some kind of hallucination or episode of mass hysteria. Martin shook his head, incredulous, as people stopped pushing at them, just stopped and turned and, once the injured fans had been carted away by PSU medics and the downed officers replaced on the line, began walking again as the containment continued to shepherd them towards the stadium. Not one of them complained about David and his baton. Not one of them apologised to Vincent for near-pummelling him into the engine of the carrier. It was as if somebody had flicked the switch that controlled their collective thought process to *Back to the footy, then.*

The helicopter peeled off, its light roaming the side roads further ahead, leaving the containment to wander through yellow street light and a drizzle that had now begun to fall.

'Amazing,' Martin said. 'I can't believe it.'

'Wouldn't go that far,' Vincent said, looking down at him as they walked. 'You took your sweet time sorting it out.'

'Got there in the end though, didn't he?' David said. 'Not too shabby after all. I feel a splash of Kouros coming on.'

'Let's ring the Chief Constable, he can give him one of his special commendations for, I dunno, doing his job?' snapped Vincent.

Martin ignored him, glanced at David. 'I mean the fans. They just . . . I mean, *look*.'

David slipped his ASP into its holder. He was still breathing heavily, his face ruddy and slick with sweat underneath his visor. 'They're used to it, kid. Long as we don't lock 'em up, they don't really care. It's all about the game.'

'Yeah. The *beautiful game*,' said Vincent.

David nodded. 'Beautiful game. Ugly bloody cast.'

They trudged onwards, towards the stadium.

The fans resumed singing.

'Coppers put the kettle on . . .'

It was forty-five minutes to kick-off.

'Amazing,' Martin said again.

'Totally,' said Vincent, and shook his head.

BUSIES

Martin sighed, Cardiff streets screaming past, the carrier's engine labouring.

'Is it always as crazy as this?' he asked.

Andrew glanced at him from the driver's seat. 'You after a tea break, Sarge?'

'Of course not. I just thought—'

'Well you thought wrong.'

'It's all gone pear-shaped again,' David said from behind. 'You might as well forget all those best-laid plans, I'm afraid.'

Martin nodded. He'd eventually managed to call on Bronze for their next deployment, the inspector explaining the loss of communications as a *glitch*, a *gremlin* from which *lessons would be learned* and an *action plan* was in place to ensure it never happened again. No mention of the nine injured officers, one of whom was now hospitalised with concussion and a broken collarbone. Nothing about the thirteen away fans who wouldn't be seeing the match after a supposedly safe containment from the pub to the ground.

Just, *Get yourselves up to the motorway and intercept a rogue vehicle*.

The intelligence had come in late: forty-odd away prominents trying to sneak in at the last minute using a privately hired coach. The flag had gone up twenty minutes ago, when the coach pinged an ANPR camera on the M4 west of the capital city.

'Now,' said Andrew.

Martin flicked the switch on the dash: sirens blared above

them as Andrew carved a route through a crossroads, the carrier rocking and pitching them in their seats, the strobes throwing indigo flickers against house fronts and waiting MOP vehicles.

'Why our serial again?' asked Vincent over the wailers. 'Are you volunteering us for everything or what? Showing leadership or whatever it is you have to do?'

'There isn't anyone else,' said Martin, trying not to sound as irritated as he felt with Vincent's constant sniping. 'Every other TSG is deployed at the stadium.'

'Five against forty or more? Excellent.'

'We've got a dog in support though.'

'Oh. That's all right, then.' Vincent shook his head, gripping the armrest.

The carrier careened westwards through the city, Martin cradling his handset against an ear, listening to the transmissions, the location updates for the coach. Behind him, amidst the rolling empty drinks bottles and week-old newspapers, David, Vincent and Alan sat quietly, buckled up in the darkness. Andrew dropped a gear, eased on to the slip for the ring road, headed towards the motorway.

Then: 'Traffic car has stopped it.'

Andrew looked at Martin. 'Where?'

'Services at junction thirty-three,' Martin said, shifting to hit the sirens again. 'The black rat is asking for us on the hurry-up.'

Andrew gritted his teeth, pushed hard on the revs.

Listing to one side and with an away team scarf tied to the radio antenna on its roof, the Volvo T5 sat in a puddle of gloom next to the motorway service station's pay-as-you-go pressure washer. The carrier's headlights lit up the traffic vehicle and a pair of wide, wet eyes above its steering wheel.

'Interesting,' remarked Alan, craning his neck to look through the windscreen.

The supporters' coach, engine idling, a dozen jeering faces pressed against the back window, was parked twenty yards further on near the shop forecourt. Two cashiers hovered at the night till, watching the goings-on intently, arms folded and the door clearly locked.

Martin jumped from the cab as the traffic officer climbed out of the stricken Volvo.

'You okay?' he asked. 'Are you hurt?'

'Thank God you're here,' she replied, her voice high and unsteady, and forced a smile but her hands shook while she fumbled the car keys into a pocket. She bent at the waist, coughing. 'I was speaking to the driver and that lot,' she gestured at the laughing fans in the window, 'they went ballistic. Chased me back to the car . . . for a minute or two I thought I was looking at a posthumous mention in weekly orders.'

'What happened to the car?' asked Martin, placing a palm on her body armour.

'They . . . they tried to drag me out but I managed to get the central locking on,' she breathed, straightening. She was the same height as Martin, and slender beneath the bulk of her uniform. 'So they started rocking the car while one of them let all the tyres down,' she said sheepishly. 'Hilarious stuff, right?'

'Did you see who did it?'

She shook her head. 'It all happened so quickly.'

'We'll struggle to pinpoint who was responsible, then,' Martin said.

She frowned. '*Sorry*. I was too busy dodging punches to write down a full description, Sarge.'

'Bastards,' grunted Andrew, withdrawing his ASP. *Shuk* went the metal as he flicked his wrist to·extend the baton.

''Least there's no damage,' offered David. 'No need for prisoners, then.'

Martin threw him a look, turned back to the traffic officer. 'I didn't mean to be—'

'I didn't mean to be either,' she interrupted. 'Look, the coach driver. He pulled them back in, shut the doors. Locked them all inside. If it wasn't for him . . .'

Martin nodded. Turned to Andrew. 'Steady, okay?'

'I'm always steady,' Andrew said, not looking at him. He had a menacing, troubling expression, was staring at the coach while repeatedly banging the balled tip of his ASP into the palm of one glove.

'Just let me deal with it,' Martin urged, and walked towards the coach.

Vincent lingered, watching them go; when he was sure they were out of earshot he stepped towards the traffic officer.

'Anything I can do for you, Charlotte?' he asked, hand moving towards her arm.

She swatted it away. 'Just fuck off, Vince, will you?' she sighed.

The away fans hammered windows, screamed and laughed, exposed penises and backsides, made the coach rock on its suspension, goaded them with wanker hand signs. The driver, a hideously obese bruiser sporting a salt-and-pepper buzz cut and old-timey tattoos on both forearms, remained distinctly unmoved by the fuckwittery on display and sat with his flabby chins resting on one hand as he chewed gum, ignoring the chaos around him and waiting for the signal to unlock the coach doors.

'We going in there or what, like?' demanded Andrew. 'Get Jabba the Hutt to open up. What we hanging back for?'

'Dog,' Martin said, pressing his earpiece into his ear and listening.

Andrew huffed, turned to Vincent. 'They could be an hour away.'

'No,' said Martin, nodding along the coach, to the Volvo. '*Dog*.'

Andrew followed the nod, saw the van pull to a stop next to the traffic car. The dog handler lurched out, scooted to the rear of his wagon, opened the cage door.

'Ah,' smiled Andrew. 'Dog.'

'That's not a dog, that's a werewolf,' said Alan, jaw dropping open.

The German shepherd strained at the leash, the handler – no small fellow himself, being well over six feet and tipping the scales at eighteen stone – struggling to control the yeti-like abomination that snarled and frothed towards them, its paws skittering on the forecourt cement.

'I'd stand back if I was you,' the handler shouted, pointing out the obvious.

Andrew checked the coach windows. No more penises. Devoid of backsides. Quiet. Still. Just a collection of wide, fearful eyes on a dog – a dog the size of a small horse – advancing towards them.

'Got to love those furry Exocets,' David said, giving the handler and the thing that led him plenty of room.

Martin signalled the driver. The big man, face impassive, hoisted himself to one side, reached down into the footwell, the jellied hunk of his shoulder shifting as he worked at something.

There was a tired hiss and the coach doors opened.

'Let her have a quick sniff,' the dog handler said, and reeled out the lead. 'Show 'em what they're up against.'

The German shepherd scrabbled up the coach steps, teeth exposed, its bark a gravelled foghorn blast. The handler restrained it next to the driver, whose hands were raised submissively, his chins trembling as he pushed himself as far away as possible from the animal. A cluster of supporters jumped from their seats, moved towards the back of the coach, shouts of 'all right, all right'.

'Good girl,' urged the dog handler, his voice a proud sing-song. 'There's a good girl, oooh, such a good girl.'

'Sweet,' laughed Andrew, tipping his head at the terrified driver. 'Look at the fat dude. He's squeezed so far into that corner we'll need to lube him out.'

Martin waited for the handler to reel his beast backwards, watching as the officer's face contorted with the effort of pulling the enormous dog from the coach.

'That should keep them quiet for you,' the handler smirked.

The interior reeked of alcohol; crushed lager cans and plastic cider bottles were scattered about the floor, newspapers, magazines and cardboard fast-food cartons completed the mess. Martin nodded a thank you to the driver. Breathed in the pungent alcohol fumes.

'Not exactly National Express, is it?' said David from behind him.

Martin couldn't see much of a difference to the inside of their own little bus, but said nothing. He turned to face the away supporters, did a quick head count, estimated around thirty of them eyeing him from seats, from the walkway.

Studied the faces studying him. Drunk. Prickly. Belligerent. Hushed.

'Glad to see I've got your attention,' he said.

'Oink oink,' came an anonymous voice.

Martin ground his teeth. Smiled at them. 'Okay. Here's how this goes. We are going to search your vehicle. We are going to search every one of you, one at a time, as you come off the coach. Whoever is in charge – and I know one of you is – you are going to remove the scarf from my colleague's vehicle and then apologise to her for your behaviour . . .'

'Bollocks,' somebody shouted.

'Not that you've got any, hiding back there,' snapped Vincent.

Martin paused. Then: 'If the apology is not forthcoming, or if we have any further issues, you will all be arrested.'

There were mutters and groans, a lone shout of 'For what?'

'If you comply, this fine gentleman,' Martin said, waving a hand at the driver, 'will return you to your home city so you can watch the match in the pub.'

A fan stood, thrust a sovereign-ringed finger at them. His Adidas tracksuit top was smudged with cigarette ash; Martin saw nicotine stains around his fingernails. 'You can't fuckin' do that,' he said.

'Actually, I can,' said Martin. 'You are all drunk. You are

a problem. You have *caused* problems. You would not be permitted entry to the stadium as a result. Your choice: apologise, go home, watch the match in the local. You still have time to make it. Or spend the night in the cells and miss the game completely.'

'What if we don't like either of those choices?' the fan leered.

Martin gestured out of the window. 'Then I will have my other colleague let his companion off its lead and we will shut the doors on you. I'm sure that will allow plenty of time for you all to make its acquaintance.'

Andrew checked through the window, at the row of disgruntled fans being patted down by David and Alan on the service station forecourt, at Martin and the traffic officer bawling out the away fan who'd identified himself as the group's organiser, at the dog handler walking the line and labouring to control the German shepherd as it drooled and snapped at thin air, yelping in frustration.

'Looks like the onion's got some balls on him after all,' said Andrew, leaning under a seat and scanning, his knobbly fingers feeling under the lip of cushion fabric. 'Took control of that lot all right.'

Vincent paused, hands poking the recesses of the baggage shelf, looked down from the seat he was standing on. 'He stamped his authority, so what?' he said, annoyed. 'Doesn't make him Winston Churchill all of a sudden. Doesn't make him his old man.'

'Well, you've got to give him credit—'

'No,' snapped Vincent. 'No I haven't.'

Andrew lowered his eyes, continued searching. 'Just sayin', like.'

They continued working in silence, listening to the dog howl and snarl outside, at the muted complaints from the supporters, at the multitude of person checks over the radio as Alan went through the supporters' details with Comms, all of them on record for something or other but nobody wanted, not even for a boring non-appearance warrant or breach of bail conditions. They toiled along the rows of seats, pulling open rusted ashtrays in armrests, stripping seat covers, checking the overhead light fittings, rifling rucksacks and plastic bags.

'Looky here,' Andrew said, peering into the side pocket of a Berghaus rucksack. He slipped a hand inside, pulled out a cardboard wrap and held it up between thumb and forefinger.

Vincent studied it. 'Gear?'

Andrew unfolded the cardboard, saw the pale brown powder, breathed in the unmistakeable aroma of stale cat piss, of ammonia.

'Speed,' he said, wrinkling his nose.

'Stop waggling it about and put it back, Thrush,' ordered Vincent. 'If the stripy sees that he'll have us arresting the entire coach for possession.'

Andrew zipped up the rucksack, wrap safely returned to its hiding place, and fingertipped onwards. Nothing but calcified chewing gum, tacky and melted sweets, bog-standard personal belongings, grime.

They'd nearly reached the back of the coach when Vincent whooped. 'Aha,' he smiled, wrestling with something.

'What you got, bruv?' Andrew said, standing and clapping his hands together to rid them of dust. 'Flares?'

Vincent was chuckling. 'Is the boy still flirting with Charlotte?'

Andrew peeked through the window again. 'Yup.'

'Good. Get Flub's attention, make sure he comes around the other side of the coach where our glorious leader can't see him.'

'What for?'

'These,' said Vincent, and pulled the tray of lager he'd found from the luggage shelf.

'*Beers*,' said Andrew, eyes lighting up.

Vincent shrugged. 'It'd be rude to turn up at Lewis's party without bringing something, right?'

David was frowning as he sidled up to the driver's window. 'What now?'

'Stop your whinging, tubs,' said Andrew. 'Look.'

He held up the slab of lager, twenty-four cans of Denmark's finest.

'Whoa!' said David. 'Quick, chuck it here.'

Andrew lowered it through the open window. 'Hide it in the shield rack for later.'

'And make sure short-arse doesn't see you do it,' said Vincent, pushing Andrew out of the way. 'I don't think it would go down very well.'

'Theft and drinking on duty?' chuckled David, trying to hide the booze under his body armour. 'You're talking stroke territory, methinks. But it'll go down well with me,' he purred, stroking one of the cans. 'Won't you, my little beauty?'

THE BEAUTIFUL GAME

The ground was almost full.

Turnstiles rolled and clanked, rolled and clanked, spewing bodies on to the concourses ringing the stadium. Home fans huddled in groups, chanted, shouted acknowledgements at other season ticket holders, made beelines for the food outlets and stalls selling replica shirts at astronomical prices. A frigid wind blew up from the pitch and through the vomitories, carrying with it the bitter tang of stale booze and then the acrid hum of urine from the overflowing toilets, the terrible bouquet hanging thick in the air of the bleak concrete corridors.

The noise from the stands. So loud already. A wall of sound and whistles, a morass of voices merged and seemingly as one.

'Bluebirds. Bluebirds. Bluebirds. Do the Ayatollah!'

Andrew tipped his NATO towards the nearest vomitory steps. 'Listen to 'em. They're ready for a tear-up.'

Martin was patting down a supporter; the fan glowered at him with arms raised, his companions muttering behind him as they waited with the stewards for their turn to be searched.

'It's just shouts and singing,' Martin said, waving the fan through. Another took his place, stopped and hoisted his hands into the air.

'I surrender,' the supporter laughed.

Martin smiled and nodded at him, turned to Andrew. 'See? Good-natured.'

Andrew waved one of the fans towards him. The man

was a squat and bespectacled fifty-something whose belly stretched his football shirt to its limits; Andrew took him by the shoulders of his puffa jacket, spun him, rifled the pockets of his jeans.

'Nothing but keys and a very thin wallet in there, boy.' The fan gave a smile over his shoulder.

'I ain't your boy,' Andrew said, gloves slapping at the supporter's flesh as he explored. 'And I think you need to steer clear of them half-time pies, fella.'

The man's mouth fell open. 'I beg your pardon?'

'Granted,' said Andrew. Satisfied, he pushed the man through to the concourse then turned to Martin. 'See what they're like?'

Martin checked the supporter Andrew had just manhandled, saw the antipathy, the mild disgust at the way he'd been treated. He glanced across to the next turnstile, saw Alan and David politely shepherding supporters through their section, Vincent standing back and leaning against a wall as he monitored both teams. Most of the fans were families: generations of supporters, husbands, wives, mothers, sons. Nathan Telemaque and his ilk were conspicuous by their absence.

Martin turned his back on the queue, looked up at Andrew. 'Bring it down a peg or two, okay? This isn't a war.'

Andrew stared down at him over the hook of his crooked nose. 'Trust no one.'

'What about never judging a book by its cover?'

'I'm not a big reader.'

Martin resisted the urge to comment. 'Ease off, please.'

Andrew swivelled his head to Vincent. Back to Martin. Sniffed. 'Whatever you say, skipper. But you give this lot an inch . . .'

'I get it.'

'Just don't come crying to me when it all goes tits up.'

'I'll try not to.'

They worked the queue, searching coats and rifling bags, Martin smiling patiently as latecomers moaned they were being held up, that they would miss the start of the match. Andrew ignored anybody who spoke to him and patted them down in silence, which Martin considered an improvement at the very least.

It was five minutes to kick-off when voices could be heard in the darkness beyond the turnstiles. Loud voices. Shouted conversation peppered with profanities and matey insults and drunken laughter.

'Heads up,' said Andrew, dismissing another searched supporter.

Vincent had moved closer, cocking an ear. 'Soul Crew?'

'Dunno. Could be. Could be the Casuals again.'

'Well, if there's a rumble,' said Vincent, tugging at Andrew's tabard, 'at least we're all wearing our *fluorescent waistcoats of justice* to keep us safe.'

'Fuckin' bosses,' Andrew chuckled, but Martin noticed that his colleague's jaw was tight, his hand toying with the ASP on his utility belt.

The shouts drew nearer, louder, the language more profane. Stewards backed away, towards the concourse wall, huddled and watched. Martin steeled himself for Telemaque and his mob to emerge from the darkness and steam them, just swamp them with numbers and leap the turnstiles and head for the away section of the stadium where they would run amok, just to feel a little better about having their arses handed to them on a plate by the UAF. He drew a deep breath, turned square on to the turnstile, set his feet a ways apart, saw David and Alan drift across, do the same, heard the unmistakeable metallic crack as either Vincent or Andrew racked his ASP behind him.

He let go of the breath he hadn't realised he'd been holding when they appeared. Five supporters. Late from the pub, no doubt. All that noise and it was just four grown, drunken men and a teenager who looked about fourteen but stood taller than Martin.

'Alrigh', ossifers?' one of the men grinned, his head wobbling a little.

Martin looked at David and Alan, motioned for them to return to their plot at the adjacent entrance. Vincent had sloped away again, mingling with the stewards, hands back in his pockets.

'Evening all,' Martin said to the group.

They fell about laughing at the cliché. Martin felt heat in his cheeks, heard Andrew mutter *What a tool*', batted the comment away and asked for tickets to be shown. He knew they weren't going to be a problem, were just a bunch of blokes, and nodded as they giggled and shoved each other and waved match tickets in front of his face.

'Come on, we're gonna miss kick-off,' the teenager said as Martin began searching him. The boy was bouncing on his heels and tugging at the beanie hat plumped on top of his head.

'Won't take long,' said Martin.

'Why you searching us, though?' asked the boy, eyes shifting from Martin to watch Andrew and Vincent check his companions. Martin wondered which one was his father, and which one had allowed the boy to sink the booze, the stink of which was now wafting from his mouth.

'Just routine,' Martin said. The teenager was still fiddling with the lip of his beanie hat, as if some invisible but incredibly annoying forelock of hair was refusing to be tucked underneath its rim.

Martin straightened. Looked the boy in the eyes.

'What?' the boy asked. Nervous now. Shifting on his feet.

'Hat please.'

'My hat? Why?'

'Just routine,' Martin said again. 'We have to check everything.'

'But I'm only wearing it to—'

'For goodness' sake, Jack, give'm the hat,' one of the men yelled. He was well spoken but the booze had rounded the clipped tones, as if his tongue was a little flaccid. 'It starts in a minute and we've still got to get the food.'

Martin rolled his eyes. Reached up, took hold of the beanie on the teenager's head. Felt something solid underneath the fabric. Some *things*.

The boy's face froze, eyes peeled upwards and fixed on Martin's hovering hand.

'Sorry,' he whined.

'I'm sure you are,' Martin said as he carefully lifted the beanie hat from the teenager's head.

Inside were half a dozen eggs.

Martin turned to show them to his colleagues, saw Andrew's eyes widen, his lip curl, his gloved hand reach up to touch the eggshell mosaic on the left breast of his tabard.

'You little bloody idiot,' the man shouted, placing his hands up to his face. He stepped towards Martin and the boy. Vincent took his arm, held him in place.

'Please don't throw me out,' the boy said quietly.

Martin turned to the man Vincent was holding. 'Are you his dad?'

The man was smartly dressed, tall and slim, his

three-quarter-length duffel coat a woollen charcoal effort that looked warm and not a little expensive. He nodded, eyes on his son, furious.

Martin sighed. Looked at the pale teenager, then across to his father. Down to the hat with the eggs. Such a stupid, childish thing to do. A pathetic, adolescent attempt at hooliganism.

'I'm really sorry, guys,' the boy's father said. 'Can you let him through? He lives for his football. Please.'

Martin saw the anguished expression, the worry. He hesitated, thinking, then sighed and waved Andrew over.

Andrew screwed up his face. 'What? You want soldiers and runny yolks or something?'

'Take his details. Run it by the command room.'

Andrew nodded. Stared at the teenager. 'Then chuck him out?'

'No,' the boy said. 'Please.' He'd started crying, his chest shuddering as he whimpered and sniffed.

'Please, guys,' the father was saying.

'We'll sort him out,' another of the men said. 'He won't do it again, we promise.'

Martin looked at the teenager as he spoke to Andrew. 'If he's clean, let him through to watch the match.'

'Really?' the teenager asked, barely able to believe what he'd just heard.

'You're taking the piss, right?' asked Andrew, and held up the hat. 'I'd rather shit in my own hands and clap than let him into the game. He would've lobbed these things at us. How d'you know that lot' – he jabbed a thumb at the group of men – 'weren't part of the UAF crowd? Eggs, see?' He gestured at his tabard, jaw jutting out.

Martin shook his head. 'Just make sure he dumps them in the nearest bin.'

The boy's father reached out to Martin as he walked over.

'I can't thank you enough. Seriously. Please accept my apologies for the . . . you know,' he said, pumping away with Martin's gloved hand in his. 'You've just made my son's Christmas.'

'Think you've just ruined Thrush's, though,' Vincent muttered, and the stewards standing beside him chuckled amongst themselves.

Martin offered a thin smile; he was tired now. Tired of the decisions and pretending to know what he was doing. Tired of not being with Sam. Tired of constantly having to second-guess this lot. And it was barely halfway through the shift.

The boy's father reeked of booze. Cider, Martin thought. He pulled his hand free, was about to offer some words of advice just to get rid of the group, was thinking about grabbing a steaming cup of coffee from one of the food stalls and finding somewhere quiet to ring his wife when he heard the referee's whistle and the crowd noise washed over them in the concourse and the boy's father's eyes widened and he lurched past Martin and towards Andrew.

'You nasty bastard,' the father shouted. 'You nasty, evil *bastard.*'

Martin turned. Saw Andrew. The wet grin.

Heard Vincent laughing behind him. Heard the drunken men remonstrate, heard 'That's out of bloody order. You lot should be ashamed', and the boy's father was now in Andrew's face, thrusting a finger towards his bent nose, telling him he was a disgrace and then David and Alan intervened and the father's friends were pulling him away, and Martin had to agree with the man.

The hat was back on the boy's head.

Egg yolk and shell pieces ran down his face and over his ears, into his fluttering eyes, his shoulders hunched and a high *eeeeeeeeee*ing noise coming out of his mouth.

Andrew was patting the top of the boy's head, the hat, triumphantly.

'Now you can go watch the match, kid,' he said.

Alan couldn't believe it.

Once they were finished at the turnstiles the new boy had trundled over and asked Alan to accompany him, earnestly explaining that he wanted to get to know everybody as quickly as possible and they *hadn't had the chance to put boots on the ground together yet.*

As if being doubled up with the sergeant wasn't enough of a chore, the Bronze public order inspector had redeployed the whole team pitchside at one corner of the Grange End and in front of the increasingly vocal home support, where – of all the wretched luck – they were standing directly in front of the boy Andrew had humiliated.

The kid's drunken father and his companions were now less focused on the game – which was approaching half-time, and which the home side were losing badly – and more on directing their ire at Alan and his diminutive supervisor. To further compound the misery, the away supporters were in the opposite corner and less than two hundred feet from where they stood. Alan had spent the best part of the last forty-five minutes shuffling and ducking to avoid the coins and other pieces of shrapnel that were being launched over the flimsy segregation fence.

It was the sort of situation most sane people would welcome with folded arms, but Alan could see Andrew further along the advertising hoardings, laughing behind his visor as he bent to scoop up the falling money and share it with Vincent and David.

'*You're shit, and you know you are! You're shit, and you know you are . . .*'

The chant had started ten minutes earlier, thousands of home fans in the Grange End repeating the line with increased ferocity, and Alan knew they were venting their frustration at the home side's woefully poor display. Then the mood darkened: the fans turned on the miserable-looking manager, the jeering away fans, the ranks of stewards with the thankless task of holding the segregation line and keeping both sets of baying supporters apart. One fan, shirtless despite the bitter cold, tried to break through and climb the twenty feet of chain-link fence but was hauled down before disappearing under a pack of bright orange tabards.

The whistle blew for half-time. Boos swept the home team down the tunnel. With no players to abuse, the supporters changed tack.

'*We're gonna do a Blakelock! We're gonna do a Blakelock . . .*'

The song rippled across the mass of heads from the back of the lower tier, was picked up as it drifted down towards the pitch, grew in volume. Alan noted that home and away fans were now singing in unison.

'Getting heated,' Martin yelled over the noise. The stripy's eyes were wide, shifting constantly to scan the crowd, the air for missiles. His face was drawn and ashen. Nervous. His body was hunched over, neck tucked in, had been like it since kick-off, a full three-quarters of an hour of adrenalin. It would hit him later. The crash. He'd be exhausted.

Alan sidestepped a full can of Diet Coke, watched it thump on the ground and burst, fizzing oily fluid and an arc of caramel-coloured foam on to the edge of the pitch.

The crowd cheered.

'*Getting* heated?' Alan shook his head.

Martin waved the other team members over. 'Let's hope the break calms everything down.'

Alan watched the sergeant unclip his mobile phone from his stabbie, check the tiny screen. The boy's face relaxed a little as he quickly read a text message.

'That Silver Command saying it's all been a big mistake and we can go to the pub now?' Vincent asked, sidling up alongside them. He kicked the empty Diet Coke can with his tactical boot; Andrew stopped it and hoofed it towards the stand.

'Keith fuckin' Blakelock my arse,' he muttered.

Martin replaced the mobile. 'My wife,' he said to Vincent. 'She's pregnant. Heavily.'

'I'm not the only one who should be at home, then,' said Alan.

David had caught up with the group, heard the exchange. 'Your missus okay?'

Martin nodded. Checked the crowd. It was thinning, a stream of people heading out through the vomitories for half-time food. He straightened. 'She's fine. Thanks.'

'No news?'

'No news. She's gone to bed.'

Alan watched them talk, narrowed his eyes. Saw Vincent and Andrew do likewise.

'What?' David asked them, shrugging.

'Fast friends now?' asked Andrew. Vincent was silent beside him; Alan could sense there would be mental calculations going on behind his black eyes.

'Don't panic . . . *Thrush*.' Martin smiled thinly. He flipped his visor up, patted Andrew on the arm. 'I'm not going to break up your little clique.'

'It's not like that, kid,' said David.

'I think it's exactly like that,' smiled Martin. He waved

them away. 'Go grab a cup of tea from the refs room. Gives you a chance to sit around and moan about me a bit more. Get it all out of your system before the second half.'

David cleared his throat. 'Tea sounds good.'

Alan was already walking away, thinking about hot drinks and relieving his bladder and being away from this madness even if it was just for fifteen brief but blessed minutes. He heard Vincent talking behind him: 'You going to get your new buddy a cuppa too, Flub?'

Then Andrew: 'Here we go, Sargey Wargey. How many sugars?'

They drifted towards the exit, towards the steps for the bowels of the stadium and the police room with the industrial tea urns that would already be half empty and their contents cooling, Alan checking his own phone, knowing it was pointless, knowing even before he looked there would be no text from his wife, no voicemail message whispering *I love you and miss you* and as he stared at the blank screen he tried to recall the last time she'd ever done such a thing, the last time she'd even looked at him in a way that told him she loved him, because she hadn't always been like this. Things hadn't always been like this.

'Last one in makes the brew,' said Vincent, hurrying past him.

Alan slipped the phone into his pocket and followed him down the stairs.

The area designated for police use by the stadium authorities was a windowless breeze-block square on the second sub-level, and in reality an anteroom to the stadium's main water station: foot-thick piping hung from polystyrene ceiling plates and snaked its way over the folding tables where dozens of ruddy-faced plods sat in various stages of undress, fanning themselves with notebooks and copies of the match operational order.

The air was hot and heavy. A low, rhythmic hum rattled cups and discarded utility belts as the pumping machinery went about its business in the room next door. The noise and the oppressive temperature were not being appreciated by the prisoners cooped up in the holding cells and waiting for transfer to the local custody hub; their constant banging on the metal doors reverberated along the corridor and into the makeshift 'police room'.

Vincent dropped into a chair, overalls unbuttoned and rolled down to his waist where he'd tied the arms into a knot at his midriff. He'd dumped the rest of his uniform and PPE in one corner with the rest of the team's equipment, ordering Andrew to keep an eye on their gear. They all knew what police were like – leave some kit lying unattended and with no witnesses about and you'd never see it again. Dirty thieving bastards. It was especially true of their own specialist equipment. Shiny things equalled good, and your bog-standard response plods were ever keen to get their hands on some TSG Gucci kit, be it a baseball cap or Taser pouch, even if they'd never touch the actual Taser during their entire career.

'Lewis is asking when we're going to arrive,' he said, and flashed his mobile.

The text message read: ETA?

David pulled on the neck of his tee shirt. 'Ten, ten fifteen?'

'Seems about right,' said Vincent. 'Long as it doesn't kick off again after the game.'

'And we don't get any bodies in,' said Andrew, eyes not leaving the mound of equipment.

'I have no intention of arresting anyone,' said Alan.

'What's new?' asked Andrew, and offered his palm to Vincent, quickly dropping it again when the high-five wasn't returned.

Alan looked askance at him. 'Must be difficult for you to guard our kit and talk at the same time.'

David chuckled; Andrew didn't move in his seat, just raised his middle finger at them.

'Ten thirty at the very latest,' Vincent said, thumb jittering over the phone keypad. 'Booze is sorted, but the food'll be gone by then.'

'You could always treat us.' Alan turned to David. 'Stop off on the way to pick up some munch with your bingo winnings.'

'*Me no comprendo*,' David said, and raised his hands in the air.

'It's Christmas, mate,' said Vincent, looking up. 'A nice gift for your pals?'

'*Colleagues*,' smiled David. 'Not pals. There's a difference. And anyway, I need the cash. Extended family and all that.'

Vincent shook his head. 'Marriage. Why bother?'

'Marriage*s*, you mean,' David said. 'Please don't forget I've served several life sentences and am on the bones of my arse money-wise.'

'We've got enough cash,' said Andrew.

Alan leaned towards him. 'I hardly think scraping together a few pounds off the floor outside is going to cover the cost.'

'Me and Vince took care of it earlier,' Andrew said, his voice flat and matter-of-fact.

Alan looked to the ceiling. 'Please don't tell me—'

'Relax, Jesus,' Vincent snorted. 'We'll treat you from the public funds we obtained.'

'I could eat something now,' said David, looking towards the door. His mind was on the food stalls two levels up; he'd spotted the burger stand as they left the pitch at half-time, the aroma of frying onions making him sniff the air with a beatific smile.

'You could always eat something,' said Alan. 'Why don't you go get that *something* upstairs?'

'Sure,' David said, shaking his head. 'Nice juicy burger with some special extra ingredient added when my back's turned, just because I'm Old Bill. No thanks. You know what they do to our food.'

'What about the boy?' asked Vincent.

'I don't think they serve that hummus shite here,' said Andrew.

Vincent threw him a look. '*No.* I mean, how are we going to get rid of him?'

Andrew blushed; he hated being told off by Vincent at the best of times, but in front of others it was akin to torture.

'Prisoner?' asked David.

'Bollocks to that,' said Andrew. 'I want to get out clean tonight.'

Vincent shifted forward in his chair, looked at David. 'You could nudge him in the right direction.'

'Why me?' asked David.

Vincent waited a beat. Smiled. 'Thought you and him were best buds now.'

'Yeah, what happened?' asked Andrew, turning now. 'Bit of male bonding while you did the pubs?'

'Give it a rest,' said David. He wiped the back of a hand over his slick forehead.

Vincent sat back, eyes not leaving David's. 'How much did you tell him?'

'About what?'

'About his old man.'

'And about us,' said Andrew. 'Thought we all agreed to sound him out first.'

David puffed air out of his mouth. 'I didn't tell him anything, all right?'

'Then why the stuff about his wife?' asked Vincent.

'Surprised me, that stuff about him being married,' said Andrew, attention returned to the mound of kit. He was grinning. 'Took him for someone who can't whistle, know what I mean, Vince?'

'For crying out loud,' said Alan. He poked David's chubby arm with a finger. 'Whatever happened, he obviously thinks he's connected with you somehow.'

'And?' asked David.

Vincent was nodding. 'And it means you can word him up. If we're careful about it, maybe get just the one in for a Section Five or something, you could let him know how appreciative we'd all be if he dealt with the prisoner. He might see it as his . . . *in* with us, you know?'

Andrew cleared his throat, hawked a globule of phlegm

into the cold dregs of tea in the nearest plastic teacup. 'Even though it wouldn't be.'

'Much as I find it agonising to admit it, Vincent has a point,' nodded Alan. 'The boy would be tied up with it for a couple of hours.'

'While we par-tay,' said Andrew, bouncing in his seat.

David shuffled his feet beneath the chair, glanced towards the ceiling tiles. He pictured the sergeant's face as he looked up at him, asked him for help. 'This doesn't sit right with me at all,' he said quietly.

'Bit late to be developing a conscience after twenty-eight years in the job, don't you think?' asked Vincent.

David lowered his gaze, stared at Vincent. Looked to Alan, to Andrew. 'Okay. How?'

'Easy,' said Vincent. 'Remember the good old days when the new boy on the group always made the tea?'

'Fine times,' said David. 'Job started to go downhill when management decided it was bullying.'

'Put a spin on it,' said Vincent. 'New boy on the group always deals with the first prisoner.'

'He won't buy that,' said David. 'He'll delegate. You know he will.'

Alan shook his head. 'Not if you let slip that it will go a long way to ingratiating him with the rest of us after his below-par performance at the protest.'

'And he'd be leading from the front,' said Vincent. 'He'll love that shit.'

'He's a career boy,' said Andrew. 'Reckon he'll bite your arm off to get his name on a charge sheet as OIC, 'specially on his first proper shift.'

David hunched over, elbows on knees, rested his jowls on his hands. Recalled the conversation he'd had with the boy again. 'He'll probably go for it.'

Vincent slapped his palms on his thighs. 'So you'll do it?'

'But not for the reasons you think,' David said wearily. 'I think he needs a break for an hour or two. He'll just be happy not to be around us for a while.'

Martin had telephoned Bronze, listened to the empty rhetoric from the inspector, bought himself a coffee from the nearest concessionary stand and sent a text to Sam as he slurped the tepid tar from the polystyrene container. If she woke, he wanted her to know he was thinking about her.

And he *was* thinking about her. Constantly. There was a horrible, nagging feeling that something had gone wrong, that he was blissfully unaware, that he would return home in the small hours of the morning to find she'd collapsed in their bedroom, that she'd tried to reach for the phone but hadn't made it, that she was gone, they were both gone, that all this – this madness and these Neanderthals he was working with and the desire to prove himself – was for nothing.

For the first time in weeks he could kill for a cigarette, and was wrestling the urge to bag a squashed Benson's from David.

He spent the rest of half-time tucked into a corner beneath the press boxes, studying the crowd as they banged the tops of their heads to *do the Ayatollah*, the ebb and flow of bodies through the vomitory stairs, the clumps of prominents sitting quietly amongst the families and children. Food and hot drinks had become more important than throwing coins and mobile phone batteries; the temperature had plummeted and people huddled together under the thin mist of their collective breath.

Four years in, and this was the first time he'd worked a

high-profile football match. The first time, and as a supervisor of all things. The thought made him shake his head.
Laugh, almost. If his father could see him now. His boy,
never the sporty type, inside a footie stadium at last, leading
a TSG group during the one football match of the season
where trouble was not a possibility but a certainty.

Martin eyed the Casuals again. Halfway up and dead
centre of the stand. A group of about twenty males, Nathan
Telemaque amongst them, stretched out on a seat, trainers
on the back of the seat in front of him. Relaxed. Bored,
even. There was something strangely quiet about them all.
Martin had expected more aggravation.

There was still the second half, he supposed. Then the
traditional running battles he'd heard about after the final
whistle. Maybe, just maybe, they'd had their fill. Were sated,
having salved the damage to their egos after their beating
from the UAF by clobbering the visiting supporters – plus
a handful of cops, which was always a bonus – in the
containment line.

He stamped his feet; his toes were already numbing from
the cold. Lowered his visor, walked out to the pitch, plotted
up in front of the Grange End again. Waited for Alan to
rejoin him. For the rest of them to show their faces.

'Bet you'd rather be doing something else on Boxing Day.'

Martin turned to the voice. It was the father of the egg
boy, calling from his seat at the front of the stand. He was
smiling, still sounded drunk, had shoved his hands deep
into his jacket pockets, appeared to have forgotten all about
the incident at the turnstiles. His son was absent, as were
his companions; half-time grub and voiding of post-pub
bladders, Martin assumed.

He nodded. *Something else*. He thought of Samanya
again. 'Right.'

The father stood, stepped forward and leaned over, placing his hands on the low wall that separated him from the narrow pathway at pitchside.

'Think we're going to have a thrashing,' the father said, wobbling slightly. 'Two–nil down already. The team just haven't turned up tonight, have they?' He added to his air of displeasure by belching; the burp was loud and forced, at odds with his neat appearance.

Martin had no interest in football whatsoever. 'It's not going well, to be honest.'

'No,' the father smiled, and looked out to the pitch, up to the floodlights. He squinted, blinked several times, swung his head back to Martin.

Martin waited as the father stared at him. The man's smile faltered for a fraction of a second, as if his cider-induced fug had momentarily cleared to allow the memory of a grinning Andrew and broken, running eggs to surface.

His eyes tapered into slits.

'Anyway,' said Martin, looking towards the security doors for his team. 'Best be getting on.'

The man's expression had changed. 'Must have drawn the short straw, working over Christmas.'

Martin noted the emphasis on *short*. 'You get used to it,' he smiled.

'Sure you do, sure you do,' the father nodded, his head loose, the nods slow and pronounced. 'You on *half* pay, then, given . . . y'know?' He gestured to Martin, waved the hand up and down. Sniggered, a mean and childish snort through his nostrils.

'Nice talking to you,' Martin sighed, stepping away.

The man was leaning further over the low wall. Martin thought if he shifted his weight any further he'd be scooping a drunken fan off the pathway. He saw the man's companions, his son, filing down the steps towards their seats and placed a hand on his radio. His forefinger on the transmit button. Ready to call on his team.

'Busy festive period for you,' the father was saying. 'Helping Santa with the presents yesterday, working here today. I don't know . . .'

Alan appeared at Martin's side.

'Problem?' he asked, arching an eyebrow as he fastened the chin strap on his NATO.

Martin tipped his head towards the stand. 'Andrew's fan club.'

'Ah. Right.' Alan looked at the man, at the other men taking their places alongside him at the wall. The son was curled into his seat, beanie hat pulled low over his sullen face.

'What?' one of the men asked Alan, arms thrown wide provocatively.

'Just ignore them,' said Alan, turning to face the pitch. 'They'll soon get bored.'

Martin checked further down the pathway, saw Vincent and David in position in front of the segregation fence, saw Andrew watching the confrontation with a lopsided grin.

'Been havin' a nice chat with your mate,' the father slurred at Alan. 'With Santa's little helper, I mean.'

The line of men hooted with laughter, nudging each other with elbows.

Alan swung around. 'Calm down. Okay?'

'Whoa, we're calm, we're calm, officer,' said another of the men, but there was an edge to his voice, and Martin sensed the mood was ugly now, that the group of males in front of them had the bit between their teeth. He closed his eyes, silently cursed Andrew for being so petty.

There was a muffled thud. Martin turned to see the father

had jumped over the wall, was now on the pathway, standing between him and Alan. He was still smiling but the hard stare of his eyes betrayed the fury bubbling beneath the friendly facade. The crowd had begun whistling, more and more of them realising what was playing out in the corner of the Grange End. Telemaque, unsurprisingly, had risen to his feet, was laughing and clapping delightedly.

'Back into the stand, please,' said Martin, raising his hand in a warding-off gesture.

'You still got your elf hat on under that crash helmet?' the man asked. 'Come on, let me see, there's a good boy.'

'Leave it, lads,' said Alan. 'We don't want any trouble tonight.'

The man shifted to look at Alan; his expression was one of angry amusement and Martin knew it was a ridiculous comment for Alan to make. He looked at Andrew, at David and Vincent. Shook his head. *Stay put. I can deal with it.*

'Let me see,' the man said again, but there was no smile this time.

His hand flew up towards Martin's face.

Martin stepped backwards.

Too slow.

His visor flipped up with a clunk. The man started tugging at the sides of Martin's NATO helmet, at the chin strap, at the flesh of his cheeks. His fingers cold and calloused.

The crowd cheered.

Martin took hold of the man's wrist, struggled, heard Alan shouting, *'That's enough, that's enough,'* tried to pull the freezing pincer fingers from his face, mindful that all eyes were now on him, that jobs had been lost and lives ruined because of complaints of excessive force, that he'd often thought it better to let them wallop you and keep your job because when push came to shove nobody in HQ ever backed you and would sell you down the river rather than defend you in a costly court case and he was thinking all this and the man's nails were digging into the flesh above his right eye when he heard a loud *oogh* and the fingers fell from his face.

Martin looked down. The man rolled on the floor at his feet, expensive duffel coat gathering dirt, hands holding his stomach, groaning.

He looked to his left, saw Andrew holding his racked ASP.

Grinning, his thick tongue visible through the gap where the rest of his tooth used to be. 'Another one who failed the attitude test,' he shrugged.

The father's companions had shifted away from the wall, the backs of their legs touching seats, hands raised as Vincent and David pointed canisters of CS spray at their faces, their shouts of *'Back off! Back off!'* audible even over the roar of the crowd. The son cowered in his seat, chest hitching as he cried again.

Supporters chanted abuse, coins began falling.

'Don't,' said Martin, stepping across to place the palm of his hand on David's bulbous shoulder. 'Don't discharge them into the stand. They'll panic.'

'Fuck 'em,' said Andrew.

'No, we won't fuck 'em,' hissed Martin. He wiped at his face, felt warm liquid spread across his temple, his cheekbone. Took a breath. Wiped the blood on his overalls. Looked across to Alan, saw the crimson splash on his chin, on the neck of his tee shirt. His blood, spattered across his colleague when the man went down. 'Alan, call in another TSG. They can take this plot while we deal with the prisoner.'

'We?' David lowered his canister, eyed Vincent and Alan. 'It's your body, Sarge.'

Andrew was cuffing the father's hand behind his back; the man was still grimacing and whinging, *My stomach! My stomach.* 'First prisoner for the team,' said Andrew.

Martin slapped his visor down, dodged a bouncing plastic bottle. 'There wouldn't be a first one if you hadn't pissed him off.'

David backed away from the stand, towards Martin. He lowered his head. 'We'll get him to the holding cells, Sarge, but you'll have to write up the statement and do the necessary in custody. You'll have to be OIC. None of us were here to witness the start of it.'

Martin held David's gaze for a few seconds, thinking it over.

'You asked for my help,' David spoke quietly, checking around him as if to make sure nobody else could hear. 'Here's your chance to show these idiots what you're made of. It's a solid public order body, plus an assault police.'

'I know.'

'Then do it justice,' David rasped. 'Airtight statement, all the gubbins about offender behaviour, how scared you were . . .'

Martin touched the cut above his eyebrow. 'It was pretty hairy for a minute there.'

'Well there you go,' David said. 'I know your dad wouldn't want this prisoner to slide. He'd be all over it like a bad suit. Never mind the fixed-penalty instant-fine bollocks: he'd make sure this bloke had his day in the dock.'

David looked directly at Martin, their visors almost touching, and nodded slowly, insistently.

'Okay,' said Martin after a moment. 'I'll sort it.'

'Top man.'

'Can you hold the fort for me?'

'No problem,' smiled David. 'I'll keep your seat warm in the van and this lot out of any more trouble.'

Martin sighed. Patted him on the arm. 'Appreciate it, Dave. Again. I shouldn't be long. Couple of hours at most.'

A slow nod from David. 'It's no bother, sarge. You take as long as you need.'

David looked across to Vincent. Saw the quick wink, the barely concealed smile, and felt ill at ease with what he'd just done. *Nice one*, he thought to himself. *Use the memory of a dead man to cajole his son into doing some work while you go to a party.*

Beside him Martin was formally arresting the father, reeling off the caution while the northern TSG arrived to replace them pitchside, their gloved hands and threats of Tasering forcing the man's companions back into their seats.

'Good work, Sarge,' Vincent said, slapping him on the back.

David watched the new boy search his face for any sign of sarcasm.

'Thanks,' Martin said, clearly a little uncertain. Then he sniffed at the air, recoiled.

Andrew hoisted the father up to his feet, wrinkled his nose. 'Jesus, what's that stink?'

'Probably you,' said Alan. 'You've buzzed all day.'

'It's fuck all to do with me,' said Andrew. 'Smells like . . . rotten apples.'

Martin took the father by his free arm and with Andrew started walking him to the security doors. 'It's the prisoner,' he said, shaking his head as he looked down.

David followed his stare. A damp patch was spreading across the seat of the man's trousers, the back of his thighs. 'Cider.'

Vincent cackled as he followed. 'He fudged his drawers when you gave him a dig.'

'Bloody hell,' whined Andrew, holding the mumbling, stumbling father at arm's length. 'This is the first time I've ever regretted batoning someone.'

David brought up the rear. He pushed through the security doors, listening to Alan moan about getting the sergeant's blood on his uniform, watched Martin struggle to help the father down the stairs, his slight frame bent sideways with the near dead weight of the drunken, battered, humiliated prisoner.

'If any of you think I'm strip-searching that bloke in the cells you've got another thing coming,' he muttered. 'I've covered myself in enough shit today.'

'Stop your whinging, lard-arse,' Vincent whispered, eyes on Martin. 'We're going to a party, remember?'

S, D AND P

'Get him to turn it down or I'll keep phoning you bloody lot!'

The neighbour hung from an upstairs window, topless, the nipple of one man-boob resting delicately on the plastic sill as he huffed and gesticulated.

'No problem, sir, we'll have a word,' said Vincent.

David and Alan chortled as Andrew hovered behind them, the tray of lager wedged sideways down the front of his overalls. He was caressing the side of one can, eyes far away and mouth already formed into a slurp.

'You want more than a word,' the neighbour shouted. They could barely hear him over the music that rocked the foundations of Lewis's girlfriend's home. 'I've got kids here! It's half ten and none of us can bloody sleep! None of us! D'you hear me?'

'Yes, sir, leave it with us,' said Vincent robotically.

The neighbour glared at him, balled his hands into fists then cursed a final time before retreating into the warmth of his bedroom. The window slammed shut, a curtain swishing back into place. A thin crack of light appeared at one side: the man was still watching them.

'Why have I always got to talk to these prick MOPs?' asked Vincent.

'Because you're so good with community relations,' laughed David, ringing the doorbell again. 'You should be on one of them poncey neighbourhood teams.'

'Tackleberry going to answer or what?' asked Andrew,

adjusting himself so the tray rested on one raised thigh. 'We're on the clock as it is.'

They'd left Martin in the custody suite at Trinity Street, David unenthusiastically coaxing the sergeant further, reminding him how great it would be for his standing to take a hit for the team. The prisoner was too drunk for process, would probably be left to sleep it off until morning when he could be charged, snapped and dabbed, so it meant all the new boy had to do was write his statement and prep the handover package for the officers coming in on the early turn. Even with the anal attention to detail he would undoubtedly apply to his evidence, they knew they had an hour, two hours at most, before he called on them to pick him up. Time had been of the essence: within three minutes of dropping him off they were screaming towards the party, blues and twos going, and passing the Kouros around to freshen up.

'At last,' David said.

The music – techno squelches and drum loops whacked all the way up to eleven – exploded out at them as the front door opened

Benjamin Lewis filled the frame. Shirtless, like the neighbour, but minus the moobs. Sweat glistened across his freakishly large pectoral muscles, around the boulders of his shoulders, on the dome of his bald head. He was breathless, David guessing that he'd been going off on one in the middle of the lounge like he was wont to do when playing the crap that now clanked from the speakers.

'It's the fackin' *filth!*' Lewis screamed, smiling, and David reflected if you didn't know him the effect could be rather terrifying. He often thanked the gods that Lewis had chosen their side; he was the only plod Nathan Telemaque had ever shown the slightest hint of deference to, probably realising – and quite rightly – that Lewis was more of an animal than he was.

His appearance was still unsettling, yet the effect was muted somewhat when David glanced down to find Lewis was wearing a pair of fluffy pink Peppa Pig novelty slippers.

'All right, Tackleberry?' nodded Andrew. 'Let us in, me arms are killing me carrying this booze.'

David coughed, glanced up at the neighbour's window. Saw the irate moon face there at the crack in the curtains. 'We're here to speak to you about the noise,' he said.

Lewis chuckled. 'Yeah, yeah, Flub. Very good. Don't worry about him next door. He beats his missus every other night, so I'll pop round in the morning and put him straight.'

'Sweet,' said Andrew, and Vincent looked at him in amazement.

'Thought you lot wouldn't make it,' said Lewis. 'Derby game and all. Those hoolies do like their post-match fisticuffs.'

Alan shrugged. 'They all cleared off home. We couldn't believe it either.'

'A miracle,' smiled David.

'Just like baby Jesus, right, Moses?' asked Lewis, smirking at Alan. 'You coming in then or what? Bit of *social, domestic and pleasure* on this frosty eve?'

He high-fived them all in turn as they trooped through the hallway, pausing only to sniff Andrew.

'You been setting fire to your farts again, Thrush?' he asked, brow wrinkling.

'Funny,' Andrew said, faking a smile. 'Just show me where to dump the drink.'

Lewis's girlfriend's home was an average suburban semi yet they'd managed to cram thirty or more people into the ground floor alone. David reckoned it was louder than the stadium: the voices, the laughter, the music, the vulgar fairy lights strung across a curtain pole. And the heat. Lewis had locked all the windows in a vain attempt to contain the noise, merely succeeding in turning the house into a multi-roomed sauna. Most of the lights were off or dimmed; a lone, tacky disco ball sat on a shelf throwing sad little primary-coloured dots on to the walls and ceiling.

'Eee, it's the strippagrams!'

A clutch of women, all lascivious shrieks and caked make-up, surrounded them in the lounge.

'Show us yer truncheon,' one cackled, lights flashing on the tips of the reindeer antlers propped on top of her head.

'I'll wear those handcuffs for you, if you like,' another said.

A plump ginger woman in her mid forties, flakes of food in her fringe and around her sweaty top lip, grabbed at Vincent's bottom.

'You, sweetie,' she slurred, leaning into him, breasts squashed on his arm, 'are lush.'

Vincent let her hand rest there, fingernails digging into his buttock.

'Any port in a storm,' he smirked.

David shook his head, gave perfunctory nods of acknowledgement to the other sweaty faces around the lounge and made a beeline for the dining room, where he was disappointed to find empty cardboard plates and the detritus of a fried-party-food fest. He satisfied himself with the last mini-cheese melt and a sausage roll that somebody had already taken a bite out of, a fact he couldn't care less about. Chewing on the pastry, he looked at the sad, sagging Christmas tree and the half-eaten sandwiches wedged between its plastic fronds, then noticed a pair of men's shoes sticking out from under the table. He leaned down and saw they belonged to Jim, their old stripy, comatose and hugging the leg of a chair while spittle dribbled from the corner of his mouth.

David kicked the shoes. Hard.

'Whaddafuck?'

'Are you awake?'

No reply; Jim huffed and hugged the chair leg tighter.

'Are you awake?'

'No.'

'Are you awake?'

'No.'

'Are you awake?'

'Christ . . . *yes*.'

David grinned. 'What woke you?'

Jim eyed him from the floor, stretching his face and blinking. 'Bastard.'

Bodies were strewn around the lounge, as if someone had liberally sprinkled the carpet with drunken off-duty plods and their partners. Every available surface was littered with wine bottles, crushed lager cans, glass tumblers and over-flowing ashtrays. Kim, Lewis's girlfriend of the moment, had commandeered the music and was now screeching along to 'Girls Just Wanna Have Fun', hairbrush standing in for a microphone and two female friends performing backing singer duties.

Vincent swigged at his lager while trying to listen to Lewis wax lyrical about Kim's bedroom acrobatics – he'd give her a seven on his *flexibleometer*, apparently – but couldn't concentrate: the caterwauling was distracting enough, but Kim's skin was looking exceptional and he was deeply jealous of the effect she'd managed with her choice of fake tan. He contemplated asking her what she was using but didn't want to upset ol' Tackleberry. The big man rightly suspected that Vincent had thrown a sticky ribbon into her a few months before they began their relationship – Vincent would actually only give her a five on Lewis's scale – and he didn't want his gargantuan colleague realising he now lived with a handover package. Andrew's little tantrums he could deal with; a lagered-up, ego-bruised and raging Ben Lewis was an altogether more troubling prospect.

'Shame we're going to miss the karaoke,' said Alan, eyeing the trio of hairbrush squawkers. 'I do like a bit of karaoke, me.'

'Starts at midnight,' smiled Lewis. 'House rules.'

'He ain't got no hymns on his machine anyway,' said Andrew.

Alan puffed air out of the side of his mouth. 'And it's so blummin' hot in here,' he muttered. 'I've got a thermal vest on under this overall.'

'Thought you'd find something to moan about, Moses,' said Lewis. 'If you won the friggin' lottery you'd complain that the cheque was torn in one corner.'

Alan made as if to speak then saw the look on Lewis's face and clearly thought better of it. He cradled his can. He'd taken one sip.

'Oy, oy,' said Vincent. 'I spy a proper stripy.'

They turned, saw Jim stumbling into the lounge, one hand on David's shoulder.

'Looky here,' said Jim. 'It's the Wild Bunch. How goes it?'

'How's retirement, skipper?' asked Andrew.

Jim shrugged. His shirt was untucked on one side, the zip on his trousers open and showing a flash of bright yellow underpants. 'S'all right,' he said, faux chirpy, but his drunken state allowed the mask to slip and show the sadness he clearly felt. 'Miss the craic a little.'

'Tell me about it,' muttered Lewis.

'How long's it been now?' Vincent asked him.

'Three months,' Lewis said. He swigged at his drink. 'They won't lift the suspension till the fuckin' IPCC make a decision.'

'I don't get it,' Andrew said. 'We all gave statements backing you up.'

Lewis shrugged. 'That's HQ for you.'

'Tell *me* about it,' said Jim. 'Least they didn't sack me over Miss Slovenia, I s'pose.'

He smiled, a shit-eating grin, and they murmured agreement, Vincent thinking how close their old sergeant had come to a spell over the wall for sexual assault. There he'd been, thirty years almost up, pension lump sum coming down the pipe, when the team had pinched a purse-dipper, some Eastern European immigrant girl who'd been lifting handbags and wallets in the city centre for weeks. As he'd been waiting to book her into custody she'd asked to shake Jim's hand to thank him for treating her so kindly during her *ordeal*. He'd done so, not caring, thinking nothing of it, a reflex action. And then she'd made the allegation to the custody sergeant. That Jim, while they were alone, had pushed her against the wall of the holding room and shoved a hand up her skirt.

Suspension followed, then months of investigation by the rubber-heelers. They found her DNA on his right hand. He became a pariah, was disowned and ignored by management, his career ruined and reputation in flames.

Turned out the girl had lied to muddy the waters, had slipped her own hand down her knickers before shaking Jim's hand and transferring her DNA to him.

It had been too much. Jim handed in his ticket and walked, antidepressant tablets rattling in his pocket as he drove out of HQ for the last time without so much as an apology or a thank you for three decades given to the job.

The six of them stood in a darkened corner, drinks in hands, forming a loose circle. The disco ball spun and pulsed, the girls screamed another song, people swayed and jerked their best intoxidance moves in the middle of the lounge.

David elbowed Jim. 'You'll never guess who our new stripy is.'

'I feel sorry for whoever it is,' chuckled Jim.

'Jurassic's boy,' said David.

Jim's eyebrows shot up. 'No fucking way. Last time I saw him was at Mark's funeral and he was only about twelve years old.'

'I think he still is about twelve,' said Vincent. 'Looks like it, anyway. He's come in on the frigging High Potential Scheme.'

'Another clueless clone, then,' Jim said. 'You dished all the dirt on his old man yet?'

'Nah,' said David. 'We don't want to upset him too soon. He's got old Jurassic on a pedestal by the looks of things.'

'Would love to be there when he finds out,' said Jim, smirking.

'So,' boomed Lewis. 'How's this new sergeant been treating you all today?'

Andrew finished his can of lager, reached behind him and slipped another from the tray. 'You're going to love him. He don't know what he's doing, that's for sure,' he said, popping the ring.

'Do any of these fast-trackers?' asked Lewis. 'They're the reason the job's fucked. None of them that have gone up the ranks have ever served any decent time on the street.'

'Not leaders, *managers*,' nodded Alan.

Vincent grinned, picked up the mantra: 'Not managers, *politicians*.'

'We should be locking 'em up for . . .' Andrew continued.

'*Impersonating police officers!*' they yelled in unison, and banged lager cans together.

'But seriously,' Lewis said. 'What's he like?'

Vincent looked from Alan to Andrew. 'Pretty unconvincing. Lost it at one point before the match, then he had a bit of a rumble after half-time and was shaking like a shitting dog afterwards.'

'Think Flub has a soft spot for him,' said Andrew.

Lewis craned his neck around. 'Aaw, bless.'

David rolled his eyes. 'Hardy-har. Bugger this, I'm off out the back for a ciggie.'

They watched David go, Lewis shouting after him, 'Can't have somebody we don't even know get their feet under the table, tubs.'

'House rules,' gurned Andrew, and tilted his drink towards Lewis.

'Indeed, my stinky friend,' Lewis nodded; their lager cans clinked together.

Alan shook his head. 'Isn't that what you've done with Kim, though?'

'Meaning?' Lewis said.

Alan shrank back a ways, lifted his can as if the warming contents were holy water that would ward off Lewis's evil spirit. 'Well . . .' he muttered, looking up at the furrowed pate of his colleague.

'He's got a point,' chipped in Vincent. 'You been together, what, three, four months and you've already moved in?'

Lewis's eyes were slits as he swivelled towards Vincent. He was quiet for several seconds. Vincent knew he knew and was weighing up the odds: take umbrage and bawl them all out, or roll with the punches. That, and the fact that Vincent could do Lewis some serious damage in the job if they fell out.

It was all about insurance, after all.

In the end Lewis shrugged. 'So?'

Vincent relaxed. 'So you don't even know her, mate.'

Lewis grinned, nodded at Kim, who was now arguing with one of her singing companions. Both had teeth bared and the profanities could be heard over the Happy Mondays track bouncing around the room. 'I don't even like her that much, to be honest,' he sighed, turning back to them with a resigned expression.

Alan was aghast. 'If you don't like her then why are y—'

'Whoa there,' Lewis interrupted. 'You need to get your head around the fact that I don't have to like a girl to like fucking her. It helps. But it's not required.'

'Long as you get your oats,' said Vincent.

Lewis clanked his can against Vincent's. 'Correctamundo.'

'Shocking,' said Alan. 'Absolutely shocking.'

Andrew sniggered, finished his can. Reached for another. Absent-mindedly toyed with the van keys in his overalls pocket as he looked around the lounge.

Lewis smiled at Alan, head bobbing to the beat of the music. He leaned down to Vincent, whispered in his ear.

'That man needs to take a chill pill,' he rasped. 'Does he know you've been spelunking in his wife's cave?'

Vincent jerked his head towards Lewis. ''Course not. D'you think he'd be standing here if he did?'

Lewis took a moment to consider this. Then: 'True,' he muttered. 'But I think he needs something to take the edge off, don't you?'

Vincent mulled it over. 'What have you got in mind?'

Lewis chuckled. 'When I give you the signal, make sure he's distracted. I'll give him a present.'

Vincent looked from Lewis, across to Alan, saw the pained expression as he watched Kim and the other girl jabbing fingers at each other, at their spittle-flecked grimaces, at the screeches and circle of onlookers and the throaty, tuneless wail of Shaun Ryder's voice.

Alan's face was a picture of misery.

Vincent smiled. 'It is Christmas, after all.'

Joseph Rhodes.

The prisoner's name.

Married father of three with no criminal record, no points on his driving licence, nary a parking ticket to his name, fine upstanding member of the community and a senior lecturer at one of the city's more prestigious private colleges. A professor in the Faculty of Humanities, no less.

At first Martin couldn't understand how they had both ended up in the custody suite. He was supposed to be out there, supervising, ensuring the away fans were safely bubbled back to their waiting coaches and specially laid-on trains, the home fans dispersed to their pubs and homes, the Casuals United crowd seen off without a repeat of the missile incident that had blackened the earlier containment. He'd let himself believe that sorting out the body would ingratiate him to the team and show them what he was made of, but in truth he'd desperately needed to get away from Vincent et al. for a short period, to have some time to gather himself after the madness of the first half of the shift. It had blinded him to the fact that he was clearly being conned.

Rhodes had looked as bemused as Martin when they were eventually transferred to Trinity Street and seemed to be in a mild state of shock: at the amount of drink he'd sunk, at letting his teenage son drink almost as much, at his boy's attempt to squirrel a half-dozen eggs into the match and how everything had spiralled out of control so quickly.

Martin was just shocked that Rhodes had behaved in such a way. It didn't sit right. Not with the man that he was. His background.

It was only as Martin booked him in, feeling more in common with the handcuffed and cowed prisoner standing beside him than with any of the members of his new team, that he finally understood what had happened.

Andrew had happened. His team had happened. And he'd allowed it to happen.

Cause and effect. His father had often told him his thoughts on what he called the police ripple. *All it takes is one bad apple, and the work of a thousand good plods is undone in an instant.* Standing beside Rhodes, Martin had wrestled with an uneasy and growing sense of guilt: the man could lose his job because of this. Lose his home, potentially his family. He would hate the police for evermore. He'd tell his family, his friends and colleagues. How his son was humiliated. How *he* was humiliated. And it would be another MOP lost in the endless PR war beloved of the bosses.

Hearts and minds. Or fiddled statistics and spin.

Martin finished filling in the custody pro forma, saved it to the hard drive and leaned back in his chair. Listened to the monotonous clanking noise from the custody suite next door, the prisoner in cell three repeatedly headbutting the steel door and screaming how he was going to murder and rape them all when he got out. Every cell was full and it wasn't even midnight – a dozen or so fans, all in various stages of intoxication; two juvies in for no bail warrants and bedded down for the morning court; one of the local toms whom he'd watched on

CCTV as he booked in Rhodes, and who was obviously coming off the brown because she was rocking and shivering on her cell bench. Throw in a few repeat shop-lifters, a woman – a magistrate, of all things – who'd blown a positive bag after being stopped driving home from a party, two prolific burglars and the predictable handful of domestic abusers – who'd decided they'd had enough of their spouses' company this Christmas so demonstrated their displeasure with fists and feet – and Trinity Street was full to bursting.

And the clubs were still to kick out.

Martin was done with the electronic paperwork. In fact, he was done all over; he felt exhausted. He checked his mobile. No messages or missed calls. He dialled David's phone, sighed as it rang to voicemail. Put in a point-to-point call to him on his Airwave but there was no answer. Gave a general call over the open channel for anybody on the team.

No response.

He closed his eyes, tried to clear his thoughts, but all he could think about was how wrong it was: the man he'd just led to a cell shouldn't even be there. He wasn't a criminal. The booze had just got the better of him.

Things had to change. That was his remit, after all.

Change.

At the cell door, he slid the suicide hatch to one side, peered through the gap. The stench of human faeces wafted out through the slot and he winced.

'What?' Rhodes muttered from the mattress he'd laid on the bench. He'd pulled the bobbled grey blanket the custody staff had provided up to his nose; the prisoner suit he'd been given to change into did little to keep out the chill. He peered at Martin with bleary, sorrowful eyes.

Martin checked the corridor: nobody about. He pressed his forehead against the door, spoke as quietly as he could but loud enough to ensure he was heard over the banging from the cell further down the suite. 'Do you know what NFA means?'

Rhodes forced himself upright. 'Neanderthal fucking authority?' he croaked. 'Like you people, you mean?'

Martin nodded slowly to himself. He didn't blame Rhodes for being anti. 'It means *no further action,*' he said. 'I'm going to enter it on your custody log before I go off duty. Sit tight, sleep it off, you'll be released without charge in the morning.'

The professor stared at him. Cocked his head. 'I . . . I don't understand,' he said eventually, looking genuinely lost. 'Why?'

For a second Martin wondered that very thing. Now he was doing this, he realised he could get himself – and the team – into a considerable amount of difficulty. He was breaking the golden rule: if you ever put your hands on a MOP, always make sure they leave custody with a charge sheet and a court date. He was taking a monumental risk letting Rhodes walk. All it would take was for him to go home, shower away the shit, then make an appointment with the nearest – and dearest – solicitor he could find and sue the force for false arrest/false imprisonment/physical assault/mental anguish/add further complaints here.

Martin sighed, placed a hand up to the cold metal of the door. 'I *should* be charging you. You should be having your day in front of the magistrate.'

'Then why aren't I?' Rhodes asked.

'Because . . .' Martin said. He held Rhodes's gaze through the suicide hatch.

Because . . .

'Because I think we've both learned a lesson,' he said eventually.

Rhodes's eyes blinked slowly, his chest rising and falling against the blanket he now held against his chest. 'Your eye . . . it was totally uncalled for.'

Martin touched the gash in his flesh; healing already, a soft scab forming. 'Not the first time it's happened to me and won't be the last, I'm sure.'

'I'm sorry, but your colleague . . . what he did to my son . . .' said Rhodes.

'I know,' said Martin. 'It will be dealt with, believe me.'

'This makes no sense,' Rhodes muttered, glancing about the cell as he pulled the blanket tight around his shoulders. 'I don't understand it.'

That makes two of us, thought Martin. 'You can make a phone call in a minute, let your family know you're safe and we're just taking care of you. I'll arrange for someone to drop you home in the morning. Season of goodwill and all that.'

'Thank . . . thank you,' said Rhodes. 'So . . . you're not going to send me to court for hitting you?'

Martin shook his head. 'Not this time.'

The professor sagged back on to his elbows. 'They'd have sacked me, you know. Work. Gone, just like that. Ten years, wasted.'

'Make your call,' said Martin. 'Then get some rest.'

Rhodes gave a nod, wide-eyed and near-incredulous. He lay down, pulled the blanket to his chin. Martin shifted his hand to the hatch, began to slide it closed.

'Wait,' said Rhodes.

'What is it?'

'The match,' Rhodes said. 'What was the result?'

Martin gave a tired smile; after all that had happened to

him, Rhodes still had his priorities. 'Your guys lost four–nil. A drubbing, I believe is the term.'

'Four–nil,' Rhodes muttered. 'Goodness me.'

Martin closed the hatch as Rhodes pulled the blanket over his head.

David decided it was time to leave.

Immediately.

He had four missed calls from the onion's mobile, and had only ignored them – along with the point-to-points plus the general calls over the event channel – because Lewis had at first cajoled him to stay a little longer with the offer of more party food. Then when that finally ran out, and David and Alan formed an unlikely alliance to demand they go pick up the new boy, Lewis had threatened to hold David's face over the hobs on Kim's range cooker.

That was twenty minutes ago, and Lewis had now moved on to other, more pressing matters: pressing himself on to Kim's best friend with the master bedroom door locked.

'You *fucker*!' Kim was screaming, one foot – wrapped in sagging tights – thrumming on the wood below the handle and slipping off every third or fourth kick so she keeled sideways to the floor.

'This is getting out of hand,' said David, picking her up again. Downstairs the music played on, pulsing up through the floor and only adding to the sense of chaos.

'Get your fuckin' 'ands off me, fatty,' Kim offered, and elbowed him away so she could continue battering her bedroom door.

'I'm inclined to agree with you for once,' said Vincent, and nodded at Alan.

David looked across to the top of the stairs, where Andrew was wrestling with a decidedly peaky-looking Alan;

his face was pale and shiny, as if he'd been laminated. Dried blood, from the sergeant's war wound, was caked around Alan's chin and collar. It was an unsettling sight.

'*I will help you, Kim!*' Alan bellowed, trying to force his way past Andrew. '"I have wiped out many nations, devastating their fortress walls and towers!" Get out of my way, you inbred! "You Ethiopians will also be slaughtered by my sword!"'

David's mouth flopped open. 'What the fuck has got into him?'

'Erm . . .' said Vincent, holding out his hands and shrugging. 'Lewis thought he needed to chill out a bit.'

'And?'

Vincent wrinkled his face. 'All I know is he said he was going to give Moses one of his tablets.'

David's eyes widened. 'You're fucking joking, right? He slipped something into his drink? *Dullas*, of all people?'

'Hey, that's all he told me. I thought he was messing ab—'

'We are leaving,' said David.

Vincent *hmm*ed then nodded. 'Good call.'

A look of relief spread across Andrew's face as they joined him in manhandling Alan down the stairs. ''Bout bloody time,' he grumbled.

'*Bastard!*' Kim shrieked and sank to the floor, sobbing as she picked at the tights that had gathered in folds around her ankles.

'*Kim!*' Alan shouted as they barrelled him down the steps towards the clutch of gawping revellers standing in the darkened hallway. 'Fight the good fight. "Go up, my warrior, against the land of Merathaim and against the people of Pekod!"'

'Remind me to kill Lewis when I see him next,' said David, placing one of Alan's arms in a gooseneck hold.

'I'll pin him down while you do it,' said Vincent, taking the other.

Andrew bent down, hoisted Alan's wriggling legs upwards. The three of them held on, taking a step down at a time, Alan squirming and arching his back as they carried him head first and backwards, as if about to deposit a violent prisoner in a cell.

'"I've seen its true face", Thrush,' Alan grinned manically at Andrew. '"Its *true face*".'

'I'm really chuffed for you,' breathed Andrew, tightening his arm around Alan's calves. 'And less of the Thrush. It don't sound right coming out of your mouth.'

'Wait,' said David as they descended. '*Wait*—'

He lost his footing, slipped on the carpeted stairs. Alan shouted in pain as David's momentum pulled them all down the final few steps and into the group of onlookers.

'Watch it,' shouted one of Kim's singing partners, but it was too late. She tried to step back as the mass of black-clad bodies hurtled towards her but, drunk and unsteady on her feet, was too slow. Vincent ploughed into her, taking her out at the knees with the soles of his boots.

David watched the woman crumple on top of Vince, the drink she'd been holding – a noxious-looking concoction that David guessed contained blackcurrant juice – arcing through the air in slow motion, the plum-coloured liquid already spilling from the rim of the glass in mighty globules.

He breathed with relief when the glass landed on the carpet next to Alan.

Laughed uncontrollably when the liquid landed on his face and chest.

'*Gargh*,' Alan croaked, and shook his soaking head. 'I'm drowning!'

'My drink,' the woman sulked, sitting upright.

Alan was licking spittle from the corners of his mouth. 'This is Sodom,' he moaned, baring his teeth as he pointed at the circle of faces above him. 'And these are your last days. *Your last days . . .'*

'Can we go now?' asked David. 'Please?'

They hoisted Alan up from the floor, his arms spread wide, his feet bunched together at the ankles, a smiling human T.

'What're you so happy about?' Andrew asked.

Alan stared down the length of his body at Andrew, a look of wonder on his face. 'I feel just like *Him*, Andrew. This is how He must have felt . . . Take me to Calvary. *Take me to the rock at Golgotha, my centurion.'*

Andrew shook his head. 'Whatever, dude.'

As they shuffled towards the front door Jim, zip still undone and garish underwear on display, appeared from the lounge carrying one of the cans purloined from the supporters' coach. The sight of his former colleagues carrying a raving Alan out of the house barely registered as odd.

'Oh,' Jim grumped. 'You're going already?'

'Yes, we are.' David yanked at the handle and threw the door open. 'Thank God.'

'Yes, thank Him, my rotund friend,' burbled Alan, craning his neck up to look at David's backside. 'Thank Him for what He has done for us.'

'That's right, lock him up and chuck away the bloody key!'

David knew without looking that it was the topless neighbour who'd given them what for when they arrived. He didn't look up but sensed the man's nipples would be on show once again, and he'd seen enough of them for one night.

'"*Your streets are an extended gutter!*" Alan shouted as they carried him towards the van. '"*And the gutters are full of blood and when the drains finally scab over, all you vermin will drown!*"'

'Fuck's sake,' muttered Andrew.

'Keep close,' said David. 'Don't let any of the MOPs see it's one of us we're carrying.'

'That music's still playing! Still playing, innit? I'll ring again!' yelled the neighbour.

Alan was on a roll. '*I tell you,*' he shouted. '"*The accumulated filth of all your sex and murder . . .*"'

'I hate religion,' said Vincent, breathing heavily as he lugged his colleague.

'I hate this job,' said David.

'Wish I had a can for the van,' said Andrew.

'. . . "*will foam up about your waists*" . . .'

Andrew unlocked the carrier, slid open the side door. They clambered in, held Alan on the filthy floor between the seats.

'. . . "*and all the whores and politicians will look up and shout 'save us'*" . . .'

'I've had enough Bible shit, Dullas,' breathed Andrew.

'It's not even the Bible,' said Vincent. 'I've just realised: he's quoting that *Watchmen* film.'

'What on earth did Lewis give him?' asked David.

'. . . "*and I will whisper 'no'*".'

Alan went limp, a tranquil smile on his face, his eyes unblinking.

'Dullas?' asked David.

Vincent swapped glances with Andrew; both were smirking.

'Dullas?' said David, his voice urgent now. He'd stopped pinning his colleague's arm to the floor of the van, was now shaking it. 'Alan, you there, mate?'

David looked from Vincent to Andrew, panic in his eyes. Nobody was smirking any more.

'Is he breathing? Check he's breathing,' urged Vincent.

'*Alan!*' David shouted, shaking him more violently. 'Alan, you okay?'

'Fuck me, has he carked it?' asked Andrew.

'How do I know?' shouted David. 'I've got no medical training whatsoever. Dullas is the first-aider on the group.'

'Can't help himself now then, can he?' mused Andrew.

David reached down, grabbed Alan by the chest pockets of his overalls, yanked him into a sitting position. Alan's head flopped back, eyes glassy and fixed, his pupils wide.

'*Alan!*' David screamed.

'Do some of that CPR stuff or . . . something,' offered Andrew. 'Y'know.'

'Mouth-to-mouth?' said Vincent, kneeling next to David. 'C'mon, Flub, we've got to try it.'

'What about an ambulance?' asked David.

Vincent leaned back, appalled. 'Are you joking? We've got to sort this ourselves. We call an ambo, the game's over, buddy. All of us, prison time.'

'He could've pegged it anyway so the game might already be over,' Andrew said.

David was sweating; he looked at Vincent, unsure of what to do next for the first time in as long as he could remember. Alan was sagging, lifeless, his head lolling on his neck, eyes staring blankly. 'Okay,' he breathed, and lowered Alan to the floor. There was a hollow *clonk* as his head bounced on the reinforced plastic. 'Mouth-to-mouth. But you can do it.'

'Why me?' asked Vincent.

'Why *me*?' asked David.

'You're buddies with him,' said Vincent.

'I'm not buddies with anyone!' yelled David. 'You were in on it with Lewis. And the onion left me in the chair, and what I say goes, and what I'm saying is *give Dullas some fuckin' mouth-to-mouth*, all right, Vince?'

'We're wasting time here, y'know,' said Andrew, yawning while he glanced at Kim's house through the open side door. 'And I could be grabbing a few more tinnies while you lot sort Dullas out.'

Vincent nodded. 'You all owe me one for this,' he grumbled.

'Just do it,' David said. 'I'll sort the defibrillator.'

'First the wife, now the husband,' Andrew cackled. 'You working your way through the entire family, or what?'

'Har-de-fuckin'-har,' said Vincent, but Andrew had a point. He looked down at Alan, exhaled and inhaled rapidly for a few seconds, then took a deep breath and held it, his mouth closed, a pained and fearful look on his face, as if he were about to plunge head first into a sewer pipe gurgling with warm excrement.

He bent forward, grimacing lips heading towards Alan's open mouth.

His fingers pinched the bulb at the end of Alan's nose, sealing the nostrils.

Vincent closed his eyes.

Fought against the urge to gag.

Steeled himself for the touch of Alan's dry and spittle-caked lips on his own.

Told himself: *It's to save a life*.

To save a life?

To save my own arse, more like.

Alan's sticky lips pressed against his own.

Vincent paused, poised to breathe out, to breathe life into his colleague, to save his life, to save them all from the indignity of internal investigations and arrest and criminal charges and financial ruin.

Bubba's prison bitch.

It didn't bear thinking about.

He let go of the breath he was holding.

Felt a hand on his right arm, fingers spidering their way around his tricep, tightening.

Felt another hand slip around the nape of his neck, fingertips caressing his hairline.

Vincent snapped his eyes open.

Alan's tongue flicked into his mouth, wet and probing. The hands pulled at him, kneaded the flesh of his arm and neck through his overalls.

'*Mmmmrrrrggg,*' Vincent cried, but the hands wouldn't let go, wouldn't let him pull away, wouldn't let him form a coherent, horrified word. He stared in terror at the closed eyelids of his once-catatonic colleague. He pulled at Alan's arms, tried to clamp down on the thick, tacky tongue that now curled inside his mouth, curled and caressed his teeth and gums and tickled his own tongue with its tip.

'Whoa!' exclaimed Andrew, as Alan wrapped one leg around Vince's midriff.

David reappeared from the rear of the van with the defib kit and first-aid box.

'What the . . . ?' he blurted, and dropped everything.

'*Ggrrimoffme!*' squealed Vincent, straining to pull away and looking like he was doing a particularly strenuous press-up.

David and Andrew grabbed Alan's arms, yanked them clear. Vincent jerked upright, his face beetroot, tottering for a few seconds before falling to the floor, hitting the exact same spot on his buttocks that he'd landed on when he tumbled down the stairs. He wiped and scraped at his mouth with his hands, ran fingernails down his tongue.

Alan was sitting up, his arms still held by an incredulous David and Andrew. He blinked, licked his lips, looked from one to the other.

'I feel so . . .' he said, an expression of utter confusion warping his face. 'I feel so . . . *up for it*.'

'"Up for it"?' asked Andrew.

'You know. *Horny?*'

Andrew roared with laughter. 'You're hilarious, man. I take it all back. All of it.'

Vincent pulled himself upright. 'You fucker. I was trying to save you . . .'

Alan gave a quick shake of the head. 'What?'

David sank backwards against a seat. 'We thought you were a goner, you muppet. What on earth do you think you're playing at?'

Andrew continued to snigger as he climbed over the seats into the cab. 'We ready to rock and roll or what?' he asked, waggling the van keys in mid-air. 'The sarge'll already have a right mardy on.'

Alan looked from David to Vincent, then down at his overalls and the tee shirt beneath it. 'I'm so dirty,' he laughed, a giggle almost. 'D'you think we could call in to my house on the way back?'

'What for? Quickie with the missus?' asked David. 'Seeing as you're so *up for it*, as you put it.'

Alan gave an exaggerated sigh. 'I think the odds are stacked against me there. But wouldn't hurt to try.' And he placed a hand over his mouth, gave a childish *hee-hee-hee* and then stopped, abruptly, and glanced down at himself again. 'I'd rather like to change my uniform,' he said, his voice suddenly serious.

David rubbed at his tired eyes, hoisted himself up into the BINGO seat.

'I don't know how we're going to explain your fruitloop behaviour to the new boy,' he muttered, and placed his head in his hands. 'But fine. We'll call in to your gaff on the way. I really don't care any more, to be frank.'

Vincent slid the side door shut as Andrew started the engine, slipped into his usual seat, and gestured towards the rear of the carrier.

'Get back down there, Dullas,' he said, scowling. 'Where you can't do any more damage.'

Lisa Redding was less than pleased to see her husband call in to the family home at such a late hour.

She hovered in her dressing gown at the top of the stairs, brooding eyes sunk into her already puffy, sleepy face, watching as first Alan then several other black uniforms stepped through the front door and hove into view, tiptoeing while her husband shushed them repeatedly before breaking into childish giggles that he seemed unable to control, something that caused her pulse to quicken with irritation. One of them, the tall and gangly specimen who'd bored her rigid at a Christmas party several years ago with his dull tales of testosterone-fuelled lunacy in Afghanistan, couldn't stop sniggering and only paused in the inanity when he looked up to see her standing silently, her chest rising and falling as she waited and stared.

'Oops,' he said. 'Look out, Al, it's your War Office up the stairs.'

She watched her husband put his finger to his mouth again; there was something odd and a little off about his movements. Then his colleague's words sunk in and he noticed her. His face lit up, a broad and devoted smile.

'Hey, Lisa,' he said, almost too cheerily. 'You look . . . I was feeling . . . Sorry but I need to change. And some of the guys need to use the bathroom, if that's okay? Is it okay? With you, I mean.' He started giggling again.

A hiss from between Lisa's teeth: 'It's gone eleven.'

She regarded him contemptuously, and was about to

launch into a withering tirade that she knew would humiliate him in front of his chums – not that she cared any more – when another figure came through the door and into the house.

Somebody who'd already *popped in* – the way he described it, the innuendo, never failed to make her smile – once that afternoon.

She raised a hand to her throat. To the necklace, where she fingered the St Christopher pendant, the pendant she now pictured swinging and banging against the pillows on her marital bed.

Vincent was standing behind Alan: Lisa saw his eyes narrow, a thin smile play on his lips. He gave an almost imperceptible nod of his head; she flushed slightly, began stringing the pendant back and forth along the tiny chain-link of the necklace.

'Is it okay?' Alan asked her, clasping his hands at his chest.

'Yes,' Lisa said, nodding, eyes fixed on Vincent. She felt a shiver, a thrill trace its way down her spine, goosebumps on her forearms, as she recalled that afternoon's exploits, and the text messages he'd sent her this evening as she lay in bed, her fingers toiling between her legs. All until that last message, of course. It had killed the mood. It was disgusting, what he had suggested. But she'd been unable to stop thinking about it. Even now, she was conjuring the image in her mind, and wondering just what it would be like to—

'Perfectly okay,' she said eventually, then turned and walked away.

Alan heard the master bedroom door click shut behind her. Despite her breezy air and the mild fog in his head, he could sense quite clearly that to try anything with Lisa now could prove to be the final rusty nail in the coffin that threatened to inter his marriage. He maintained the jaunty tone, smiling as he pointed out the location of the downstairs loo to his colleagues. Andrew disappeared to relieve himself; David lined up for the next spot.

'Your car window's been put through,' Vincent said to Alan.

'Yes, I know,' he replied.

'That'll cost you a pretty penny.'

'Yes,' seethed Alan, the giggles gone. '*I know.*'

'I didn't notice it . . .' Vincent started, but stopped himself quickly.

'You didn't notice it what?' asked Alan.

'When, y'know, when we first pulled up.' Vincent said. 'Anyways, I'll use the bathroom upstairs. I'm bloody busting to go.'

'Carry on,' said Alan. 'Don't forget to wash your hands, there's a good boy.' He laughed at himself, then stopped and cocked his head, unable to remember what he had just found so amusing.

Alan watched Vincent take the stairs two at a time, then turn left at the top, towards the bathroom. He contemplated following his colleague up the steps, towards Lisa and their bed. He mulled it over for a full minute, until Andrew reappeared and ruined his concentration by breaking wind and chuckling about his effort. *Maybe tomorrow*, he thought, and made his way through the kitchen to the utility room and its piles of clean washing.

Alan found the spare overalls, the tee shirt, changed quickly, mindful of the time and that the sarge was already nagging them, that they needed to get back into the city centre for kicking-out time at the pubs and clubs, that Lisa needed to get back to sleep, and he was thinking about all of this when he recalled why he had been so down today, the things he had been worried about, and he sensed something wasn't right, that the answer was probably right under his nose. He walked back into the entrance hallway where David was zipping up his overalls and Vincent was bounding down the stairs saying 'That's better' and Andrew was opening the front door and it was only then that it hit him, hit him despite the fuzziness and the gaps in his memory, hit him so hard that he almost doubled over. It took all his strength to remain upright, all the willpower he could summon just to walk in a straight line back to the van, all his remaining energy just to clamber in and make his way to the seat at the very back of the carrier where he slumped into the saggy fabric and shook in the darkness.

'You all right now?' David asked, studying him.

Alan nodded, kept nodding.

He dipped his head, dipped it up and down mindlessly as the rest of them busied themselves, as the carrier engine grumbled into life, as Andrew stamped on the accelerator and the van pulled away from the front of the Redding family home and all this was distant to Alan, distant and abstract and not really registering because all he was thinking about was Lisa and why she'd been so aloof of late, why she'd been so off with him and curtailed their physical relationship, why it felt as if he was missing something, being made a fool of, being taken for a chump by everyone around him.

Most of all he was wondering how on earth Vincent – who'd never been to Alan's house before, as far as he was aware – knew where to find the upstairs toilet without asking.

BOXING DAY, 2333HRS

'So go on, then,' Chloe says and offers her right hand which is palm down with the thumb extended out as far as possible, so there's a small declivity at her wrist, a tiny skin-bowl with the half-gram of powder sitting within.

She feels the music thrumming the floor, the walls, her chest, hears the shrill voices of girls gossiping in the adjacent cubicle, one of them arguing with somebody on a mobile phone, shouting, *Yes you did, you said you'd be here and you're fucking not and you're probably with her, aintcha?'* before sobbing uncontrollably and she wishes Chloe had a tooter, this feels far too intimate, too personal because it's been a while but better this than railing lines off the filthy toilet and anyway Chloe's an old friend, it'll be fine, she's sure it'll be fine so leans down to the hand, which is hovering over the back of the cistern, presses one nostril closed with a finger and snorts the coke, gets that involuntary have-to-twist-your-head-to-one-side moment as the insides of her nose, the back of her mouth, go cold for a second and the bitterness makes her throat spasm. She looks up at Chloe whose eyes are closed, her head nodding to the *whump-whumpwhump* of the bass line and she sighs, remembering – as if she really could've forgotten – just what nights were like with her, before she moved on and moved in with Paul, before she became Miss Respectable.

She swallows the mucus drip, shivers.

Tells Chloe how good the gak is and Chloe just grins, nods with her eyes still closed, so she grabs her highball glass of vodka and lime from the toilet seat, takes Chloe's hand, pulls open the cubicle door, pulls her out where the Ladies is crowded, rammed with teenagers fussing over hair, bra straps, lippy, Kohl eyeliner, faces pressed up to wall-length mirrors, straightening halter tops and babydoll dresses as they chitter-chatter and bicker in the fug of perfume and body spray and sweat, the sodden remnants of tissue paper clinging to sandals and high heels and the filthy tiles of the toilet floor.

She brushes her fingers against the end of her nose, convinced there'll be off-white granules still dusting the tip.

Chloe shakes her head, laughs.

Tomorrow. Tomorrow is going to be just awful, she knows this. Knows why she stopped these nights out, knows she'll suffer through work and then Paul will have to suffer her just like she's been suffering him lately and she finds herself staring at the floor, at the misshapen lines of toilet paper, wondering if she really loves him any more, wondering if moving in together was really such a great idea and now she's tweaking, the coke and the booze making her feel drunk and euphoric and just a little off-kilter and Chloe is tugging at her arm and still laughing and shaking that bright red hair of hers.

Nodding.

Nodding at Chloe and they're at the bar, she can barely recall getting there, Chloe's stretched forward across the countertop, flashes from the ceiling strobes zinging off her sequinned dress as she yells their order to the blond surfer-type standing at the pumps, almost nibbling his ear she's so close and he's not looking at Chloe, he's looking at *her*, smiling like he has been all night, at first she thought it was because she knew him from something at work, spent the first hour trying to recall where they'd met but couldn't and then it dawned on her that he was interested, flirting with her every time she bought drinks, pouring her freebies each time which is why she is now in this state but it's nice, isn't it, knowing you've still got what it takes and he's, what, nineteen at the most, eight years younger than her and still keen, still watching her as Chloe hands over another cool, tall V&L.

Squinting, she examines the contents of the glass before lifting it to her lips, sips the drink, eyes the surfer and the image is there, she tries to bat it away but it's there and maybe, just maybe she would, Paul would never know, would never know about the nice, pointless shag she's used to blow away the relationship cobwebs and she closes her eyes and imagines it, imagines what she would do to the surfer, what she would let him do to her and she pictures it, swaying there next to the dance floor, flopping her head to the deep bass beats and swirling synths, pictures it and rubs the cold rim of the glass against her lips, her cheek, her throat, her drunken daydream playing out and reaching its climax and she lifts her eyelids and stares at the surfer, smiling.

Tells Chloe she wants to leave.

Sees the exaggerated sigh, the heave of her friend's chest, hears her call her an *old lady*, a *straighthead*, irritated now, already lost in the surfer so she slings the rest of the vodka into her mouth, ice cubes tinkling against her teeth, drops the glass to the bar, blows a kiss to the blond guy who's already sussed he's on to a loser and she's about to vanish, is already switching his attention to her old friend.

So she tucks her clutch bag under her arm and leaves, drops down the steps, concentrates on placing one patent high-heeled foot in front of the other, the chilly night air taking her breath away, so cold she can feel it at the back of her throat as she inhales, a high keening sound replacing the dance music in her ears.

'Just another half-hour,' Chloe's calling from the door of Liberty's. 'Come on, Becca, this barman's really mad for us. Come on . . .'

She wraps her arms around herself, doesn't answer, lowers her head as the group of men in fancy dress barrel past her: Batman, a cowboy, a pirate, Austin Powers, a Smurf and what she thinks is supposed to be one of those Jedi people from the *Star Wars* films, the guy wielding his toy lightsaber at her, all of them stopping to make comments, *'Where you going, love? Don't you want to play with my sword?'* and as a police van trundles past in low gear the men fall silent, think better of it, turn towards the club, Batman's cape billowing in the light and chilly breeze.

She sees faces pressed up against the police van windows, watching her. Nearly waves at them but it's too much effort. Too cold to lift her arms from her body. All she can think about is food, taxi, sleep.

Just trying to walk.

Just walking is effort enough.

She opens the door, steps carefully into the kebab shop, heat on her face from the grills behind the counter, salivating at the juicy grey meat rotating – like the shop itself, her eyes unable to fix on one point – on its spit, the photos of fantastically juicy burgers and fried chicken, the aroma of freshly cooked chips, a flat-screen on one wall showing foreign football, the Turks or Algerians or Moroccans with their bright yellow tee shirts and tired smiles watching her from behind the counter.

'Yes, please?' one says, his dark eyes looking her up and down then back to the television. She tries to focus, can see dried grease, dull finger marks, across the right breast of his tee.

She orders, waits. Smacks her lips, head bobbing, weaving, hair brushing the counter.

Then the carton is slid in front of her and she pays and it's manna from heaven, she's digging her plastic fork into the coils of fatty lamb and pitta bread, shoving salad and barbecue sauce into her mouth as she staggers to a table in one corner, smiling stupidly to herself, smiling at the two girls sitting opposite, then it's head down, eyes closed, tucking in.

Paul. She thinks of Paul.

The coke. She knows if he were here she wouldn't be able to contain herself, wouldn't be capable of keeping her hands from pawing at his jeans before dragging him into the toilets to carry out her second questionable act in a cubicle tonight.

She's chuckling to herself when the kebab shop door swings open and heads turn because in strut four or five of them, loud and brash and full of their own self-importance, the Turks or whatever they are produce over-egged smiles and matey nonsense and she lowers her head further, takes a last forkful of meat, pushes the carton away from her, pushes too hard, watches as it slides towards the opposite edge of the table.

She reaches for it, misses.

A hand stops it, cool as you like.

And a voice says: 'Are you who I think you are?'

She looks up to see who the hand belongs to and it's *him*.

GOOD BANTZ

They were parked outside the stadium, right in the centre of the disabled car park, right where it had all gone awry earlier that evening, where the placards and sticks and bottles had long been swept away, Martin knowing it would be quiet there at last and he could finally say his piece.

They'd listened as he talked, watched as he'd jabbed his finger, nodded and chewed their gum as he'd laid down the law. They were all chewing gum and reeked of aftershave; the carrier hummed of peppermint and Kouros and the subtle whiff of cigarette smoke, Martin presuming David had sucked on a couple while he was out of the picture. He didn't mind, in fact he understood it completely. What he hadn't been able to understand was why David had failed to answer the job mobile, that none of them had picked up his point-to-point calls on their radios, that not one member of the team had replied when he gave a general broadcast over the air. They'd brushed it off with the usual grumble about being in a poor reception area and Martin had snorted, pulled a *what do you think I am, stupid?* expression, had really set about them but his composure and assuredness cracked when David asked him if he'd finished then advised him to call Ops Room to check the time they put the complaint in.

It crumbled completely when he was told by the FIM that all four of them had rung Ops to grumble how the radios were in fallback for over an hour, and they were unable to transmit or receive. The job had been logged with 02 so they could check if the nearest mast was operating properly.

'See?' muttered Vincent. 'Cheap-shit Airwave comms from the last bunch of mugs in government.'

Andrew was nodding. 'You had trouble getting hold of Bronze for an hour tonight. Remember? When the containment went bendy?'

'Bloody rip-off,' mumbled David. 'Costs every force a fortune, and we might as well have tin cans and string.'

Nobody spoke for a while. The engine clicked and ticked as it cooled beneath the bonnet. Alan's deep and laboured breaths sounded from the darkness.

Martin swung around in the passenger seat. 'We start afresh,' he said. 'As of now. No more bollocks, no more pissing about. I am here and I'm here to stay, so you'd better get used to it.'

Andrew twitched his eyebrows, staring out of the window. His fingers drummed on the steering wheel.

'Any objections?' Martin asked.

'You're the skipper,' Andrew replied.

'*You're fucking right I am!*' Martin barked, leaning towards him. 'I'm the skipper, the stripy, the onion bhaji, the sargey, and you lot will shape up or fucking well ship out, do you understand?'

No response.

'Are we clear?' Martin asked, one arm draped over the back of the front passenger seat. He looked at each of them in turn, waiting until he saw the bob of their heads: Andrew in the driver's seat, Vincent in a chair directly behind, David in his so-called BINGO seat. And Alan. Sitting in the gloom at the rear again, amongst the shields and fire extinguishers, the bulkhead light throwing a shadow across his pallid features.

None of them looked directly at him.

'Then let's move on,' Martin said.

Andrew cleared his throat. 'So what next?'

Martin shifted to face front, lifted his boots on to the dashboard. 'City centre for some high-viz patrol,' he said, and looked at the FM radio sitting in front of him. 'I thought we'd have some of those *banging choons*, as you call them, while we do it.' He reached forward, switched the radio on.

Andrew grinned when a Kings of Leon tune twanged from the speakers. 'Sweet,' he said and gunned the revs, the slick tarmac of the stadium car park flowing underneath the wheels of the carrier as it turned towards the city centre.

It was just as busy: thousands of post-Christmas revellers, a mix of club punters and football fans who'd decided to drown their sorrows at the home team's thrashing, but the atmosphere was less tense, far less uncomfortable. There were no calls, their PRs and in-carrier Airwave set wonderfully quiet, the FM radio dialled to a station with no mindless DJ chatter. It was just music, and good music at that, classic tracks from the seventies, eighties, nineties filling the van, their heads silently nodding along to the songs. People even waved and smiled at them as they trundled by, one group of ladies demonstrating their high spirits by gleefully flashing their breasts, which Andrew had a slight episode over and had to be cajoled into driving on, drool on his bottom lip.

'There's your favourite tree,' chuckled Vincent, tapping Andrew on the shoulder.

City Hall was drifting past the windows, its clock tower and glorious Portland stone frontage washed in the soft glow of dozens of floodlights, the fountains and pool sitting on the lawn in front of the entrance portico. Alongside the temporary ice rink was a Christmas tree, the centrepiece of the council's annual Winter Wonderland event – it towered above the carrier, a seventy-foot pine blanketed with multicoloured lights.

Andrew smiled. 'I could have slotted the tosser for doing that.'

'What happened with the tree?' asked Martin, leaning down so he could look up at it through the windscreen.

Andrew raised a hand. 'Don't say anyth—'

David roared with laughter. 'When Thrush was a proba-tioner, his tutor gave him a call about a theft on the City Hall lawn. Something about people stealing the lights from the Christmas tree. So off Thrush toddles, with instructions to make sure all the lights were present and correct.'

'And were they?' asked Martin, realising what had happened.

'Yarp,' said Andrew. 'All five hundred and seventy-seven of the mothers.'

'Four hours!' David was holding his shaking belly. 'Four hours he stood there, counting every single bulb. Ops Room were watching him on CCTV the whole time . . .'

'Bastards set me up, didn't they?' muttered Andrew. 'Me tutor faked the incident on the computer, worded Ops Room up so they gave me the call. I froze me knackers off going round and round that tree.'

Martin laughed. 'Didn't you suspect it was a wind-up?'

'Nah,' Andrew said, taking a right at a set of traffic lights. 'I was new, wasn't I? Didn't know the ropes, didn't want to rock the boat, so got on with it. Y'know?'

Martin nodded at that. 'Sure do.'

'What about you?' asked Vincent from behind him.

'Me?' said Martin, looking over his shoulder.

'Anybody yank your chain when you joined up? Or don't they do that to the High Potential student officers?'

'You must have dropped a bollock or two,' said David.

Martin shrugged. 'First burglary I went to, a commercial job, high-value theft of computer equipment, we had quality prints on a pane of glass that had been removed. My tutor put it to one side while we checked the office.'

'And?' asked Andrew.

'I stepped on the glass. Shattered it. Destroyed the dabs completely.'

'What a cock,' Andrew blurted, David and Vincent laughing from the cheap seats.

Martin laughed along with them. 'And . . . I can't believe I'm telling you this. But I locked up a shoplifter once, walked him out of Tesco – he was nice and compliant – and popped him in the back of the van while my buddy was finishing taking details from the manager—'

'No offence, Sarge, but this is supposed to be a funny story,' said David.

Martin closed his eyes. 'But I'd shoved him in the back of a painter and decorator's van that was parked next to ours.'

'No way,' said Andrew, staring at him in astonishment.

'Yeah. When my buddy came out, and once he'd stopped pissing himself, we opened the door and found the prisoner sitting on a tin of emulsion with a puzzled look on his face.'

There were roars of laughter, Martin chuckling at the memory.

'Don't worry,' said David, wiping at his eyes. 'We won't tell anyone.'

Andrew nodded. 'What happens on the van stays on the van, innit?'

'Glad to hear it.' Martin smiled, and the carrier chugged

onwards, circling the city centre, and the laughter grew loud and long as the talking continued, as the piss-takes and war stories came tumbling out. The slipping of random words – Vincent had used *gusset* on at least three occasions at Magistrates – into taped interviews and evidence at court. The time when David had delivered a death message about a husband's passing away at work to the wrong woman in the wrong house. Their habit of pasting finger-print ink on the mouthpiece of random office phones at HQ, leaving civvies and rankers with black goatees when-ever they answered a call. Vincent, miffed at being kicked off a plain-clothes department, leaving a dead fish hidden above the ceiling tiles that resulted in very expensive air conditioning contractors being called in when the stench polluted the entire station. The fun they had on night shifts getting back at the pikeys, by driving on to their caravan site at four a.m. and sitting there for ten minutes with two-tones blaring. The time when Andrew, on a drugs search, forgot to wear latex gloves when picking up an acid tab and ended up tripping out for three hours, eventually locking himself, completely naked, in a cell, where he sat cross-legged and demanded everyone call him Osama bin Laden.

Amid the sniggers and banter Martin felt the last dregs of poisonous atmosphere dissipate, the headache behind his eyes ebb, his shoulders relax for the first time since he left for work. He felt the tension go.

Martin knew they were as relieved as he was. Another shift almost done. Another shift where they would go home safe to be with their loved ones. And a turning point for him, he felt.

He'd survived.

Made it.

Possibly, finally, made a connection with these old sweats, too.

'Er . . . Sarge?' said David eventually, and raised his finger in the air.

'Yes, David,' said Martin, his voice tired and rough.

'All right with you if we grab some munch now? We're all a bit starving after that poxy packed lunch.'

'D'you ever think of anything other than food?'

David looked out the window, deep in thought. He turned back to Martin.

'Not really, no.'

'Refreshments it is, then,' chuckled Martin. 'Or munch, if you must.'

'Refs,' Andrew said, and swung the carrier around.

In the shadows at the rear of the van, Alan sat quietly.

REFS

'Nice and easy, like,' Vincent breathed into Andrew's ear.

He'd spied the blonde woman leaving Liberty's about five minutes earlier, pushing her way past a gang of lads dressed in stupid costumes, had stared out of the window at her as they eased past in the van, as she wrapped her toned arms about her torso, Andrew muttering some comment about her little black dress looking like wrapping paper. Vincent ordered Andrew to follow her but keep it casual, keep their distance.

It was clear she'd had quite a few. She had that overly cautious and mildly amusing gait that pissed women who don't want people to know they're pissed usually adopt: steady, ever-so-careful steps that are nothing to do with the high heels and the difficulties they cause when walking. Measured, over-controlled paces that scream drunk and embarrassed about it.

The onion had no clue about them following the girl, much in the same way that he had no clue about their reasons for involving him in the banter. He'd mistakenly assumed it was a bonding session, that they were letting him in at last, when in reality it was a carefully contrived effort to distract him – along with the gallons of Kouros and sticks of gum – from the fact that they'd been on the piss, and that Alan was still off his tits and barely able to form a coherent sentence.

Vincent watched the boy, busily scribbling into his notebook as the carrier eased along in first, Andrew following the blonde, Vincent's lips whispering instructions that nobody else could hear over the bleep and drone of the Airwave set fixed in the dashboard, the faint music still playing on the FM radio. She paced up Park Place and past the New Theatre, hesitated, swaying at the traffic lights at the junction with Boulevard de Nantes, made a dash through a gap in the black-and-white line of hackneys, horns sounding, stumbled slightly as she reached the opposite pavement.

Mid twenties, I'd say, thought Vincent. *Probably fifteen years younger than Alan's wife with her pussy that drips like a fucked fridge.*

He imagined the blonde's tight little arse hoisted up on his sofa, her face buried in the cushions as he pistoned her. Felt a stirring in his groin. Resolved to ditch Mrs Dullas at the next available opportunity if things panned out as he planned with this new woman.

There's something about her, all right, he thought.

She left Park Place, picked up the pace as she turned into St Andrew's Crescent, wandered under the railway bridge with its panels of rust and student politics graffiti, and followed the raised pavement as it curved left into Salisbury Road and the city's student area.

'The Parthenon?'

Vincent nodded. 'Yup.'

Martin raised his head from his notebook. 'Is that where we're eating?'

'Yup,' said Vincent again, because he was pretty sure where blondie was heading. The Parthenon Kebab House was the only takeaway in this street, the only takeaway within a mile radius, and the woman had dodged the taxis on the boulevard, had ignored the hackneys that had passed her since, so wasn't looking to go home as yet. And she seemed to be on a mission. Vincent figured she either lived around here – but she didn't look like your typical student, and most of them had disappeared home for Christmas anyway – or was heading for some post-beverage sustenance that she would regret as soon as she cranked open her eyes in the morning.

Andrew was hanging back, letting the woman pull ahead, just as he'd been ordered. Vincent watched as the girl skipped further up the street, heading – and he almost punched the air – towards the kebab shop.

'Hurry up,' said David from behind them. 'I could eat a scabby horse.'

Martin smiled, leaned his head back towards him. 'You probably will be.'

The blonde disappeared inside the Parthenon. Andrew slowed to a crawl, watched through the takeaway window as she studied the menus with a screwed-up face, her body swaying, one leg flopped at an angle at the knee and her high heel kinked to one side.

'Game on,' Vincent said.

Andrew killed the engine. 'I've got the dollar.'

'You can get the orders in, then,' said David, sliding open the side door.

Martin stretched, his joints clicking, and switched off the FM radio. 'I hope they do some kind of salad combo.'

'What are you, a lesbian?' Andrew smiled, and climbed out of the cab.

'Charming,' said Martin, and rolled his eyes.

They pushed through the entrance door, Andrew loud and shouting *oi-ois* to the staff who grinned and *hey, guys*ed them in return, Vincent, stepping back, hovering near the tables where a handful of patrons hunched over their late-night meals.

Martin glanced around at the tired decor, the shabby paintwork and chipped countertops. The smell of grease and burnt chips hung in the air. He inspected the discoloured photographs of the food on offer, suspecting that anything they purchased would bear scant resemblance to the pictures. He also suspected it was a carve-up, and that the food venue had been decided while he prepped the paper-work for his prisoner. There was nothing for him here. He scanned the price list: nearly six pounds for a nasty-looking chicken burger.

'Yes, my friend?' asked one of the fellows behind the counter. He was squat and hairy, shorter than Martin, with perfect teeth and a black buzz cut. Grease marks smudged the yellow fabric of his tee, mostly around the right breast area. Martin assumed he had an itchy nipple or something.

'Do you do, y'know, just salad?' he asked, feeling a little self-conscious.

Itchy Nipple Man's head recoiled, as if Martin had just admitted a fondness for penetrating the odd goat of a weekend. 'Just . . . salad?' he asked, eyes tapered.

Andrew strode centre stage. 'Don't worry about him, Abdul,' he barked. 'Bung some of that lettuce in a bun. He'll manage with that.'

Martin suspected Itchy Nipple's real name was nothing like Abdul but the man said nothing so Martin said nothing and eyeballed Andrew's warped and gangly image in the stainless-steel splashback behind the grill area: the usual gurning grin, flicking his shaved head here and there like a shifty villain on the make.

'All sauce?' asked Nipple Guy and Martin nodded, not really caring. The food was free, after all, thanks to Andrew. Martin turned around with his carton, tuning out Andrew who was managing to further abuse Mister Nip while simultaneously ordering three king-size lamb doners and a relatively healthy chicken shish for Vincent.

He saw Vincent leaning over one of the tables, talking to a woman. She looked familiar, and it took a moment for him to realise that it was the girl he'd seen climbing out of the taxi earlier that evening. She'd looked a good deal smarter when he last saw her, and was looking up at Vincent with panda eyes, her lipstick smeared at one corner. Drunk and emotional. Blonde hair matted on one side, as if she'd been twisting it with a finger or running it through her lips.

Vincent was talking to her in hushed tones, crouched down next to her now, one arm resting on the tabletop, a cheeky grin above that. Martin couldn't make out what he was saying over the crazed foreign football commentary, but whatever it was it was working. The woman was smiling; sniffling and screwing up her face as she tried to concentrate, tried to act less drunk than she clearly was, but smiling all the same.

Martin glanced at Andrew but he was arguing with the guy behind the counter. He looked across to David and Alan: David leaning his bulk against the counter and watching the game, Alan rigid, a pained expression cutting across his features, eyes boring into Vincent as he chatted to the girl.

Vincent clearly couldn't help himself.

Martin wondered if he should have a word.

Fuckin' Martin an' his fuckin' faggoty ways, thought Andrew. *'Do you do salad?' Fuckin' salad? This be the best doner house in the city bra and the onion's doing his hoity-toity nonsense. Throwing his veggie weight about and expecting me to pay for it. Expecting me to pay for it after bawling us all out in the van not half an hour ago.*

He'd pushed the stumpy fucker out of the way, told Abdul what the score was, watched as the salad 'n' sauce combo was slid across to the stripy who'd minced off to one side to stare at Vincent and the woman.

Andrew knew Vincent had his moves going already. Warm as toast, he was. *Warm as fuckin' toast, man.* Andrew laughed and turned back to the counter, saw the stocky Arab with shit smeared around his tit still giggling along with him.

'Three king-size doners for the lads,' Andrew bellowed, jabbing a finger at the staff member. 'Plus a chicken shish.'

'All salad and sauce?'

Christ, Andrew thought. *He must get bored of saying that. But more fool him for coming here in the first place. Shoulda stayed home, weaved rugs in his mud hutch or somethin'.*

'S'right, Ahmed,' Andrew said, and the guy's name was probably not Ahmed but did it really matter? Andrew had probably shot a few of his cousins back in the day. Yomping around the villes out there in Nad-e Ali district, sniffing out the T-Ban in the sand. The bloke didn't flinch, wouldn't have corrected him anyway. 'Everything 'cept those fuckin' pickled chillies for me, my man. My guts, y'know?'

He rubbed a hand across his belly, shook his head with a rueful grin.

The staff member laughed and Andrew laughed right along with him as though they were fast friends, except he knew they would never be anything of the sort, that if this was a delivery to the nick that they'd ordered over the phone there'd be some *special sauce* waiting for them on the food. It had happened plenty of times before. He knew of an entire shift in a station down west who'd ordered a Chinese takeaway on a night turn, only to wake the next day with every man and woman shitting for Britain.

Andrew made sure he watched as the guy jammed his hairy fingers into the refrigerated trays lined up behind the glass: shredded lettuce, limp discs of cucumber, couple of tomato slices, some raw onion. He piled them on to the cartons, on to the sweating meat.

'Bring it on, buddy,' Andrew grinned. 'Bring on the animal sphincter.'

'Garlic?' the man asked, as if adding a ladle of milky breath-death to the chilli and barbecue efforts he'd already glooped over the kebabs would be the final nail, a little more than Andrew could handle.

'Lob it on there, Hamed,' he said with a wink.

'Your wife not be happy,' the staff member offered.

Andrew was blank-faced, gave the man his best *who the fuck d'you think you are to mention my personal life, let's not cross the fuckin' boundaries here, buddy* stare and the guy hunkered down, got on with it.

Andrew knew he was right, though.

I'll stagger in at shit o'clock, he thought. *Stagger in and want my oats and Claire will roll away, half asleep but still capable of rolling away and pulling her tee shirt down to cover her saggy arse just because of what happened before work.*

No fuckin' entry, Andy boy.

David was willing Andrew to stop giving the staff gyp; his stomach griped continuously, empty now. The morsels he'd scraped together at Lewis's house party hadn't touched the sides.

And he was stuck with Alan again. He was thankful his colleague had calmed down a tad – a lot, actually, especially since the visit to his house and the clean uniform – but the lingering effects of the Mickey Lewis had slipped into his drink were clearly evident. He was miserable, that was a given, but there was something else. Alan seemed distracted, distant. Ill, almost. He wasn't even grumbling any more: not about the choice of food, the damage to his car, not even the football on the television. David had shepherded Alan away from the boy, as far away as possible within the confines of the takeaway, to take up one side of the counter beneath a widescreen showing a match that Fenerbahce were winning three–one.

Alan hated football. Whined whenever it was discussed in the van. Waxed lyrical about the rugby, about *a game for real men*. Bored them senseless with stats about Wilko and Warburton and Shane Williams and the origins of the All Blacks' haka.

This time there was nothing.

It was making David nervous.

'Look, the poof's game's on the telly,' said David.

Alan was silent, unmoving. Watching Vincent.

David sighed, glanced up at the television, caught the referee blowing for half-time. He'd had more than enough football for today. He watched an advert for Toyota cars flash on to the screen, some generic piece he'd seen countless times on ITV but this one had a voiceover from a husky foreign female who sounded like she had lady-wood from looking at the 4 X 4's bodywork. It made David want to take one of the things for a test drive.

He looked across the takeaway at Vincent, at the woman he was chatting to. *He's pulling the same old crap, and yet she's still lapping it up, the daft cow.* Falling for it just like they all did with him because, and David was happy to admit it, Vincent was an exceptionally good-looking bloke. Whenever he spoke to his eldest daughter, David's message was always the same: *You ain't going out till you're twenty-one, girl. And when you do, don't drink yourself into a stupor. Don't put yourself in any danger.* He always pictured Vincent as he said it.

Much as he liked the guy, Vincent was – what they called in the trade – a complete and utter cunt.

Vincent couldn't place her.

He'd been crouched at the table talking to her for nearly ten minutes and it still hadn't clicked. Where he knew her from. The gym? Work? Definitely not the local supermarket, though. He'd done a few of the till girls there, even that customer service supervisor, what was her name? Deb or Bev or Beth or . . . Anyway, she'd been a right stuck-up ice queen in her little green outfit and I'm-rather-important headset but wanted all sorts of weird stuff after a shedload of wine. Moral compasses and all that. A right dynamo that one, and not a little crazy. Your typical uptight career woman who lets it all go when they're bevvied up. *Completely lose control, they do,* he thought. He'd stopped short of hitting her, even though she'd been begging him to do it while they fucked, so had just yanked on her hair and half strangled her to keep her quiet. He hadn't wanted to leave any marks even though she'd taunted him and called him a pussy.

What was her name? he wondered. *Ah, as if it matters. What a wildcat though. What a night.*

This one . . . Vincent thought she looked a bit rough at the moment but knew she was too well groomed to be a checkout chick. Totally drunk, but a nice girl. Coy too. But she was giggling in all the right places. It was pretty easy, if he was being honest. There was an element of inconvenience because she was so pissed he had to do all the talking, but he sensed it would be worthwhile in the end.

'Come on,' he smiled, mildly irritated that he still couldn't place her. 'Tell me. Are you who I think you are?'

Vincent knew it wasn't his local. He'd been very careful there, especially after the two bar girls he was fucking found out about each other and knuckled up over him that one time. Vincent thanked Christ the landlord had binned them for scrapping under the optics; he wouldn't have been able to take anybody new in there at all.

The blonde just shrugged and lolled to one side drunkenly. Vincent knew she was on the verge of passing out, she'd caned it so much. He knew he had to get a move on. Hoped Andrew had the food sorted. He needed to hurry up. The girl was alone and mullered, and there was already a flicker of interest, so wouldn't take much coaxing.

'I saw her earlier,' said Martin. 'Is she all right?'

Vincent hadn't noticed him shuffle up alongside them. He saw a carton in one of the stripy's boy-hands, a clump of lettuce hanging out of a burger bun within.

'I think we should give her a lift home,' Vincent said, not looking up at him, annoyed the midget was sticking his oar in. 'Drop her off before we head into town for the rest of the night.'

He was preparing to mentally record her home address for future reference.

'I want to get into the city centre soonest,' Martin said, picking at some bread and placing it into his mouth where he chewed suspiciously.

Vincent looked up at him this time. It wasn't far for him to shift his neck. 'She's on her own,' he said quietly, insistently, turning away from the woman. 'She's so drunk she doesn't know what she's doing. And her flat is on the way,' he lied. 'What if it was your daughter?'

Vincent saw the sergeant go into that strange trance-like state of his for a few seconds, a state that reminded him of Da Silva whenever he had to make a decision on the spot. As if he was mulling it over when in reality the boy was bricking it about making a decision.

You'll fit right in with the rest of the senior ranks, he thought.

Eventually Martin sighed. 'Okay. But make it quick, please.'

'Cool,' Vincent said. *You fucking weakling*, he thought. *Where's your backbone?*

Martin sloped away; Vincent heard the front door open and shut.

'Let's get you out of here,' he said to the girl and offered his hand.

'Wherewe . . . wherewegoin' . . . ?' she mumbled, confused. Vincent caught a flash of wariness in her eyes but it was a tiny moment, gone in an instant. She slipped her hand into his. He squeezed it, felt the soft, damp skin of her palm. Smiled and looked into her shiny, rolling eyes.

He glanced across to David, saw him tucking into his kebab, juice on his chin. Felt Alan's stare. Checked Andrew near the door, keys to the van in one hand and the rest of the food cartons balanced in the other. He grinned at Vincent, winked.

Vincent returned it.

'Come on,' he said to the woman, gently pulling her up

from the table. 'We'll take you home. Now, where is it you live?'

Coiling a grey slab of meat into his mouth, David climbed into the carrier.

Sandra would murder him if she knew what he was eating – she constantly berated him about his blood pressure, his smoking and his alcohol intake – but at that moment in time he could not care less. David could eat two of these bad boys, and was contemplating shooting back into the shop to spend some of his bingo winnings on a spare; he'd hide it at the back of the fridge and eat it cold in the morning.

He dropped into the BINGO seat, got nice and comfortable. He had no intention of doing anything other than stuffing his face, enjoying another Eddie, then seeing out the rest of the shift with a nice quiet snooze on the circuitous route they would undoubtedly take – thanks to Martin and his sickeningly keen stance on *maintaining community reassurance* – on the ride back to the station.

'You're going to have to move.'

Alan. Clambering into the wagon. His voice flat, emotionless.

David looked up at him, amber fat glistening on his lips. 'I'm a bit busy here,' he said, swallowing a stray sliver of onion. 'And this is my seat.'

Alan was bent over at the waist, his hair brushing the roof of the van. 'Look,' he said, jerking a thumb over his shoulder.

David leaned to one side, checked around Alan and through the open side door of the carrier. 'What does he think he's doing now?'

'Vincent is giving the girl a lift home.'

'What for?'

'I . . .' Alan said, then stopped. He seemed far away, as if struggling to continue the thought. 'Public safety.'

Yeah, right, thought David. He glanced at Martin, who was standing on the pavement with his head lowered towards the carton of food gripped in his tiny hands.

'For God's sake,' David muttered, and closed the polystyrene lid on his food.

He pushed himself up, Alan following him to the seats near the rear doors. David grimaced as Alan sat next to him. Watched silently as Vincent helped the drunken woman up the steps and into the carrier.

The girl was paralytic. Utterly incapable. Vincent was grinning and giving strange little nods to himself, quick little nods with his head shaking up and down, muttering, *'Yeah, yeah, yeah.'*

'This,' David said, staring at Vincent as he eased the woman into the BINGO seat, 'is a very big mistake.'

Vincent slid the carrier's side door shut, gave a little shimmy.

David turned to Alan.

The man's eyes were on Vincent. His food remained unopened on his lap, gripped between the white tips of his fingers.

'Alan?'

'What?'

'Are you sure you're okay?'

Alan's food carton creaked, cracked, as his fingers squeezed.

'Just eat your kebab, David,' he breathed.

'Smooth operataaah . . .'

Andrew turned the key in the ignition as he murdered the song. Vincent gave him another wink.

The stripy was pacing the pavement outside, *yes, sir*ing into his job mobile as he took more instructions from Bronze public order; he looked at the van as the engine snarled into life.

Andrew gave him the thumbs-up: *all ready to go, skipper*.

He turned around in the driver's seat, watched as much as he could before he had to drive off, losing the light from the kebab shop. Vincent was shushing the woman who'd now slumped forward in David's favourite seat, was sitting next to her, cuddled up and gently rubbing her left thigh with one hand, the other slipped around her waist.

Andrew could see Vincent was squeezing at her flesh through the fabric of her tiny dress. The woman was making noises from underneath the hair that hung down in front of her face, but whatever she was saying was unintelligible to Andrew.

He smiled. Dug a couple of forkfuls of meat from his carton on top of the dash. Chewed and watched as the new boy jumped into the passenger seat, salad carton held in his little paws.

'We fit?' Andrew asked, arching an eyebrow.

'Info is Telemaque and about a dozen other prominents are doing the bars,' Martin said. 'Head for the city centre. We'll show a presence at kicking-out time.'

Andrew was only half listening as he adjusted the rear-view mirror so he could catch some of what Vincent was getting up to.

'After we drop the girl off,' he said.

Martin sighed. 'Yes. After that.'

The carrier's tyres screeched as Andrew pulled away from the kerb.

'Sade,' said Martin.

'You what?' asked Andrew.

'That song you were singing. Sade, yes?'

'Thought you'd be a bit young for that one.'

Martin smiled, placed the food carton on the seat next to him. 'My wife. She likes all the eighties stuff. The Cure, Depeche Mode, Spand—'

He paused. Reached into a pocket. Dug out his mobile.

'My wife,' he said again, eyes wide and on the tiny screen.

Andrew waited for him to finish. Gave up waiting.

'How quaint,' he mumbled and stamped on the accelerator; the engine strained. He left the student area behind, humming the song quietly as he watched the dark shapes in the rear-view mirror.

He wished Andrew would slow down a little.

Vincent knew the man was excited but the van was throwing him about, making it difficult to do the right thing with the woman. His hand was hovering at the side of her left breast; every bump in the road was causing it to swing and knock against his fingertips, a nice li'l game of tit cricket, a pastime he and his teenage friends created one evening before they ventured out to the clubs and which he'd never stopped playing since. Vincent estimated her to be at least a C cup, which was nice, and with each knock he totted up his runs.

'It's okay,' he whispered to her, the back of the BINGO seat hiding him from Flub and Dullas. He checked the stripy; Vincent was positioned sideways on to the front of the carrier, his torso covering the girl and his hands, just in case Mr High-Flyer suddenly turned around. It was pretty dark back here, but if the onion managed to catch an eyeful it would look like Vincent was supporting her as the van rocked and rolled.

Wouldn't want a drunk MOP to keel over and hit her head, after all.

The pitch and yaw of the van, the hum of the engine, they were sending her to sleep. She folded herself into him before slowly sliding her head on to his lap.

'You'll be home soon,' he said, pulling her hair from her face. He very much liked where her mouth was. His fingers stroked the fine hairs that quilted the skin behind her ear, moved down to her back, her hips, brushed the hemline of her underwear through the dress.

The woman murmured something, something that sounded like the name *Paul* and her hand squeezed at Vincent's leg, shifted up his thigh towards his groin.

'There, there,' he said, heart singing.

He took a tentative squeeze of her breast, a nice relaxed handful. Waited for any reaction, for her to spring upright, slap him in the face. There was nothing.

With his other hand he undid the buckle on his utility belt.

Lowered the zip on his overalls.

Pushed her hand inside.

'That's it,' he murmured. 'That's right.'

Vincent grinned into the rear-view mirror, at Andrew's bulbous eyes, as the woman's fingers instinctively began to rummage around.

He was finished, had demolished the flaccid and peppery meat, its accompaniment of rancid greens and overripe tomatoes, its viscous coating of sauces, and had jammed the plastic fork through the polystyrene lid.

David dropped the carton to the floor, sated. Belly full,

bloated, he shuffled into the seat, folded his arms over his midriff. Let his head flop back on to the headrest and closed his eyes.

He began to drift, the engine noise lulling him, becoming distant, a white noise in his ears until, moments later, he was gone. Snoring quietly.

Not hearing the whining.

It sounded like a dog. A dog whining from some distance away, and as if it was in considerable pain.

Next to David, Alan's face was twisted and ugly, slit-eyes watering as he stared at the back of Vincent's head. The kebab carton was crushed in his hands. Meat hung from the sides, dripping pinkish sauce on to his uniform.

And the noise was coming from his mouth.

The onion had gone strangely quiet, which was a good thing because Andrew knew he would have difficulty speaking if the new boy fancied a chat. He could not believe what was going on behind him. It was gloomy, and he was getting it in the flashes of passing street lights, but it was enough.

He'd been driving in a huge circle, giving Vincent time. Giving himself time to enjoy what he could see of the show. Doing the loop around the northern fringes of the city, where the road network bordered the neighbouring force. He eased up on the revs, dropped down into second, let the carrier cruise on to the bottom of the road that flanked the capital's crematorium before winding up through the mountains.

'Smooth operator,' Andrew said quietly. His eyes were fixed on the rear-view mirror, using peripheral vision to guide the van as best he could. He didn't want to miss anything.

Nothing at all.

Andrew was dribbling and he didn't even realise.

The van cleared the crematorium, the blackened spout of its chimney sweeping past Martin's window, Andrew wishing he was in the back with Vincent. With his best friend.

With the woman.

He thought of Claire, of his miserable life at home, of the stupid decisions he'd made, of the ruin that faced him if he did a Flub and divorced her. The fat fucker barely had two pennies to rub together and yet he still kept walking down the aisle.

Andrew's eye began to twitch.

The carrier climbed the mountain road. The interior of the van darkened further, but not before he caught the woman's hand moving beneath the folds of Vincent's unzipped overalls. He swallowed.

A spasm in his eye, an uncontrollable flutter.

Andrew thrust his boot on to the brake pedal.

Pulled on the handbrake.

'What? What?' yelled Martin, jerking his head back and forth to check through the windscreen, through the passenger window, eyes wide and fearful.

'Fuck this,' said Andrew, and booted open the driver's door. Left the engine running. Jumped out of the cab. Ran around the front of the van. Ripped open the sliding side door. Ignored the shocked expression on his sergeant's face.

'Move over, Vince,' he grunted, his voice hoarse. He climbed into the van.

Vincent swung around, overalls sagging around his buttocks, the woman's hand squeezing at his erection even though she was still flopped forward in the seat, blonde hair covering her features.

'Piss off, Thrush!' shouted Vincent.

Andrew was undoing his utility belt. 'My turn.'

Vincent looked; Martin had shifted around in his seat, was squinting into the gloom.

He snapped his head to Andrew. 'You had to fuckin' spoil it, didn't you?'

'*Paul*,' the woman moaned.

'What's the problem?' asked Martin. 'Is it the woman?'

'Mind your business, Mart,' said Andrew, licking his lips as he stared at the half-naked blonde.

'Who do you think you're calling M—' Martin started to say, but stopped and dropped his mouth open a ways as his eyes adjusted to the murk.

Vincent supposed it was a bit of a scene for the boy. The girl was completely naked bar the dress bunched into a belt around her midriff. Her hand still gripping his penis. Vincent's arse out to the wind and overalls now around his ankles. Kebab cartons strewn around the floor.

Not exactly The Last Supper, *is it?* he thought.

'Look, I can explain,' Vincent said, but Martin was already clambering out of his seat, dropping to the frozen road, walking round to the side door.

'You are *finished*,' Martin said, pointing at Vincent from the opening.

Vincent went to speak, didn't know what he was going to say, knew deep down that it didn't matter what he said now because he wouldn't be able to extricate himself from this one, didn't have anything on the new boy, had no insurance whatsoever as far as this was concerned.

Then something connected with the side of his head, something hard yet fleshy. It knocked him to the cold van floor.

Raised voices. *'What the fuck?'* screamed Andrew.

Vincent shook his head. Focused.

Saw Martin's eyes shift slightly, fix on something.

Widen.

His expression one of horror, of revulsion.

Vincent rolled to one side, looked back at the woman.

Felt his innards tighten as he saw Alan behind her, behind the woman who had been flipped around on to the floor on all fours, the woman whose face was buried in the BINGO seat with Alan behind her, overalls down, his fingers digging into the flesh of her skinny hips, his top lip drawn back, face slack and sweating, vein pulsing across his forehead, eyes vacant, muttering something, muttering something over and over and over.

Vincent craned his neck, listened.

Listened as Alan spoke, as he rocked and thrust into the woman.

As he chanted the one sentence repeatedly.

"'Be still, and know that I am God. Be still, and know that I am God. Be still . . .'"

Alan flailed elbows – Vincent realising what had hit him – and snarled at Andrew as he pulled at him, saw David, bleary-eyed and horrified, emerge from the darkness at the back of the van. Alan snapped spittle-flecked teeth at them as they dragged him off, threw him to the floor next to Vincent, landed blows to his face and neck as his softening penis swung between the pallid skin of his thighs, Alan screaming, *'Now you can have her, Vince, now you can have her seeing as you're so keen on my second-hand goods!'*

The woman slumped on to her haunches, face misshapen and pale, staring at Vincent.

Tears falling from accusatory, hate-filled eyes.

Vincent reached towards her. Reached a hand, wishing he could take it all back, wishing he could go back in time and do it all over again, wishing he could go back far enough to stop what happened at a time when he didn't know any better, when he couldn't know any better, when those around him dealt him the hand that shaped his life and made him behave this way.

And then the carrier's Airwave set went off.

'Shit, we've got a call,' David yelled.

The new boy was pasty-faced and quivering, still standing at the side door of the carrier, head snapping from David to Andrew, down to the vile tableau in front of him, to the woman, to Alan who was now buckling up his utility belt and adjusting his epaulettes.

Alan staggered to the back of the van.

David watched as he sank into the seat next to the shield racks, dropped his head into his hands.

The woman was crawling about the van floor. She picked up a high-heeled shoe, slipped it on, sobbing as she moved, as she struggled with the rolled-up dress, 'Ah-huh ah-huh . . .' she moaned as she tried desperately to cover herself up.

'It's a code red at Liberty's,' David said, looking at Martin. 'The Casuals . . . Telemaque . . .'

'We've got to get out of here,' said Vincent, zipping up his overalls.

'We've got to get rid of *her*,' said Andrew.

'I've been asleep ten minutes,' David yelled, looking from Vincent to Andrew, to Alan's shivering shape. '*Ten fucking minutes*, and you do *this*?'

He couldn't think straight. Couldn't work out what was the best move. His head was filled with images of losing another wife, of missing yet more of his kids grow up, of jail time, of appearing upstairs at Crown, of being sent down for a ten-stretch just for being in this van on this night.

No matter that he did nothing; the fact that he *did nothing* while it happened would be enough to put him behind bars for a very long time.

He kept staring at Martin, willing him to say something. Wishing he was more like his father, because – and David knew this without a shadow of a doubt – the boy would never replicate his old man. David knew now that the kid didn't have it in him.

Martin was a good person at heart, with the best intentions.

But he was over-promoted.

And he was lost.

David could see it in his face.

Fuck this, he thought.

'Get in the driver's seat,' he barked at Andrew. 'Vince, get her dressed, quick-time.'

He leaned over the seats into the cab, grabbed the handset from the Airwave kit. Transmitted to Ops Room, told them they were en route to the city centre, sergeant plus four, TSG Central van. He turned, saw Vincent had fastened the woman's bra, had tidied up her dress, had suffered a rake across his cheek from her fingernails for his efforts.

'Get her out,' he said.

Vincent nodded, hand up to the bleeding scratch mark on his face.

She was ushered down the steps at the side of the carrier, out the door, *ah-huh ah-huh*ing as she stumbled on to a grass verge at the side of the mountain road. Vincent was holding her elbow, unable to bring himself to look at her.

'Come *on!*' David shouted, as Andrew climbed into the cab and revved the engine.

The front passenger door opened. David turned to see Martin slide into his seat. There was a stillness about him. He said nothing, just stared straight ahead, as if he didn't want to acknowledge what he had just witnessed.

David quickly checked the van floor. The woman's bag.

Fuck.

'*Vince!*' he yelled, scooped up the handbag, leaned over the seats and past Andrew to toss it out of the driver's window.

Vincent let go of the woman's elbow. Ran back towards the carrier, to the handbag on the floor just outside the driver's door. The woman walked unaided a few paces then sat heavily on the frost-covered grass. Her head hung low on her shoulders, between her knees.

Vincent picked up the bag, not realising it had opened as it landed. The woman's personal belongings scattered everywhere as he jogged back to her.

'Bollocks,' he said, stopping momentarily to check about the icy grass. He couldn't see anything. Too dark.

He sprinted the last twenty feet, stopped and held the bag out to her.

'Here,' he said. 'Take it.'

When she didn't respond, or lift a hand to him, he shook his head.

'*Vince.*' David's voice again.

'Fuck it,' Vincent grunted, and turned away, tossing the bag over his shoulder.

Numb.

Martin felt numb.

It was a waking nightmare and he felt like he had just before his father had slipped away.

If you don't look, it isn't real.

Except his father's death was real.

This was real.

He turned to Andrew but he was eyes straight ahead, one hand gripping the steering wheel while the fingers of the other operated the strobes and wailers, using the buttons on the dash.

The radio was still screaming, further units required at Liberty's nightclub, several officers injured, the Ops Room woman's voice calm as you like.

In his right hand Martin held his mobile phone.

He'd felt it vibrate not five minutes before. While he was standing at the side door, while it all happened. A burst of short throbs. Three missed calls from Sam's mobile.

He looked at the phone again. Read the text message he'd received outside the kebab shop. The text message that had made him freeze. That had made him oblivious to all that was going on behind him.

Please come home. Baby on way. I love you.

Martin gagged. Leaned forward a little, checked the van's side mirror.

The girl was staggering along the grass verge, lit by the

strobes of the carrier – of his carrier – her chest hitching, mouth open, eyes wide and seemingly pleading.

As they hit the downward slope and rounded a corner, before she disappeared from view, Martin saw her raise a hand in the air.

As if to beckon them back.

CONFLICT
MANAGEMENT

Alan walked towards them, arms hanging at his sides, ignoring the new boy's shouts, shrugging off the hands that grabbed at his protective vest, his fluorescent waistcoat, trying to pull him back.

Glass crunched beneath his boots. Uniform helmets lay amongst the glittering shards, amongst the hundreds of flattened cigarette butts, the overturned tables, the twisted, dented chrome of bar stools. A splotch of blood here, a smear there. Blue lights pulsed all around him. Sirens wailed in the distance, but moving closer. His radio blared and mixed with the bass thumping through broken windows, with the terrified screams of female onlookers, the shouts and profanities and murderous threats coming from the mass of brawling men on the courtyard outside Liberty's bar.

A chaotic ballet of flying fists and stamping trainers, of spittle and rage and drunken swings into empty air, of shirtless torsos and grappling police officers and the thick necks of door security, the scene lit by a hundred camera phones.

Alan walked into the middle of it all.

And just let it happen.

Just let go.

He thought of *penitence, repentance, self-abasement*, the words floating across his vision, lit by the neon glare of the sign flickering above the entrance. They comforted him, cushioned him against the first punch, a ferocious ridge of knuckles connecting with his cheekbone and rocking his head backwards. The man – Nathan Telemaque, his pocked face a twisted mask of rage above the torn collar of his jacket – shifted his weight, drew back his other arm, took aim, eyes glittering, teeth clamped together, and struck Alan again.

His jaw snapped sideways; blood in his mouth where a tooth nicked his tongue.

Reparation, he thought. *Atonement, contrition.*

Alan looked up at Telemaque. Wished he could embrace him.

'"Their sins and lawless acts I will remember no more",' he said, unsure if he was talking about Telemaque or himself.

Telemaque cocked his head, hesitated, face still set with anger. Then Alan saw his shoulders loosen, relax, the shadow of something he couldn't quite describe – was it compassion? – pass across the man's features.

'"I am he who blots out your transgressions",' smiled Alan, '"for my own sake."'

Telemaque studied him, chest rising and falling. It was as if they were cocooned together, removed from the chaos, sheltered by an innate understanding. Two old sweats too long in the tooth to be doing this any more.

Alan reached out to the man. Hand shaking.

Then: 'What the fuck you on about, scuffer?' Telemaque sneered, and punched Alan square on the nose.

It spun him, and he reached up, felt warm blood on his hands, running over his lips, heard the crunching, crackling sound of bone fragments shifting as he pressed with his fingertips, a sickness in his guts.

Alan opened his eyes, saw them. David looking at him, studying him almost, motionless and not a little sad. Vincent and Andrew restraining Martin, their reproachful eyes telling all. Martin, struggling against the hands that held him, straining to intervene.

Alan understood.

Turned back to face Telemaque.

'Do it,' he said, words slurring through the syrupy blood around his tongue.

Arms flailing, Telemaque pummelled him, pounding at Alan's head and neck and broken, ruined nose, and he could feel the man's hot breath on his face, could see more of them advancing on him, enraged, shirts ripped, eyes blood-shot with drink and fury so he lifted his face to the dark heavens and thought of Lisa and their children and all that he had now lost.

Then David's voice: '*He's had enough*,' and Andrew spitting '*Fuck 'im*' and David shouting '*He's one of us*' and Alan heard the unmistakeable sound of batons being racked out, of high-carbon steel connecting with clothing, with flesh, heard footfalls and more screams and as the slapping stopped felt an arm on his shoulder and looked down to see Martin at his side, saw David and Andrew and Vincent beating the men away, ASPs arcing through air, clearing the courtyard.

'Let's get you back to the nick,' said Martin, squeezing at Alan's jacket.

Alan blinked, the flesh beneath his eyes already swollen and blackening. He swallowed blood, glanced about at the crowd, at the exhausted, beaten divisional cops, the soiled uniforms and damaged facade of the club, the men pinned to the floor with hands cuffed and legs thrashing, the fight still not gone out of them.

He nodded. Began to walk.

'We always look after our own,' said Vincent from behind him. 'No matter what.'

Alan stopped. Turned around.

'Problem?' Vincent asked.

'*Don't*,' yelled David.

It knocked Vincent to the ground, the punch, and nobody except Vincent moved. Even Telemaque, cuffed on his belly on the floor, stared in amazement at what he had just witnessed.

Alan waited a moment, fist clenched at his side, the laughter and cheers from the crowd of onlookers drowned by a thunderous heartbeat in his ears.

'All right,' he said quietly, and stepped towards the van.

27 DECEMBER, 0042HRS

Cold.

So cold it's confusing at first, when she wakes, when she cracks her stiffened eyelashes open, because her flesh seems like it's burning, seems so hot, and as she rolls on to her back she wonders if she's woken on a beach somewhere, is *catching some rays* as Paul calls it, is just waking from a deep and dreamless and wonderful nap and in a moment will feel sand between her toes, hear the ocean hissing softly at the shoreline, feel Paul's warm hand falling gently on to her shoulder.

She smiles faintly. Wants the feeling to last. Wants to lie there, to revel in it.

'Paul?' she says, but the voice she hears is coarse, guttural. Not hers.

She swallows; her throat clicks and catches, the back of her tongue pasting itself to the roof of her mouth and making her gag.

She forces her eyes to open.

Sees the black of the night sky. The prickled silhouette of the treeline. The sloping road with its coat of glittering frost.

Realises. Remembers.

The grass beneath her hands, she clutches at it. Digs her nails into the frozen topsoil, feels the blades snap and crumble as she rakes her fingers. Hears that rasping, calloused voice again as it shrieks her boyfriend's name, hears it echo down the mountainside and fade away to nothing.

She sobs as she rolls to one side, pushes herself on to an elbow, the effort exhausting, her arms shivering uncontrollably, the spasms in her legs causing the heel of one shoe to plough a miniature furrow in the earth.

It's so cold.

So cold it feels as though it's reached into her bones, freezing the marrow.

Her bag. Her clutch bag. She blinks, laboured breaths puffing from cracked lips in short, tremulous bursts. Looks around. Can't focus. Can't seem to concentrate.

Can't see the bag.

She knows she has to get off this mountain. Knows she has to call somebody. Anybody. Her mobile phone is in the bag.

It takes all the strength she can muster to stand, every muscle and sinew screaming as she pushes herself upright, the skin around her joints so tight she feels it will rupture and split through the effort, through moving too quickly. She pulls on the hem of her thin dress, yanks it down with a trembling hand, desperate to cover up, to warm her white-blue thighs. Takes one step. Stumbles. Flaps at the still air in front of her. Regains her balance. Hugs herself. Her damp hair hugs her neck, making her colder still.

Downhill. Easier for her. She lurches downhill, down the gentle gradient, her smudged and watering eyes scanning the ground, searching for her clutch bag, willing it to appear, praying she doesn't have to turn around, doesn't have to climb back up the slope to find it. She doesn't think she'll be able to do it. It's too far. Too hard now.

She's fifteen feet from the road, shrouded in the shadow of spruce and fir and winding ivy when her shoe catches on something.

She looks down. Her eyes adjust to the darkness.

'Oh,' she breathes.

She's standing above a shallow drainage ditch.

The bag lies on the mound of soil that curves over at its lip.

'Oh . . .'

She bends, picks up the clutch bag, whole body shuddering. It takes her a full minute to work the clasp, her fingers seemingly incapable of following orders, her eyes unwilling to set themselves on one spot.

Her heart races as the bag opens.

And it's empty.

No mobile phone. No house keys, purse, money, make-up. Nothing.

She throws her head back, releases a raw and wretched cry, screams until her throat itches, until she has to drop the bag and scratch at her own neck.

'Pleasepleasepleasepleaseplease . . .' she moans, rocking herself, hands clasped between her breasts; despite her freezing skin her fingers still feel cold pressed against her chest. She doesn't have the energy to search. Doesn't know where to start. Doesn't know what to do any more.

She doesn't even know where she is.

She waits. Thinks it best to wait. Wait and see if she discovers the right thing to do. Stands amongst the branches, pine needles spiking her numb shoulder, shaking, arms enfolded around themselves. Easier this way.

Easier.

So she waits.

When she first hears the noise it barely registers. A high-pitched yet distant whine, the sound of wind shifting through the forest behind her. Yet the whine grows in volume, coming closer, coming from the other side of the mountain, and she turns away from the hedgerow and the trees and cranes her neck towards the road and sees diffused whiteness flickering and lighting up the crest of the hill.

She reels forward. Lifts a hand.

Knows.

The headlights burst over the summit, drop down, the small car moving at speed, moving at speed in low gear and causing the engine to bellyache. She staggers, wills her legs to work, pushes herself up the slope towards the road, towards the car with its driver who won't see her in the murk if she's this far away, tucked in amongst the roadside foliage, won't see her at all and will pass her by and leave her alone again unless she hurries. Unless she tries.

Unless she makes it.

She's ten feet from the road as the car nears her. Arms aloft, mouth open, throat so dry and cold. The headlights bathe the verges in a dazzling halogen glare, lighting up the frost, the bare beech trunks, the rivulets of ice in the gutters.

Lighting up her face.

The engine noise drops, the car slows.

She bends at the waist, eyes closed. 'Thank you . . .' she whispers.

And the car accelerates away.

She stares after it, its rear lights red pinpricks that shift across her vision, fading slowly into the blackness until disappearing from sight completely.

'No,' she says quietly. She repeats this one word as if somehow it will bring the car back. As if it will place her mobile phone in her hands, take her off this mountain.

As if it will erase the night that has taken place.

She repeats it with each step, each step that takes her closer to the road, closer to the spot where they left her, where the car just slowed before driving away.

Where she sees a flat, rectangular shape lying in the carriageway.

She cackles uncontrollably. Curses herself for walking in the wrong direction. It was there all the time. Not five feet from where she woke up.

The cackling slows, descends into sobs, the relief almost unbearable, as if it might crush her with its weight. She thinks of Paul, of her parents, of her friends and colleagues and even the ridiculous, once-inconsequential things she might never have seen or done again if she'd frozen to death on this mountain. Because she could have.

She could have.

It was so close.

She shudders, reaches down, fingers brushing the mobile. Picks it up. It feels lighter than usual so she turns it around, sees she's just picked up the flip-top cover, shakes her head, looks down and sees it.

The rest of the phone. The cracked screen. The crushed and useless keypad.

And she realises why the car slowed down.

It's so cold.

She looks downhill, where the car's rear lights shrunk and vanished. Sees the faint amber glow on the skyline, the hazy yellow dome of pale light. Of thousands of street lights.

The city.

It must be.

She folds her arms inside her dress, lowers her head.

Walks.

DEBRIEF

Water dripped from overhead pipes, thrummed on the roof of the carrier.

Everyone gone. The rankers, support staff, comms girls, overtime bandits, mutual aid vans. Da Silva, finished and off duty. The command room shut down, its terminals and telephones and radio points switched off and silent, waiting for the next event to swamp the city. The parking bays in the basement, empty but for their own private vehicles.

Everyone gone but them.

They sat in the carrier, not moving. Listening to the steady *tok tok tok* as fluid from the air con leaked on to the metal panels above their heads, a rhythmic percussion that drummed and reverberated through the cabin.

Tok tok tok.

Tok tok tok.

A miserable metronomic pulse.

Their collective revulsion marked in bpm.

It was David who moved first. Slowly lifting himself from his favourite seat, shuffling over to the sliding door, opening it. Facing each of them in turn, holding each gaze, silently urging them, nodding when they nodded at him before dropping down from the carrier, on to the sodden concrete floor of the basement.

As if waking from a deep slumber, they followed him. Faces drawn and pale under the harsh glare of bulkhead lights pinned to thick support struts. Eyes blinking, hollow and red and underlined with dark crescents. Watching as

David walked slowly to the storage cages, the grilled boxes heaving with lost property, with stolen property, with abandoned pushbikes and power tools and beaten filing cabinets and a solitary, listing swivel chair. Waiting as he unlocked a storage cupboard, reached in, removed brushes, a mop, detergent.

They set to work with Martin still sitting in the front passenger seat, worked around him in silence, brushing out the floor of the van, the footwells in the cab, the seats and Taser cabinet and the shields and equipment racks. Wiping down the steering wheel, the headrests, the windows, the radio kit.

Cleaning. Removing. Hiding.

Nobody talked.

After a while, after a long while, Martin joined them. Stood before them as they scrubbed and swiped and polished things away. A mobile phone held in his small hand. His features pained, his eyes darting from one colleague to another, as if searching for answers that he knew he was never going to get.

David stepped towards him, looked down at the boy, the boy who was trying so hard to be like a man he didn't really know, a man who, in his pomp, when he was beating on prisoners and planting drugs and skimming money from pimps, Martin wouldn't want to know. A man who could trump pretty much any of the heinous things he or Alan or Andrew or even Vincent had done in their time – until it came to the woman.

Until tonight.

David could see the torment behind Martin's eyes. The conflict. The urge to do the right thing, to unhook his PR and point-to-point the Night Silver to confess all, battling with the innate sense of self-preservation, with the prospect of his nascent career in tatters, of losing his wife and unborn child, of going away for a very long time.

He watched as the boy studied his mobile.

Read and reread a text message.

When he took the rags, the detergent, from David's meaty and sweating hands a tear fell from Martin's right eye. He held David's eyes with his own for a moment.

'What happens in the van stays in the van,' he said eventually.

David nodded.

Martin drifted away and set to work without another word.

In a way, David felt desperately sorry for him. The boy was a tourist, a seagull. Yet in the course of one night and despite his best intentions, despite railing against it, Martin had become all of them. Him, Andrew, Vincent, Alan. He'd walked with dinosaurs and it had changed him for ever. The irony was he'd also become Da Silva in the process: tainted from the outset, burdened with a guilt that would haunt him for the rest of his service.

Old sins cast long shadows.

Two sides of the same tarnished coin, and Martin was both.

He'd wrestled with his conscience and his conscience had lost out.

And without even realising it, he'd become his father.

Nobody said a word when Vincent, face caked with blood and swollen from Alan's punch, leapt from the body of the carrier, his eyes wild and filled with horror. No one offered anything when he placed his hands to his head and walked in circles, boots throwing up water, soaking the legs of his overalls. Not one of them stopped working when he moaned *No no no no noooo* and punched the green button to open the shutter, sprinted to his car, started the engine, reversed from the bay with tyres keening amidst the spray of surface water.

Vincent disappeared up the ramp and out into the night air.

David glanced into the carrier.

Alan was missing.

He checked the basement, the kit rooms, the locker area.

Found his uniform in a heap outside the shower cubicles. Could hear the spray of water, see steam fogging the entrance.

David stepped into the mist.

Saw Alan curled into a ball on the tiled floor, scalding water soaking his naked, shivering body, hands clasped tightly to his chest, eyes closed, rocking as he muttered to himself.

"'Forgive us our trespasses . . . Forgive us our trespasses . . . Forgive us . . .'"

David watched for a moment

When he'd seen enough he walked away.

He drove with his boot jamming the accelerator to the floor, seventy in thirty zones, running reds at junctions, taking roundabouts the wrong way, the car engine shrieking, the city falling away behind him, heading north, heading towards the crematorium, punching the steering wheel, punching his fist to his forehead, to his bruised and bloody face, knowing there was probably nobody left working, there never was nowadays so he didn't have to worry about being stopped, didn't care about the traffic black rats or sector officers anyway even if they did appear in his rear-view mirror and he couldn't believe it, couldn't believe he'd forgotten, cursed himself for allowing his memory to blend all those nameless faces he'd wooed and fucked into one opaque morass of features that meant nothing to him any more, that meant nothing to him at all until now, until tonight, on that mountain road, on the frozen mountain road he was now screaming along not two hours since they dumped the woman there, abandoned her, discarded her just like he was discarded all those years ago and he gnawed at his knuckles, hunched over the wheel, peered through the windscreen for her, quick-panned his eyes across the landscape, over the grass verges and banks of trees, felt the ache form in his temples, felt so utterly foolish for forgetting about last year.

Last year.

With her.

Vincent slowed the car at the spot where he'd walked the woman to the roadside.

Stopped.

Climbed out. Staggered across the grass, across to the treeline.

Jerked his head back and forth, searching.

Searching.

'*No*,' he moaned, breath misting before his tired eyes.

She was gone.

Gone.

He chewed on his knuckles again. Trudged back to the car.

Saw the crushed mobile phone lying in the roadway near one of the wheels.

Looked back towards the city.

David was sitting on the step at the side door of the carrier, elbows on knees, a lit cigarette between fingers that hung between his thighs. Smoking on police premises: a minor infringement in the grand scheme of things.

The new boy squatted next to him, a borrowed Benson hanging from his mouth, eyelids fluttering as grey smoke drifted up his face.

David watched, eyes narrowed, as Vincent climbed out of his car.

'Anything?' David asked.

Vincent shook his head.

'No,' he said, almost to himself.

David was about to push him further when Vincent strode towards the lift, pressed the call button, waited for the doors to open, hands against the wall, head lowered.

'No,' he said again. 'No, no, no.'

Andrew jumped down from the back of the van, mop in hand.

'Vince?'

The lift doors hissed open.

Vincent pushed himself upright, stepped in, reached out to jab one of the buttons.

'Vince?' asked Andrew, palms upturned, questioning.

'It's all over,' Vincent said.

The doors slid closed.

27 DECEMBER, 0227HRS

She places one unfeeling foot in front of the other and leaves the shadows of the park behind, moves through the cones of amber street light and the parked cars and the dead and chilly silence of the road then pauses at the bottom of the steps, places a shivering hand on the frosted rail, steadies herself. Breathes. Breathes deeply to calm herself. Looks up at the building, at the brightly lit sign above the entrance doors.

For a second or two she thinks about turning and limping away. Away from the building, this place of shelter and supposed safety. Thinks about walking, walking until somebody, anybody, finds her somewhere and holds her and wraps her in their arms and shushes her, knows instinctively what has happened, knows just what to do, tells her everything will be all right, everything will be fine now because at last her ordeal is over.

It is over.

She climbs the steps. Lifts a quivering, clawed hand to her eyes and wipes at the streaked mascara with the heel of her palm. Runs ragged nails through her blonde and grubby hair. A pathetic attempt to make her look less pathetic.

She would laugh if it wasn't all so horrible. So grotesque.

On frozen feet she ascends the steps, the ache in her hips and stomach swamped by a lurching, tumbling sensation in her chest as she finally succumbs to shock, to the cold, to the exhaustion.

She falls to her knees. Grips the metal railing.

Lifts her head, neck straining, mouth letting slip a low moan.

Squints at the brilliant light of the sign, the sign that was all she could think about as she forced herself onwards for miles, for hours, for ever.

The sign that reads WELCOME TO TRINITY STREET POLICE STATION.

She lowers her head and cries.

Cries and hugs herself and rocks as she pushes herself upright, pushes through the entrance doors, her skin burning with the sudden hike in temperature.

The foyer is empty, silent. Her eyes skim walls covered with Neighbourhood Watch posters, rows of low and vacant chairs, a lone potted plant in one corner, the facade of the public service counter, its glass smeared and chipped and tinted so she can barely see into the bowels of the station.

She waits. Thinks. Thinks as best she can. Breathes the warm and musty air, feels the carpet beneath her toes, the soles of her feet. Feels her skin tingling as it comes back to life, as it regains feeling.

She breathes deeply, calms herself. Rakes her fingers through her hair once more, straightens her dress. Palms away the make-up around her eyes.

Walks to the counter.

Presses the buzzer.

The desk clerk is in no hurry. He yawns as he appears around a corner, an uninterested, bored expression on his chubby face as he ambles towards the glass, not even looking at her. She can tell he's been sleeping.

'Yep,' he says, leaning down to the countertop so he can speak through the small gap at the bottom of the glass. He rubs at his reddened eyes with pudgy fingers.

'I need . . .' she says, and her voice cracks.

'You *need*,' the clerk mimics, one finger exploring a nostril. 'You need what, love?'

She swallows. 'I'd like . . .'

'Are you going to finish a sentence or shall I go back to my book while you mull it over?' he says, irritated now, then he does look at her. Shifts his eyebrows upwards. 'Bloody hell, you've had a good night, haven't you?'

She catches herself laughing. Laughing at the madness of it all. Stops when the clerk laughs along with her. Hears a faint *ping* from somewhere behind the desk, in the greyness of the station.

Looks past the desk clerk to see the light above the lift doors is illuminated, that the doors are opening. She hesitates.

Sees the uniformed figure step out.

Sees his eyes widen, his face drain of colour.

Feels her heart stop.

Thinks of the kebab shop, the mountain, her empty clutch bag, everything rushing back to her. Remembers the summer before, the residential course, her first time away from Paul and the lies she fell for, the bogus flattery, her naivety and stupidity leading her to another man's bed.

To *him*.

Vincent Vinyard.

Standing before her, ten feet away, separated by the glass, his chin quivering, hands outstretched, frozen in mid-air as they reach towards her.

'You newbies,' she can hear the desk clerk saying, his tone gently mocking. 'You'd better get your head down, Bex. You're on the response car in the morning.'

Her eyes don't leave Vincent's when she replies.

'You'll have to buzz me in, Pete,' she says to the clerk. 'I've lost my warrant card.'

Glossary

ACPO – Association of Chief Police Officers. Private limited company. Provides forum for chief police officers to develop policing practice in England, Wales and Northern Ireland.

ANPR – Automatic Number Plate Recognition. System that can read number plates on passing vehicles, and immediately check a database to see if the vehicle is stolen, uninsured, has markers for drugs etc. Fitted to most traffic police vehicles.

ARV – Armed Response Vehicle. Crewed with Authorised Firearms Officers to respond to firearms incidents or other high-risk calls. Occupants fond of grooming products, gym work and sunglasses.

BCU – Basic Command Unit. Policing territory; forces are divided into several BCUs, each covering a designated area. A BCU is usually commanded by a uniformed Chief Superintendent.

CBRN – Chemical, Biological, Radiological and Nuclear. Acronym relates to equipment used by police to protect against a terrorist attack using any one of these weapons.

EGT – Evidence Gathering Team. Similar to Forward Intelligence Team (see below). EGTs are deployed during varied public order events to photograph / video incidents and individuals for 'post-incident arrests'.

ESSO – Every Saturday and Sunday Off. Derogatory term for officer – typically of the higher ranks – who works Monday to Friday in an office.

FIM – Force Incident Manager. Typically an inspector based in the force control room. Solely responsible for immediate, critical decisions on a vast array of incidents across the force, from firearms calls to fatal accidents.

FIT – Forward Intelligence Team. Officers deployed to gather and record evidence at demonstrations, major incidents, sports events. Frequently deployed in advance of TSGs, PSUs etc. to assess any risks.

MOP – Member of the Public. The air the police breathe.

NATO – North Atlantic Treaty Organisation. Acronym used by police to describe the military-style public order helmets/visors they wear.

NBPA – National Black Police Association. Interest group of the Black and Minority Ethnic (BME) staff of the UK police service.

NCALT – National Centre for Applied Learning Technologies. Officers are rarely trained by living, breathing humans any more – instead, they are provided with software 'packages' such as the NCALT system, where they can learn how to pursue a stolen car or disarm a knife attacker from the environs of the station sergeant's office.

OIC – Officer in the Case. Primary investigator in any case, responsible for collating approximately four hundred pages of evidence which the CPS will ultimately refuse to proceed with.

PCSO – Police Community Support Officer. Uniformed but non-warranted police staff, with limited powers in a non-confrontational role.

POLSA – Police Search Advisor; specialist search-trained officers deployed at Major Crime scenes, Missing Person searches etc. The officers you see on the news, fingering blades of grass.

PR – Personal Radio. The bane/saviour of many an officer.

PSD – Professional Standards Department. The people who police the police.

PSU – Police Support Unit. Teams of BCU officers trained in basic public order, often drafted in from normal duties at short notice to assist with football matches etc. A fondness for regularly working eighteen days straight is key to a successful stint as a PSU officer.

RV – Rendezvous.

SMT – Senior Management Team. Higher ranks, usually Inspectors up to Chief Superintendents, who run BCUs.

TSG – Territorial Support Group. Specialist public order officers. Deployed for public order containment, terrorism response, BCU support, armed response, amongst others. The Millwall Football Club of police. You don't like them, they don't care.

Acknowledgements

Thanks, and appreciation to:

Jason Arthur, Karolina Sutton, Tom Avery for his patience and painstaking work during the edits, Caroline Ross and Teddy Kiendl for the days away and evenings of wine, Russ Litten for the email support, Rob and Shelagh Middlehurst, and Barrie Llewelyn. A special mention for my ex-colleague Lady Lynne Dwyer, who provided most of the weapons-grade filth that appears in the novel.

I would also like to thank everyone at William Heinemann and Curtis Brown.

And to the boots on the ground: don't let the bastards grind you down.

MIKE THOMAS

Pocket Notebook

Meet Jacob Smith, your good-old British policeman. But Jacob's no ordinary beat bobby. He's a tactical firearms officer; a handsome, popular, financially secure specialist. He's a connoisseur of fine cinema, and he likes to keep himself in shape, hence the large steroid habit – and the even larger amount of money he owes his dealer. Did we mention he's partial to women's feet? The girlfriend who's desperately trying to shrug him off? Or his parents' dark past?

Now Jacob's family and friends are starting to worry – and his police superiors are increasingly taking notice of the way he conducts himself. Life is beginning to get rather complicated. But Jacob's pretty sure he's got it covered. After all, he's recorded everything meticulously in his regulation pocket notebook . . .

'Stuns like a truncheon, grips like a pair of handcuffs, crackles with charge like a taser ... terrifying.'
NIALL GRIFFITHS

'This arresting tale doesn't miss a beat ... While Pocket Notebook might become cult reading in police circles, it certainly isn't about to become a recruit training manual.'
INDEPENDENT

'A cracker of a read. Needless to say, Smith is heading for an especially bloody end. It's who he'll take down with him that provides the suspense, and the horror.'
MIRROR